D0423013

THE LITTLE WOODS

THE LITTLE WOODS

McCormick Templeman

schwartz & wade books · new york

Text copyright © 2012 by McCormick Templeman
Jacket photograph copyright © 2012 by Albert Delamour

All rights reserved. Published in the United States by Schwartz & Wade Books, an imprint of Random House Children's Books, a division of Random House, Inc., New York.

Schwartz & Wade Books and the colophon are trademarks of Random House, Inc.

Grateful acknowledgment is made to the Penguin Group (USA) Inc. for permission to reprint excerpts from *The Odyssey* by Homer, translated by Robert Fagles, copyright © 1996 by Robert Fagles. All rights reserved. Reprinted by permission of Viking Penguin, a division of Penguin Group (USA) Inc.

Visit us on the Web! randomhouse.com/kids

Educators and librarians, for a variety of teaching tools, visit us at RHTeachersLibrarians.com

Library of Congress Cataloging-in-Publication Data
Templeman, McCormick.
The little woods / McCormick Templeman.
p. cm.
Summary: Entering St. Bede's Academy halfway through her junior year, Cally Wood is thrust into the complex social world of the upper echelon, but she is more interested in Iris, a girl whose recent disappearance is similar to that of Cally's own sister ten years earlier.
ISBN 978-0-375-86943-3 (hardback) — ISBN 978-0-375-96943-0 (glb)
ISBN 978-0-375-98349-8 (ebook)
[1. Missing persons—Fiction. 2. Boarding schools—Fiction. 3. Schools—Fiction. 4. Social classes—Fiction. 5. Mystery and detective stories.] I. Title.
PZ7.T2557 Lit 2012
[Fic]—dc23
2011047345

The text of this book is set in 11.5-point Augustal.

Book design by Rachael Cole

Printed in the United States of America

10 9 8 7 6 5 4 3 2 1

First Edition

FOR QUILL

PART ONE

Sinews no longer bind the flesh and bones together—
the fire in all its fury burns the body down to ashes
once life slips from the white bones, and the spirit,
rustling, flitters away . . . flown like a dream.
But you must long for the daylight. Go, quickly.
Remember all these things.

—Homer, *The Odyssey*
(translated by Robert Fagles)

CHAPTER ONE

THE LAST TIME I SAW my sister we played hide-and-seek. My dad was still alive then too, and heart attacks were something that happened to other people. My mom wasn't drinking back then. Or maybe she was. It's hard to know when you're a kid.

We were supposed to be playing in the yard, but I knew Clare had gone inside. From my perch up in the oak tree, I saw her slide open the back door and sneak through. My dad was trying to find us, and I didn't want to be the only one playing inbounds, so I climbed down, darted across the yard, and crept in after her. I found her in the den, her pink Keds poking out from under the heavy curtains. I thought I might hide with her; we usually did that, but for some reason, that day it wasn't allowed. Sensing me, she pulled back the thick fabric, and meeting my eyes, she shook her head. Not today. Today I

1

would have to find my own hiding place. She held a finger up to her pencil-thin lips, and then, closing her eyes, she drew the curtain, disappearing behind it.

It was ten years old, that memory of my sister, and the last one I had, though I knew there must be others somewhere. I must have stood behind the car waving as she and my dad drove off for California. I must have helped her pack. I must have at least hugged her goodbye and inhaled the scent of her for the last time—strawberry ChapStick mixed with soap. But I don't have those memories. I don't know where I put them.

That summer my dad had a conference to go to in Sacramento, and Clare had a camp friend nearby. The mother of this camp friend was a teacher at a boarding school called St. Bede's Academy, and my dad thought it would be great for the girls to have the run of the place while it was empty. *How liberating,* he'd said. He was always going on about how kids these days were too constrained, too protected, unable to roam wild and free like he'd done when he was a boy.

Whether Clare enjoyed the freedom was something we'd never know. On the third night of her visit, she and her friend vanished from their beds. Their bodies were never found.

My aunt Kim, my cousin Danny, and I were sitting at their kitchen table when I told them I'd been accepted at St. Bede's Academy. Kim looked up from her pile of bills and stared at me like I was an alien species. Danny continued munching his Cocoa Puffs.

"Tell me you're joking," Kim said, but she knew I wasn't.

Mom had recently broken a six-month sober stint, and her appearances at home were becoming increasingly sporadic. Soon she would take off again, and I didn't plan on waiting around for her.

"You can't change schools in the middle of the year like that."

"Yes I can. I've already been accepted. Kim, it's a top school, and they're giving me a full ride," I said. "Because of Clare."

My aunt winced.

"*That* school?" Danny stopped munching and froze. "You want to go there?"

"It'll get me into a good college. Besides, I don't want to be home anymore."

"Cally," Kim said before taking a drag off her cigarette. "You can always stay with us. You don't want to go to that place. Danny, tell her she's being crazy."

Danny's eyes met mine. My cousin was a big guy—close to three hundred pounds—with eyes like mud. He was also my best friend. "You sure about this?" was all he said.

"I'm sure," I said, though I wasn't. How could I be?

Danny nodded and gently placed a hand on his mom's arm. "Cally knows what she's doing. She goes there, she could probably get into Stanford or something. Let her go if she wants."

Kim winced again and stubbed out her cigarette.

It wasn't that I needed permission—Mom had already signed everything that needed to be signed—but Danny and Kim were important to me. Maybe I wanted their approval. Maybe I wanted them to stop me.

But no one did stop me, and a month later, I took a plane

down to California and a bus up into the Sierras. It was a gorgeous campus with rolling green lawns surrounded by a dense, rich forest of poplars and pines. The buildings looked like miniature castles, and for the first time, I felt incredibly fortunate to be given this chance. Maybe St. Bede's didn't have to be just my escape. Maybe it could be something more. Maybe it could be my opportunity.

I was met by Mrs. Harrison, the headmaster's wife, a sweet redhead with bouncing curls. She called me sugar and looped her arm through mine. When I'd spoken to Dr. Harrison on the phone, I'd told him I didn't want the other students to know about Clare. I didn't want to be that weird girl with the dead sister. I'd been her enough already. I wanted to be someone new. Dr. Harrison had seemed relieved—what headmaster wanted something like that dredged up after ten years?—but immediately upon meeting me, he offered his condolences and told me his office was always open. Then he handed me my orientation packet and pointed me toward my dorm.

My dormitory was called McKinley, and I was lingering in its dimly lit foyer, searching through my packet for my room assignment, when someone stepped into the hallway.

"Um, hello?" she said, her voice scratchily feminine as she held a hand up to her eyes as if it would allow her to see me better. "I was just about to turn on the lights."

"Hi," I said into the darkness. "I'm Cally Wood. I'm new."

She stood for a moment, small and wispy, and I remember now that I thought she must be a student, and a younger one at that. But then she switched on the light and I saw that her face had the sharp demarcations around the cheek and jaw of a woman in her early twenties.

"Welcome," she said, holding out her hand, but something in her eyes told me that I was not, in fact, welcome, that there was something she was doing in her apartment that she wanted to keep on doing, and that she didn't want to have to deal with me. "I'm Ms. Harlow. I'm your dorm head."

"Hi," I said, shaking her hand.

"Well, let me show you around," she sighed, and brushed her waist-length honeyed curls over her shoulder, only to have them fall forward again.

I followed her through the dorm as she pointed out the showers, the laundry, the common room. She moved languidly, one of those people with a deep inner stillness that always scared the shit out of me. She wore ratty sweatpants with a red *Harvard* curving around her left quadriceps and a white T-shirt that was so old it looked silky and chic. I could see her lavender bra through it, though I kept trying not to. At last we reached my room.

"Four-oh-six," she said, shrugging. "Why it's called four-oh-six when there's only one floor is beyond me."

"Oh," I said, attempting to laugh out of politeness, but only half committing, so it sounded weird and vaguely rude. She squinted at me like I'd just stuck to the bottom of her shoe and now she'd need to decide how best to scrape me off.

"Your roommate's name is Helen Slater," she said, opening the door. "But she won't be back from winter break until tomorrow morning, so you've got the place to yourself tonight."

I said thanks and smiled at her, and she smiled back, but not really, and that was that. I closed the door behind me and leaned against it.

The room was cozy, with warm hazy-yellow walls, two wooden sleigh beds with matching desks, and a sliding glass door that looked out onto an upward-sloping, intensely green lawn. I felt like a gnome hiding in an underground bunker.

My roommate's side was subdued but lived-in. A navy-blue flannel comforter smoothed neatly on the bed. An Egon Schiele print. A few music posters: Leonard Cohen, Bauhaus, Billie Holiday. A smattering of interesting books showing a clear preference for French existentialism. There was a framed photograph of a remarkably pretty little girl wearing makeup and a beauty pageant sash. I hoped this person was not my roommate. She wore a tiara. The girl with the navy comforter and the Bauhaus and the Sartre probably didn't wear tiaras or frame pictures of herself. Or maybe she did. I would find out soon enough.

I stepped into the closet and poked my head inside. The cedar planks were lined with what looked like decades of ball-point graffiti. It was too dark to make out much more than *Ashley Sodor is a Tit Queen!* but that was enough. I unpacked, stuffing T-shirts into drawers, haphazardly draping things in the closet, pretending not to notice when items slipped off hangers and puddled on the floor. I tossed my paperbacks onto the shelves above my desk and threw shampoo and soap into a bathroom basket, which I placed near the door. When I'd finished, I sat on my bed and wondered what I was supposed to do. How did a boarding school girl act? What was going to occupy all the time I would have spent doing slightly illegal and potentially dangerous things with Danny?

I was hungry as hell, so I headed for the dining hall—a crosshatched L at the far end of campus, according to my map. The walk was eerily quiet. Just the odd pair of girls wandering back from dinner arm in arm, intent on not seeing me.

I paused outside the dining hall, then steeled myself and opened the door. Inside, they swarmed like terrible aphids, laughing too loudly, prancing and strutting like all high school kids do, but there was an intensity to them I found un-settling. The boys were especially daunting, trying to sit casu-ally at their tables, passing condiments when you could tell they wanted to go apeshit.

I opted for the soup, which, after surveying the situation, I realized was a poor decision. Soup required sitting. There'd be no ducking out with a sandwich now. I slunk through the rows of tables, looking for an opening. There were seats, of course, but no openings. The din grew louder, and I tried to swallow over the burgeoning lump in my throat. I sat between a pale red-haired boy and a heavy boy wearing a stern expression and a Cthulhu shirt. They ignored me and each other.

I ate my soup, all the while watching a man across the room. He was blond and handsome in a B-list-celebrity way, and he had a dog at his feet—a golden retriever that seemed to be named Tinker. As more and more boys passed, flicked their chins out, and called, "Reilly, what's up?" it became clear that he was faculty or a coach of some kind.

One of the boys who stopped to say hello was intensely easy on the eyes. He was black with vaguely Asian features, bright eyes, and the most incredible body I'd ever seen—broad shoulders and smooth, muscled arms. Nothing extravagant, just everything exactly as it should be. I couldn't take my eyes off him, and without warning he turned and stared directly at me. I looked away and tried to seem preoccupied with my soup, but I must have been completely obvious, because he laughed—a deep, wonderful sort of laugh—and then headed to his table.

I finished quickly and realized I'd no idea what to do with my tray. I stood awkwardly and tried to look around for a place to bus it without looking like I was looking. The last thing I wanted was to appear confused. I walked toward a little room, an annex of sorts that emitted a glow like kitchen lighting. I was just walking in when a pair of long, slender hands slid the tray away from me and set it on a conveyor belt. I followed the hands up to find a teacher with the face of an elven princess. She had arresting blue eyes and ice-blond hair that fell in wispy waves to just below her shoulders.

"You must be Calista Wood," she said, grasping my hand to shake it.

I knew who she was. I had seen her a million times in my dreams, and in the newspaper photograph I kept hidden in a shoe box in my closet at home. She was older now. Ten years older. In my photograph, she was crying, crumpling into a spasm of grief, but in real life, she was fresh and bewitching, and her eyes held no pain. When I wished on stars and birthday candles, this was what I wished for—to be that fresh and empty.

"Yeah," I said, trying my best not to have a weak wrist, looking for recognition in her eyes.

"Welcome," she said. She smiled unevenly. "I'm Ms. Snow,

but please call me Asta. I'm your advisor." I knew that already. Dr. Harrison had told me as much. Presumably he'd placed us together because of some ill-conceived notion that she could help me heal, as if such a thing were possible. "You look scared," she said.

"I do?" I asked, my carapace slipping. There was a sparkle to her eye and a warmth to her smile that intimated that astoundingly wonderful things might happen in her presence.

"It's okay," she said, gently guiding me toward the dessert table. "They all look like you when they get here. You're going to be fine."

"I am?"

"You're going to be better than fine. You're going to have fun." Her eyes lit up and suddenly it seemed like it could possibly be true. "I'm going to make sure of it."

"People don't normally come midyear, do they?" I asked as I watched her wrap some cookies in a napkin.

"Not usually, no." She laughed and handed me the little package of cookies. "You should be really proud of your acceptance. I've seen your PSAT scores. Very impressive. Now, take these back to your room and try to get some sleep. Tomorrow's a big day."

"Thanks," I said, stroking the rough red paper napkin. "I'll see you around, then."

"I'll see you tomorrow. I have you in biology." She smiled. "And in assembly. We sit together in advisee groups."

"Okay," I said, my voice disappearing somewhere inside my throat.

She laughed—a great, open-throated joyous laugh—and

every muscle in my body seemed to relax. "Look at you. So shy. Don't worry, okay? You'll like it here. I promise."

I smiled and nodded, then made a quick exit. Holding the cookies at my side, I headed back to the dorm, determined to go directly to sleep even though it was only seven-thirty. In my absence, the dorm had changed considerably. Girls. Lots of girls with high-pitched, chattering voices. I tried to push through, but the hallway was thick with them, carrying duffel bags or nibbling dinner leftovers. It seemed every few steps I took, two girls erupted into screams and threw themselves at each other, three weeks apparently more time apart than they'd been able to manage. I weaved through them and made it to my room, ready to slip into my pajamas and turn out the light.

Inside I found a gangly redhead going through my underwear drawer while a gamine with huge eyes and a bleach-blond pixie cut spat a viscous black substance into my green mug. Their eyes widened when they saw me, and the blonde covered her mouth. The redhead casually shut my drawer.

"Jesus, this is awkward," the redhead said, looking something like a praying mantis.

"I'm, um, just gonna get my backpack. Sorry."

"Oh my God, no!" squeaked the blonde. "This is *your* room." There was an incongruous globule stuffed in her cheek, slurring her otherwise clarion voice.

The redhead approached and extended her hand. She slumped a bit at the shoulders, possibly an attempt to hide her prodigious altitude, and she smiled sharply, as if reminding herself to hold something back. She wore a formfitting blue sweater and a gray flannel skirt. Her metallic-orange hair was pulled back on one side by a barrette. It hung to her shoulders, thick and intractable. I pulled my oversized Bikini Kill T-shirt farther down over my skater shorts and did my best to brush the hair from my eyes.

"Fredericka Bingham, but everyone calls me Freddy," she said, shaking my hand. "And I just want you to know that under ordinary circumstances, I don't hang around in other girls' rooms looking through their underwear."

"Don't believe a word," Blondie said, and then spat into my cup. "That's practically all she does."

"Wait, Bingham?" I said, recalling a name from a welcome letter I'd received. "Aren't you the student body president?"

"Yeah. I'm going to be a politician, so obviously I'm going to have to have you both killed. You can understand how this might look."

"Of course," I said very seriously, and Freddy smiled for real with big joyously gapped front teeth.

"Don't worry, Noel will be first to go. This is Noel, by the way."

"Nole?"

"Yeah. Noel. Written like the Christmas song, but pronounced like the grassy Kennedy-assassination one," she said, nodding and tugging on her sleeve. She had dressed herself in a sort of punk rock menagerie, fishnet peeking out here, waffled long underwear tucked under there, and she had ringed her eyes in thick black liner. I was impressed.

11

"Her parents named her after Noël Coward, isn't that bourgeois?"

I nodded, completely lost.

"He was a playwright," Noel said, rolling her eyes. "My parents are total assholes. They named my sister Albee, but she changed it to Helen when we were, like, five."

"Wait, your sister . . . is she . . . ?"

"Your roommate. But don't worry, we're nothing alike," Noel said, smiling, then spat again.

"My—my roommate?" I stammered. "I thought she wasn't back yet."

"She's not." Freddy laughed. "Not until tomorrow."

"She's doing Outward Bound, and they got stuck somewhere, can you believe it?"

"And so we came to use Helen's room so Noel could dip. It's disgusting but she does it to wean herself off the cigarettes she smokes over breaks. Anyway, we saw all your stuff," Freddy said, shrugging. "I know. I know. Normal people would have left, but we started snooping. I hope you're not mad. We heard about you, and we were curious."

I took a seat on my absent roommate's bed.

"They never let people transfer midyear," Noel said, her eyes wide. "My God, your test scores must be off the charts."

I shrugged. "They said they had a slot to fill."

"They always have a slot to fill." Noel shook her head and spat into my cup again. "Someone always chunks it and gets sent home for some reason or another. You're more likely to be eaten by wolves than make it all the way through St. Bede's."

"We're lacking hard data on that, but it's basically true,"

Freddy said, taking my green cup away from Noel, who leaned back and set her snowy head against my pillow. They looked at me, and I knew I was supposed to speak, but I had no idea what to say.

"So then you're my welcoming committee because I got high test scores?" I asked.

"How high are they?" Noel asked, her voice breathy, nearly reverent.

"High," I said. "I've got kind of an eidetic memory, you know, like photographic. It's not a classic one, but if I look at a list of information, I can usually recall it for a while. It fades eventually, but it's useful for tests."

"You don't retain any of it over the long haul?"

"Some of it, yeah. I remember definitions. My cousin and I went through a phase where we'd get really high and memorize the dictionary—well, Danny mostly got high, and I mostly memorized, but lots of that stuck. Whatever, standardized test scores are meaningless."

Freddy gasped.

"Helen's going to love you," Noel snorted.

I adjusted a sock that was creeping uncomfortably down my ankle.

Their eyes lingered on me, and I felt gawky and strange.

"You know about the whole no-cell-phones-no-Internet policy, right?" Noel chirped.

"Yeah." I shrugged. "I hate cell phones anyway."

Freddy nodded and smiled like I'd just passed a test. "We do too. And anyway, service is spotty at best here, so it's actually not such a big deal."

"Wait," I said. "Did you just say no Internet?"

"Yeah."

"I knew about the cell phones, but no Internet? What the hell?"

Freddy pursed her lips. "It's not banned like cell phones are, but it's strictly limited. Basically there's one computer with Internet access in the library. You can use it if you need to, but the signal's always going in and out, so it's actually a waste of time."

"So there isn't, like, a computer lab or anything?"

"Oh, there is." Freddy nodded. "State of the art, but it's only for writing papers and making spreadsheets and stuff. There's no Internet in there whatsoever."

"God," I said. "Are they trying to make us feel isolated or what?"

"It's actually a good policy," Freddy said, thrusting out her jaw. "It means we do research the old-fashioned way. St. Bede's has a phenomenal library. And we don't have to worry about the Internet plagiarism problem some of the other top boarding schools have had. So really it's good."

"Yeah," I said. "Sounds great. So are you guys juniors too?"

"Mmm, no. Helen and I are," Noel said, taking my cup back and massaging the handle. "But Miss Bingham here's a senior, and Pigeon's a sophomore."

"Pigeon?"

"Yeah, you'll meet her later. She's, well . . ." Noel rolled her eyes at Freddy. "She's just Pigeon. You can't really describe her."

"Don't any of you have normal names?" I asked.

"What do you mean?" Noel laughed.

"I don't know," I said, laughing too now. "No one here's named, like, Heather, or Kristen, or anything."

"Sure they are. Take Kristen Mitchell or Heather Whatserface. But they don't really *do* anything, so no one really talks about them."

"Do you guys live in McKinley too?"

"No. We live in a nice dorm. No offense," Noel said, and stretched out farther on my bed.

"This is primarily a sophomore dorm. We have singles in Prexy, which is where most of the juniors and seniors live, except for the ones who want doubles, or ones like Helen who are too lazy to fill out their room request forms. They live here."

"It's good for you," Noel said. "It's nice to have a roommate when you're new so you don't get lonely. That's why it's required for freshmen and sophomores."

"So the other girl left, then?" I asked. "The girl who used to live here? Did she get kicked out or something?"

Freddy and Noel exchanged looks, and something heavy settled onto the room.

"Iris," Freddy said. Noel looked at her feet. "She ran away."

"In the fall," Noel said, her voice cracking. I noticed that she'd gone pale. "She was . . ."

"Enough about Iris," Freddy said, getting up and smoothing her skirt. "She was a pain when she was here, and she's a killjoy now that she's gone. It's getting late, and Noel and I have to go."

Noel looked up at Freddy with questioning eyes and then nodded. "If you want, come sit with us at lunch tomorrow. Do you have first or second?"

"What?"

"Lunch." Noel laughed, the color slowly bleeding back into her cheeks.

"I don't know. How do you know?"

Freddy smiled sideways at Noel, who spat one final time into my cup, then set it on her sister's desk.

"If you see us, just come sit with us, 'kay?"

They left me in my room, dusky light trickling in through the curtain as it wavered in their wake. I changed into my moose pajamas and crawled under my big plaid comforter.

I wondered what Clare would think about my coming to St. Bede's. I wondered if she knew I was here. I wanted to tell myself that I could feel her presence—that I was somehow closer to her—but I'd never believed in ghosts.

CHAPTER TWO

WHEN THE ALARM CLOCK WENT off at seven-forty-five, my eyes felt like sandpaper and my tongue tasted sweet-rotten, like decayed fruit. I brushed my teeth, pulled on a black T-shirt and my shorts even though I knew it was too cold for them. Somehow I'd already managed to lose my brush, so I ran my fingers through my hair and hurried off to breakfast. I kept my eyes down, and alone at a table in the corner, I ate my bowl of cereal in record time.

I had English first period. I didn't like English. My English teachers always hated me, partially because I could be kind of obnoxious with my vocabulary, but mostly because I tended not to do the reading. They were also usually grizzly old men, so I was thrown off when I walked into junior English to find Ms. Harlow. In the morning light, she looked about fifteen with her white peasant top and her low-slung bell-bottoms.

She turned from erasing the blackboard and sat on the edge of her desk. She looked peaceful, ruminating, and I was pretty sure she had a belly ring. She was going to hate me even more than those grizzly old men did.

I was just settling into my seat when a distraction of monumental proportions walked in. He was pale and slight, with sable eyes and matching hair, and I thought I could just make out the slant of his hips above his trousers. If I couldn't, it wasn't for lack of trying. He was one of those boys who make you dizzy when you look at them, and when they smile, it feels like you've just stepped into a too-hot bath. It's nearly unbearable, but then it feels good.

I was so taken with him that it was a moment before I noticed the girl at his side. She was black with a cherubic face and a statuesque body. She seemed to be all curves, and her hair poofed away from her head in a magnificent mass of black curls held back by an emerald-green band. Her eyes curved up at the corners like a cat's, and her brows arched finely above them. The boy stroked her hand as he held it, and he stared at her like she was the answer to an impossible riddle. So that was kind of a buzzkill.

"Jack. Sophie." Ms. Harlow smiled, jumped down from her desk, and sauntered over to greet them each with a languid sort of hug. "It's so good to see you guys. How was your break?"

I tried to eavesdrop, but other students were filtering in now, and their conversation dissolved into murmurs.

Ms. Harlow started class with a freewriting exercise, which I'd always considered something of a cop-out; then she asked if any of us wanted to read ours aloud. Unfortunately some of us did. A boy with bleached-blond hair and a puka-shell necklace read something about surfing. A girl with thick, pouting lips read a poem about suicide. I looked over at Jack and Sophie. They seemed to be playing hangman. Maybe they could be my friends.

When the readers had finished, Ms. Harlow clapped leisurely.

"Great stuff, guys. Great stuff. So I've got a question for you all. What makes some writing good and some writing bad? How do we take something that is essentially subjective and make it objective? How do you know if something is literature?"

Oh God. Her eyes roamed the room and I could feel them settle on me. *Oh please, God, no.* I stared down at my college-ruled sheet of doodles and pretended to concentrate. What was literature? *Hmm. I am formulating my opinions, and I'm not quite ready to speak, so I hope no one calls on me yet.*

"Miss Wood?"

I looked up.

Pushing a blond ringlet behind her ear, she gave the impression she was at a Cat Power concert rather than standing in front of a classroom full of students. "Welcome, Cally. So tell us, what does literature mean to you?"

"Honestly . . ." I could barely hear myself speak over my heartbeat and I had no idea what I was about to say. "Honestly, like, this question is so important to me that I almost don't even know what to say about it. I mean, what is literature? How can we know, you know, because it's, like, really super subjective. I mean, who am I to say I hate Shakespeare or whatever? I mean, who am I? And that is, like, the real thing, isn't it? Literature makes us ask ourselves who we are and what we want to know or whatever. It's all about identity."

Oh my God. Had I really just said that? The room was completely silent until Jack fairly burst. "Did you just say you hate Shakespeare?" He laughed. Everyone else looked horrified.

Ms. Harlow wrinkled her brow, clearly disconcerted, and then searched the room for someone who wasn't ridiculous. Her eyes settled on Sophie.

"Miss Taye?"

"Sure, um," she said, her voice strong and clear. "I guess I agree with Cally. Identity is fluid. There's a continuum, and however far away from a white patriarchal view you situate yourself on that continuum is going to influence your view of literature. Makes sense to me."

My God, had she just taken what I'd said and made it sound cogent? I smiled at her, and she winked at me. When class ended, and Ms. Harlow called me up to her desk, I was sure I was going to be kicked out for being an idiot, but instead she handed me a copy of *The Odyssey*.

"We read it in the fall, and I don't want you to miss out. It's a yearlong syllabus, so you're responsible for everything." She smiled, pleased with herself. "I like to teach the books out of chronological order because I feel *The Odyssey* is easier for a high school student to penetrate."

"Wait, I have to read *The Odyssey* and *The Iliad*?"

"I'm not asking anything of you I haven't asked of your classmates. St. Bede's is rigorous, Cally." She gave me a treacly smile. "It's best not to get too far behind."

I nodded and left.

Outside, a gentle rain was falling, and the grounds looked ridiculously lush. Jack and Sophie walked ahead of me, linked arm in arm. With a shock, I realized I was following them, and I had no idea where I was supposed to be going. I reached into my bag and pulled out my schedule and map. It looked like maybe I was going in the right direction. Jack and Sophie stopped ahead where the path split. They embraced quietly and just stood there hugging. I walked past them and tried not to make myself noticed. Then I heard a scuffle of feet and a female voice.

"Hey, new girl," I heard someone call, and when I turned, I saw Sophie coming toward me. "Wait up."

She took my arm in hers like we were old friends.

"I'm Sophie. Are you going to Spanish?"

"Yeah, how'd you know?"

"There's nothing else down this way. I'm in that class too. We can sit together."

We walked the rest of the way, arm in arm. She smelled like lilies.

"It must be scary," she said, "starting midyear."

"At least I'm handling it super well and not, like, making a fool out of myself or anything."

She smiled at me. "That *was* some crazy stuff you said back there."

"Thanks for saving me. I'm not great at talking in class."

"If you don't like talking in class, Spanish is going to be a doozy for you. I'll try to run interference."

"Thanks," I said, trying not to blush. I wasn't used to girls going out of their way to be friends with me, but then, Sophie clearly wasn't your average girl.

"*No problema,*" she said, laughing.

The rest of the morning was far from pleasant. It turned out that the Spanish teacher actually expected us to learn Spanish, and it seemed that most of the kids in the class already knew it. I'd spent the past few years quietly napping while my Spanish teachers played telenovelas on rolling TVs. It was clear I had a lot of catching up to do. I'd always relied on being competent without having to study, but if the rest of my classes were like Spanish, it was going to be a challenge to maintain my extraordinary laziness while at St. Bede's.

When class was over, I felt like I might cry. Sophie put her arm around me and smiled.

"Welcome to St. Bede's," she said. "What do you have now?"

"Um. Chemistry."

"Here, I'll walk you. Jack has chem now too. You guys should be partners."

"Is Jack your . . . your boyfriend or whatever?" I asked, trying not to blush.

"He's not my boyfriend. He doesn't date."

"Oh," I said, not sure I understood. "Do you mean he doesn't date girls? Like he's gay?"

"Not really. He's sexually ambivalent. You know, like Morrissey." Then she stopped and smiled, warm, friendly. She patted me on the back. "Have fun in chem. Just don't let Jack handle anything explosive, and you'll be fine."

The all-American surfer guy from the dining hall the night before turned out to be my chem teacher. His name was Mr. Reilly, and I could tell right away that he was going to be an enormous douche bag. When I walked in, he was flirting with a skittish redhead who was clearly quarterbacking the St. Bede's anorexia squad. He leaned into her and smiled, and she trembled, looking terrified and excited all at once, and then he flipped his head back and laughed.

"Shelly, we're gonna get you out there one morning."

"I don't know, Mr. Reilly. I get really seasick." She tittered.

When he saw me, he stepped away from the little redhead, a complacent smile playing on his too-full lips.

"Hey," he said, strutting toward me. "I'm Mr. Reilly. You must be the much anticipated Calista Wood."

"It's Cally."

"Ah. Kali, goddess of destruction."

"No, just Cally. No destructive tendencies."

"I feel you." He nodded. "Take a seat."

Jack waved and motioned to the empty spot next to him.

"Jack Deeker," he said, extending his hand. "Glad to finally have some help here. My last lab partner went AWOL in October, and I suck ass at chemistry. You any good?"

"Yeah," I said.

"Wow," he said, laughing. "Modest too."

Up close, he was ridiculously toothsome, and he smelled

so good—like fresh cut grass mixed with the mating musk of some exotic ungulate—it made my face ache.

"You okay there?"

"Yeah. Just some, um, allergies. I'm Cally Wood. I'm new."

"Yeah. I know," he said. "We don't get a lot of skate punks at St. Bede's. You kind of stick out." Glancing down at his book, he turned to the section we were supposed to be working on.

"I do?"

"Kind of. If you get a chance, you should let those shorts know it's not 1987."

I flipped him off and he grinned.

"Nah, I'm just messing with you," he said. "How could I not notice you after what you said in English class?"

"That bad?" I cringed.

"Look," he said, pointing to the book. "I know you're supposed to be some kind of genius, but let's just say the jury's out until we see what you can do with my chemistry grade."

After that he was all Erlenmeyer flask this and micropipette that until the bell sounded, and after packing up, he asked me if I wanted to walk to lunch with him. Bounding up the wide steps in the center of the school, he gave me the rundown on what to have for lunch.

"At first, things are going to look pretty good. Edible at least, but trust me, stay away from everything except the rice and the pasta. Even then it's best just to go into the toaster room and make yourself a sandwich. Whatever you do, avoid the soup at all costs."

Following Jack's lead, I made a cheese sandwich. Bologna

would have to wait until I could ascertain whether it would be a controversial choice in my new environment.

"Let's go to the balcony," he said.

As I followed him, I caught sight of Freddy and Noel. Freddy waved, then seemed to take in my company. She pulled her hand back and just smiled in my direction. Noel laughed and Freddy kicked her under the table. I motioned that I was going out to the balcony, and Freddy nodded, clenching her teeth.

Jack hadn't seemed to notice the girls, but once we got outside, he exhaled deeply and raised an eyebrow at me. "Don't tell me you know those two already."

"They were in my room last night when I got back from dinner."

"I'd avoid them if I were you."

"Why?"

"Because they're overprivileged lame-asses." He pulled his knees to his chest and bit into his cheese sandwich.

"Aren't you privileged, though?" I asked. "I mean, you're here, aren't you?"

He shook his head. "Sophie and I are on full scholarships. She's brilliant, and I'm just really really good at soccer. I end up on academic probation every semester. It's really embarrassing. But hopefully you and that chemistry grade are going to turn things around for me."

"I don't know. I have a pretty bad work ethic."

"But you transferred in midyear. No one does that."

"I'll see what I can do."

I liked Jack Deeker. He had a straightforward sweetness about him that reminded me of Danny, though Danny had a good 150 pounds of flab on Jack and definitely wouldn't be caught dead playing soccer.

Just then Sophie came around the corner and gave me a little wink.

"I see you've met Cally. Isn't she adorable?" She lifted a lock of my hair and showed it to Jack as if it were a new sweater. "This hair. Those eyes. It's like a pixie mated with Anaïs Nin! I think we should keep her. Do either of you have a cigarette?"

Jack looked around, then slid a hand into his pocket, retrieved a cigarette, and slipped it to Sophie.

"What dorm are you in?" Jack asked.

"McKinley."

"Mmm." Sophie looked me over, then smiled to herself. "You're taking Iris's place, then."

"She's the girl that ran away, right?" I asked, and then took a bite of my sandwich.

Sophie and Jack exchanged looks.

"She didn't run away," Sophie said, her voice lowered to a discreet level.

"Stop being creepy." Jack intervened. "She ran away last October. Everyone's still a little freaked out about it, and Sophie's convinced we're in the middle of an Agatha Christie and we're going to find her body in a dumbwaiter any day now."

Sophie punched him on the thigh.

"If she ran away, then where did she go, Jack?" Sophie challenged him. "Why haven't they found her yet?"

Jack rolled his eyes. "Because she doesn't want to be found."

He turned to me. "Don't let her freak you out. The police were all over here back in October, and they decided she bailed. She'll turn up, probably on a fucking billboard hawking designer perfume. Sophie just likes the drama."

"Have you met Helen yet?" Sophie cringed.

I shook my head. "Is she really that bad?"

Jack crinkled his nose. "You're going to meet her fifth period and then you can decide for yourself."

"How do you know I'm going to see her fifth period?"

"You have bio with her," he said.

"But how do you know I have bio then?"

"Jack knows everyone's schedules," Sophie said. "He's kind of OCD about stuff like that."

"I looked at yours in chem. The better question is why the hell are you taking two sciences?"

"You're taking two sciences?" Sophie cringed. "Oh God. You're going to fit right in with the Slater twins. You're practically a triplet."

"They said if I took chem and bio I wouldn't have to take an art, and I really really hate art."

"What kind of person hates art?" Jack laughed, incredulous.

"Two sciences?" Sophie sneered. "Gross."

"Sophie's no one to talk. She skipped eighth grade and takes math at Dublin Community College."

"Yeah, but math is fun. Science is for nerds," Sophie said.

Jack flashed me a wicked grin and then took an enormous bite of his cheese sandwich. I spent the rest of lunch out on the balcony with them, wondering when Sophie would smoke her cigarette, only to realize that something as innocuous as smoking was bad business at St. Bede's Academy and would, I surmised, require an after-hours stealth mission to what they referred to as the side of the hill.

Honors history was taught by a man who barely seemed to know he was in the room, and who somehow managed to make China's Cultural Revolution seem about as dramatic as a trip to the dentist. I tried to take some notes but then gave up in favor of examining my fellow students. They were a diligent and focused bunch, with the exception of Sophie, who was blatantly reading a science fiction novel. I hoped we could be friends.

As soon as we were given our assignment (150 pages of *Eastern History, Eastern Thought*), Sophie headed for the door, but I found her waiting for me just outside, her arms crossed in front of her like a schoolmistress's.

"I'll walk you to bio. I have chem down there. There's something we need to discuss."

"That sounds very official."

"Listen, I don't care what Jack says. Iris didn't run away."

"Okay, my interest is piqued," I said, turning my attention to Sophie. "What happened to her?"

"She was murdered."

"Right." I laughed, but then I saw that she was serious. My books suddenly felt very heavy on my back.

"I'm not joking," she said. "And if you ask me, the police never took her disappearance seriously. There were all these signs that seemed to point to her running away, so everyone just assumed that's what happened, but I don't buy it."

"What signs?"

"Well, first off, she started failing her classes. You didn't know Iris, but Iris didn't fail stuff. Math, art, physics, you name it, she was brilliant. She was my main competition for two years, and then suddenly last spring—poof—it was like she wasn't there. You don't spend half your life busting your butt and excelling just to decide one day that you don't care any-more."

"You do if something bad happens to you."

"Exactly," she said, snapping her fingers repeatedly.

"But that just lends credence to the whole running-away theory, doesn't it?"

"Not necessarily. See, there were other things. She started getting sick all the time. It seemed like she was always camped out in the infirmary. Only, she didn't really seem sick to me. She seemed like she was avoiding something.'"

"What was she avoiding?"

"I don't know, but I started wondering if maybe she was in some kind of trouble. See, Iris didn't come from money, but last year she started dressing like a model. She was on an academic scholarship like me. Her parents definitely didn't start buying her designer clothes all of a sudden, so how'd she get them?"

"Did she have a job?"

"She did a work-study as Ms. Snow's lab assistant, but that's a pittance."

"So what are you saying?"

"I don't know. I just think there are a bunch of pieces that don't necessarily add up to a whole, and if I were you, I'd watch my back."

"Why me?"

"Oh, I forgot to mention—because Helen killed her."

I tripped over a rock, stumbling forward onto my hands and knees. I heard a smattering of laughter erupt behind me. I pulled myself up, dusted off my shorts, and kept walking.

"Sorry," I said. "Did you just say my current roommate murdered her previous roommate?"

"Yeah," Sophie said, laughing. "I just thought you should know."

"It *was* thoughtful of you," I said. "Do you have, um, evidence that Helen killed Iris?"

Sophie shook her head. "Just a gut feeling."

We entered the Hardwicke biology building, a redbrick Georgian number in stark contrast to the Gothic gray architecture that dominated the rest of the campus. Inside, everything was white and shiny and unnecessarily curvy.

"Well, thanks for the heads-up, I guess," I said, still trying to decide if I was being hazed.

"I'm gonna be late," she said. "We'll talk later." She gave me a quick wave, then left me alone in a corridor lined with glass cases displaying various bones and models.

"Okay," I whispered to myself. "What the hell was that?"

When I walked into the biology lab, I drank in the cool laboratory rush of fresh oxygen, marble-covered work spaces, and metal spigots ready and willing to spurt air at my bidding. There were only a few kids in their seats, and only one of those stood out. Though I could see a resemblance between her and Noel, they were far from identical and seemed almost to be carved from different material. She was unlike anyone I'd seen so far at St. Bede's. Alarmingly beautiful, she emitted a sort of sixties chic. She wore her long dark brown hair swept up from her chiseled face, achieving a slight poof at the top of her head. Her dark blue eyes were offset by what looked like fine black eyeliner, and there was a wildness to them that I found immediately disconcerting.

Helen looked at me starkly, coldly, and it was obvious that she knew who I was. And then her face lit up, and she pushed herself out of her seat and moved toward me, the cold exterior falling away to reveal a delicious, caramel warmth. Approaching me, she grasped my hand, and then she led me to her lab table. All eyes were on me. Audrey Hepburn had been summoned from the grave specifically to shower me with affection.

"Cally, right? I'm Helen, want to chop up dead things with me?" Her voice, scratchy and low, called to mind sixth-grade boys and unrequited crushes. "I saw you talking to Sophie Taye outside. What's she been saying about me? She hates me, you know. I think I, like, made fun of her pencil box in ninth grade or something. I was kind of a bitch then. I heard you caught Freddy going through your stuff. You could get her impeached if you wanted. So where are you from, anyway?" She fell back into her seat like a stream of fresh water languishing into a marble fountain.

"Yeah, um," I said, sitting, feeling clunky. "I met Freddy and Noel last night."

"Noel told me. We're twins, you know, but as you could probably tell, she got all the ugly genes. She's coming to bio. She can't stay away from me. Kind of a stalker."

I felt someone's eyes on the back of my neck and turned to

find the dark-skinned boy from the night before sitting in the last row. I almost had an aneurysm when he smiled at me.

"That's Alex Reese," Helen whispered. "He's kind of the big man on campus. Captain of most sports, straight-A average, head prefect too."

"What's a prefect?"

"They're like liaisons between the students and faculty. It's prestigious. It helps you get into college. Freddy's one too, and Tanner, have you met Tanner yet?"

I shook my head.

"He's boring and blond and fratty. Freddy has a thing for him, but he's been going out with Cara Svitt since her freshman year."

"Got it," I said, doing my best not to appear overwhelmed. I stole another look back at Alex, and he laughed quietly to himself. Then he leaned back in his chair, his arms, a symphony of delicate tendons, crisscrossed behind his head. My Lord, I was starting to like this school.

Asta entered laughing, pale green chiffon swirling around her, two adulating girls in tow. Everyone seemed to perk up a bit when she entered. The girls took their seats and Asta leapt up to sit on her desk. Looking around the room, she met each of our gazes, seeming to delight in our very existence. And then she laughed again—that deep, growly sort of laughter that came from her chest.

"My God, don't you all look morbid. Is it really that bad to be back?" As she spoke, I could feel the room lightening, feel my muscles relaxing. "I hope everyone had a great break," she said. "I hope you're all well rested and ready to take on a new semester. I've been here the whole break working." She grimaced. "But Dr. and Mrs. Harrison just got back from Belize, and they've got some amazing samples I'm going to bring in. We're going to have a really fun semester, I swear." She crossed her legs, revealing delicate ankles. "We're going to take on the infamous Drosophila melanogaster in genetics lab. Three cheers for fruit flies!"

Freddy and Noel trickled in late, waved to me and Helen, and took a seat at the table in front of us. Asta raised an eyebrow at them. "And let me remind you that I do not tolerate tardiness. I've already spoken at length about my reasons for being rather strict regarding this, and rest assured the first day back from vacation is no excuse. Now today we shall revisit the swine, because I feel I owe it to you, considering what happened in the fall." She hopped down from her desk and began handing out fetal pigs.

"Delicious," I said, trying not to gag.

I tried to focus, but it was difficult not to stare at Helen. It was like being in the same space as a movie star.

"You'll be pleased to know that I didn't go through any of your stuff," Helen said, taking up a scalpel and jauntily slicing into the gray-pink flesh.

"That was big of you. Don't cut that part. I think it's the spleen."

"Poor piggy," she said, pretending to pout. "So Cally, or do you go by Calista?"

"Um," I said, still kind of dazed. "Cally."

"I'm going to call you Wood. Are you nervous about living with me?"

"Why would I be nervous?" I said, but I stumbled over the words, and it was clear Helen couldn't help laughing.

"There are always rumors about me. Did you hear the one about me killing my roommate?"

Heat and blood rushed into my cheeks.

"That's a classic. Don't get me wrong, I'd love to think of myself as the femme fatale, and it's true that I didn't care for Iris, but I'm perfectly certain she's alive somewhere, if not well, because, let's face it, the girl was bananas. She's probably in an institution gnawing her arm off as we speak."

A very small black girl with very large glasses rolled her eyes and raised her hand. "Ms. Snow, I'm finding it difficult to concentrate with all the talking."

"Sorry, Drucy," Helen muttered.

Asta approached, smiling at me with a maternal softness before turning her gaze to Helen. "Miss Slater, as fascinating as I'm sure your insights into the lab must be, I'm going to have to ask you to keep them to yourself."

"Okay," Helen said, unflappable, and went back to work.

Asta lingered a moment, sitting neatly on the edge of my work space.

"And how are you getting along, Miss Wood?"

"Me? Fine. Fine. I'm, um, yeah."

"Let me know if you need any help with anything. St. Bede's can be a touch fast-paced, so don't worry if it feels kind of crazy at first. I'm sure you'll fall right into step, but if you should need anything, my door is always open." She smiled and gently patted me on the shoulder.

"Your test scores must be ridiculous, Wood," Helen whispered after Asta walked away. Then she looked at me as if she were only now seeing me for the first time. She shook her head and laughed. "I think we're gonna have a fun semester, Wood. I really do."

Sports tryouts were directly after school. I didn't have tons of experience with team sports. I enjoyed watching them on TV with Danny, and I wasn't exactly bad at them, but my phenomenal laziness had prevented me from excelling at any. Unfortunately, at St. Bede's, laziness wasn't an excuse, and sports were mandatory.

Noel caught up with me walking out to the field, a large stick slung awkwardly over her shoulder.

"Are you shooting for varsity?" she asked.

"I have no idea what I'm doing," I said, noticing that everyone else was wearing boys' basketball shorts that read *Dartmouth* or *Yale.* I looked down at my Dickies and shrugged.

"Are you any good at lacrosse?" Noel asked.

"I don't even know what that is."

"Good, then you're coming with me. Freddy, Helen, and Pigeon are on varsity. My sister's the captain, and you'd think that would get me on the team because of, like, nepotism or something, but it never does. Come on, we'll try out for JV."

"Which one's Pigeon?"

"Over there," Noel said, pointing out a dark-haired slip of a girl walking with Helen and Freddy.

"She's cute."

"She's a nightmare," she said.

I was given a lacrosse stick, and we hopefuls were broken into three lines, the center girl given the ball. Then we were supposed to do something involving running down the field and putting the ball into the goal. I managed to avoid the line of girls who were supposed to do something with the ball, and spent the afternoon sort of lurching down the field, hoping not to fall into ditches. When I watched Noel descend upon the unmanned goal and miss it by a good three feet, I knew that neither of us would make JV. Rather than humiliate ourselves by being the only upperclassmen on third team, we decided to pursue independent walking as our sport—something I was pretty sure Noel had made up on the spot. She said someone named Ms. Sjursen would sign off on it for us.

"Will that count?"

She thought a moment. "I think so. She's a little bit senile, but she's good with lists. She runs the equipment center and just sits there marking stuff in and out all day. She can just mark us in and out as well. Plus she likes me. I bring her cookies sometimes."

We were walking by the varsity field on the way back to the dorm when I first met the disaster I would come to know as Pigeon. She was sitting on the bench, picking at her nails and biting her lower lip, when she saw us and waved. She jumped up and ran over, faster than I've ever run.

"Oh my God, are you Calista?" she yelped when she reached us.

She was lithe and bronze with huge brown eyes and dark

36

hair pulled back in a tight ponytail. There was something a little off about her. She wore her lacrosse kilt buttoned high and tight at her waist when the other girls wore theirs slung down around their hips. And she was unattractively thin, all her edges firmly demarcated as if she were perpetually posing as an awkward nude.

"She goes by Cally," Noel sighed.

"Did you guys make JV?" Pigeon asked with a soft lisp, looking me up and down in a way that I could describe only as impolite.

"We decided to do independent walking instead," Noel said, smiling at her like she was a benighted child.

"Oh my God, what, like just walking around?" She laughed too loudly and made a face at my shorts. "Where did you get those shorts? They're enormous. Are you being, like, ironic or something, because I don't get it. So walking around? Just walking around? That's not even a sport. Did you get it okayed with someone?"

I backed away from the sheer force of her, though she was so small I feared a light wind might topple her.

"Pigeon, you're in," an exasperated girl called from the field.

Pigeon jerked her head around to the girl, shrugged, gave my shorts one more pained look, and loped back to the field.

"Wow," I said, finally exhaling. "So that was Pigeon, huh?"

"Yeah," Noel said as we continued on. "That was Pigeon."

"She's kind of like an eight-year-old on crack."

"Oh, just you wait."

"Where's she from?"

"Spain. Her parents are descended from Spanish royalty or

something. It's not that she's a bad person or anything, but ten minutes alone with her and you will want to kill yourself."

"And she's a sophomore?"

"Yeah."

"So why do you guys hang out with her?"

"Helen loves her. She thinks she's hilarious. She just showed up to lunch one day dragging Pigeon along and insisted we integrate her. We all thought it was some kind of elaborate joke. I mean, you never know with Helen. My sister eats Sno Balls for dinner and I still don't know if she's just being eccentric. But she was adamant about Pigeon and, well, here we are."

"They still make Sno Balls?"

"Yeah. She's so weird."

Noel headed off to her dorm, and I took the long way back to mine, skirting the edge of the woods, listening to the whistle of the wind in the pines.

Walking around St. Bede's, I couldn't help thinking of Clare. With every step I took, I wondered if the ground beneath me had been touched by her feet, so big back then in her pink Keds and her purple socks, turned tiny with time. I imagined that now I would be able to hold one of them in my hand. That wasn't supposed to happen. Big sisters were supposed to stay big.

Had she played hide-and-seek in the empty hallways of what was now my dorm? Had she drawn her looping flowers on the chalkboard of my math classroom? Early that night—the night they'd disappeared—a fire had started in the woods. The campus went to bed thinking it was under control, but it wasn't, not really. At some point the wind blew the wrong way, and the whole forest lit up like a Christmas tree. When they evacuated the school, when they came knocking at the door, the girls weren't in their beds. They found no sign of forced entry, and Ms. Snow had heard nothing while she slept.

They had wandered off into the woods, they said, two little girls stealing away from their beds just past midnight, to play some unknowable children's game. They must have ended up in the woods, they said. They must have ended up in the heart of the fire. Those were the actions of normal children, they said, of difficult children, but Clare hadn't been a difficult child.

I wasn't there, so I didn't see the frantic search, the inevitable failure. I missed the heroism of the firefighters who put out the flames, who saved the school and the town from destruction. I missed the aftermath and the fruitless hunt for remains. My dad was there soon enough, of course. The heartbreak of it, the futility, was probably what killed him in the end. I was hundreds of miles away, and a child, so what did I know? But part of me had never believed that Clare would do something so stupid, so dangerous. Part of me would always hear a string of chords just beyond the range of sound, a leitmotif that ran through my life, whispering that the truth of what had happened that night was someone else's secret.

Later as I was dressing for bed Helen asked me if I wanted to "take a Saturday night" at her house.

"I don't know what that means," I said, pulling on my yellow moose pajama bottoms.

"The first weekend of the semester, a lot of the parents are still around, so after Saturday classes, we can go off campus. The others are going out to dinner with their parents and then staying the night with my family at our lake house. You can come too. You can even come to dinner if you want."

"Um, I don't know," I said. As far as I was concerned, the jury was still out on Helen, and I didn't want to end up the butt of some joke.

"Some of the boys are going to come over later that night too. Alex Reese will be there."

"That guy from bio?" I could feel myself blush.

"Should I sign you up, then?" she asked, flopping back down on her pillow. "I'll fill out the request for you. You won't have to lift a finger. And Noel and I will drive you. My parents got Harrison to let us keep a car on campus for emergencies. Special dispensation."

"Yeah, I guess," I said, climbing under the covers. And then my body went rigid. "Wait, we have class on Saturdays?"

"Did you even read the viewbook before you applied?"

I shook my head and turned out the light.

"Oh, Cally, my Cally. Welcome to hell."

CHAPTER THREE

SOMETIMES I HEARD THE OTHER kids complain about what a drag it was to be at boarding school and how they wished they were back home. I felt similarly, only I didn't want to be back home. I just didn't want to be at St. Bede's.

I could tell that other kids missed their families, but I didn't miss my mom. I missed the idea of her, but not the actuality of her. I loved her, but she was gone most of the time, even when she was there. It wasn't her fault. She had lost a child and a husband in the same year, and she had been left with nothing, unless you counted me, which I didn't.

St. Bede's kind of sucked, but it wasn't so bad, considering. Back home, I had a few guy friends, but school had been pretty awful. I was shy, and a little weird, and when I was younger, before I figured out I needed to do my own laundry, my clothes were sometimes dirty. Kids could tell when there was something wrong with you—when there was something wrong with your family—and it was like you were an injured member of the herd. They shunned you, because when the lions came, you'd be the first to have her leg torn from her body, and no one wanted to be standing next to you when that happened.

But Danny was in my grade, and he was a loner too, because of his weight and his love of explosive devices, so we always had each other's backs. Only Danny was hundreds of miles away now, and when I tried to call him, his cell phone always went to voice mail. I left messages on the home phone, but no one ever called me back. Kim worked nights and slept days, so we were never on the same schedule, and she tended to switch off the ringer. Still, it wasn't like her not to return my calls.

To occupy myself, I focused on stalking Alex Reese, which I thought could be a pleasant semester-long pastime. I set about trying to engineer our independent walking route so that our path might cross his as much as possible.

Saturday morning I stood in the dining hall dribbling honey over my Cheerios and humming to myself.

"You should put some more honey on that, Wood."

I looked up to find Alex Reese, and down to find my Cheerios absolutely smothered in honey.

My cheeks burned. He knew my name? I had to think of something to say.

"Sometimes you gotta carbo-load, you know? Big game coming up."

"A big walking game, Wood?"

I was pretty excited that he knew what sport I did—or rather

42

that I'd weaseled my way out of proper sports—but I tried to play it cool.

"I'm just doing walking because I'm so good at sports that I didn't want you to feel, like, threatened."

"Oh really?"

"Yeah. New girl comes to St. Bede's, schools your ass in soccer, it would be embarrassing, so I thought I'd just forgo the whole sports thing this year. And to be honest"—I lowered my voice—"I put someone in the hospital last year because they were looking at me funny on the field."

"Uh-huh."

"When I get pissed, I'm like an animal, man."

He laughed and took the honey from me, his fingers brushing lightly against my wrist as he did.

I tried not to watch as he spread the honey on his toast, but then I tried not to seem like I was trying not to watch, because that was for sure weirder than just watching.

"You're kind of odd, aren't you, Wood?" he asked.

"Yeah." I smiled. "Kind of, yeah."

"Okay, well . . . ," he said. He made a strange face, as if trying to take in the full scope of my weirdness. Then he smiled at me, and my stomach surged. *Please, God, don't let me puke on his shoes.*

"See you around," he said, and winking, he strode out of the room, leaving me alone with my viscous Cheerios. I shrugged and then tossed some Cocoa Puffs in for good measure.

*   *   *

I was all set to go as soon as possible that afternoon, but we had to wait for Noel. She did a work-study as Ms. Snow's lab assistant and, according to Helen, was not very skilled at her job.

"Noel's a mess," she said. "I don't know how you could ever want her to help you organize anything. The other day, Asta had her help her with something at the house, and somehow Noel nearly set the place on fire making them tea. My sister is hopeless."

When Noel finally arrived, she looked harried and confused, but was quick to declare herself the driver. In their parents' much-too-nice car, we headed out to their lake house, which, they explained, was no more than a short hike through the woods behind school but could be reached by car only on a steep and narrow road that curved around the lake. The twins seemed to think this added a good thirty minutes to the journey, but we were there in less than fifteen.

Noel drove wildly, and she smoked while she did. Every once in a while, Helen would gently snatch the little white cylinder from her sister's mouth and take a slow, whimpering drag, then gently replace it. I tried to read my detective novel, but my stomach couldn't manage the curves. I folded back the corner of my page and opened my window, drinking in the fresh pine scent.

"You're going to love Richard. Isn't she going to love Richard, Noel?" Helen, all sparkling and perfect, turned around to smile at me.

"Who's Richard?"

"Our father. He's amazing. And Magda's okay too," Noel said.

"Magda's a bore."

Magda, I surmised, was the mother, and she was waiting for us in the driveway when we pulled up. Little more than an afterthought when set beside her daughters, she had wan orange hair that she wore swept up. Richard Slater was young and terribly good-looking. He wore a tailored Italian suit, and he flashed me a smile before being tackle-hugged by his daughters. I was left staring at Magda.

"You must be Cally," she said as if my name tasted sour. "Welcome. Welcome."

She took me by the arm and led me into the house, a modernist spectacle, several stories tall with steep gray steps that led down to a boathouse and then to moody gray water below. Despite its mass, the house was warm and open, with light streaming through windows and flowers bursting forth from most surfaces. Something involving birds of paradise and purple hyacinths awaited us in the loggia.

Magda took a seat on the daisy-print sofa and motioned for me to sit beside her. She turned her rigid body toward me and appraised me like she might a new set of pearls.

"So the girls tell me you're from Oregon. We're from San Francisco, of course, this is just our little vacation spot, but we do love it."

"It's really beautiful here, and your house is . . . wow."

"Thank you," she said, leaning forward, dimpled chin on ruddy knuckles. "I hope you're adjusting to boarding school. I know it can be a bit of a shock. What do your parents do up in Portland?"

"Um," I said, shifting in my seat. "My mom's between jobs."

45

"I see. And your father?"

I tried to swallow over the lump in my throat, to push my way past the familiar longing in my chest.

"He died when I was seven."

A perfunctory gasp from Magda. "My condolences, of course."

"Heart attack," I said like a child who'd memorized words she didn't understand.

"Well," she said, patting my knee, but then it was clear she had nothing else to say. Wrapping a blue cardigan around bird shoulders, she stood abruptly. "We should find the girls. I'm going to go check the toiletries. You head into the kitchen. I'm sure they're in there, getting into the wine already." And with that she disappeared around a corner and shut a door behind her.

I walked along the hall, my Converse squeaking on the red baked tile. The twins were not in the kitchen but another girl was. She smoked and seemed to fairly drip off the counter on which she sat. She was oddly, disconcertingly beautiful in a way that made no sense. Her hair was an ugly grayish blond, more gray than blond. Her lips, too full and caked with cherry-red matte, were shaped by nature and accentuated by character into a brutal pout, and her skin was nearly translucent.

"You're the roommate," she said, her voice a little too nasal. "I'm the neighbor."

"Hi."

"I'm Chelsea . . . Vetiver. Chelsea Vetiver. I tell you that because people say I don't make sense unless you know both my names. What do you do, anyway?" she asked, slipping off the counter.

I laughed but saw that she was serious.

"I'm in school. I'm seventeen."

"Well, so am I, but that doesn't, like, define me." She opened the fridge and stared distantly at some item within. "Okay, so you don't do anything now, but what do you want to do with yourself?"

"Like when I grow up? I don't know." I shrugged and thought about the book I'd been reading. "I guess I'd kind of like to be a private detective, you know, like Philip Marlowe. Like in those novels."

"Detective novels," she said as if she were explaining the color wheel to a slow child.

"Yeah." I shrugged again. "I guess so. So what do *you* do, then?"

"I'm an artist. I make art. Some might even call me an art star."

"Really?"

"No." She removed a jar of expensive-looking marmalade from the fridge and unscrewed the cap. She almost dipped her finger into the orange goo but at the last second wrinkled her nose and looked around for a spoon, which she located in a drawer near the pantry. "Maybe someday. Right now I mostly take photographs and do things to them."

"Like what?"

"Do you know anything about cameras?"

"No."

"Then it wouldn't make sense and I don't have time to explain it," she said, chewing on the end of the spoon, which had previously contained a little dollop of marmalade. I laughed again, but she just stared at me. "I'm going to take pictures of you sometime. I was going to use Helen but she's too peachy. I want something a little dark, a little ghastly, you know?"

"I'm not too peachy; I'm just not a nudist," Helen said behind me.

"I didn't hear you come in," Chelsea said.

"You know me. *On little cat feet.*"

The two girls hugged like porcelain dolls.

"How's school?" Chelsea drawled.

"Horrible."

"Serves you right for being too dumb to get into Exeter."

"We didn't apply," Helen mouthed at me, shaking her head.

"Let's go outside and have a cigarette. My brother sent me some Gauloises from France. He's such a candyass."

Forgetting about me, the two of them swayed out the screen door, and I realized that Chelsea Vetiver hadn't been smoking. She was just the kind of girl who always seemed to be holding a cigarette.

Dinner was pizza eaten standing up around the kitchen counter, Magda staring at me as if I were a virulent strain of encroaching fungus, Richard dashing into the room now and then to grab a slice and make a mildly funny joke and then dashing off again to take care of some amorphous kind of business in his home office.

"He's an investment banker," Noel whispered as if that meant he cured cancer, and I nodded and tried to seem impressed. The girls would perk up whenever he entered, and seemed to deflate in his absence.

Freddy and Pigeon showed up just as I had solved an argument over who should have the last piece of pizza by taking it for myself. They looked flushed, like maybe they'd been drinking with dinner, and they carried grocery bags, one of which seemed to be clink-clinking with wine bottles.

I avoided drunken teenagers, Danny and his Strawberry Hill Boone's excepted, because where there were drunken teenagers, there tended to be an inordinate amount of groping and puking. It was clear, though, that things would be different at the Slaters'. I had the impression alcohol was condoned, encouraged even, by the parents who practically extolled the virtues of adolescent drinking—stopping just short of using the phrase *on the Continent*. Everyone adjourned to the loggia, and Helen's parents poured us each a modest amount of red wine. I waved mine off.

"Antibiotics," I said.

"So, girls, what's all the gossip?" Magda asked, staring over her wineglass.

"Well," said Freddy, leaning back and giving her wine a little swirl, "I'm starting to think being president is no fun. I want a dictatorship."

"Next on to the White House, am I right, Miss Bingham?" Richard laughed and poured himself a plentiful glass of red.

"God willing."

"That's the spirit," Richard said, taking a seat across from me. He had sharp, clean good looks that he'd passed down to his daughters and a set to his jaw that made him seem jaunty and fun. Guys like him always creeped me out.

"We're all holding out hope," Noel said, sipping lightly.

"And how are your parents, dear? Still spending a lot of time on the Continent?"

There we go. Where was I? What was I doing with these people? I felt like a foreign exchange student struggling to understand inscrutable customs. I wondered if it would be rude to excuse myself and head up to bed. But just then, a knock sounded on the glass loggia door, and I jumped a little in my seat.

"My God, Calista. You are such a chicken," Pigeon said, laughing. "It's only the boys. Don't worry, I won't tell them about how you are such a chicken."

Alex Reese strolled through the front door with Brody Motley. My heart simultaneously leapt and constricted. I'd forgotten about the boys. I wasn't ready for this. I was one step away from crawling into my moose pajamas. I'd thought I was in girl territory. I'd thought my actions were allowed to be sleepy and safe. Now I was going to have to sit up straight and tuck in my tummy, worry about how my boobs looked and check for crap in my teeth. I didn't have that kind of energy.

I liked the idea of being around Alex Reese, but I didn't want to be too obvious, so I set myself talking to Brody, a hockey-player type with shaggy brown hair and a sweet way about him.

The parents went up to bed after the boys arrived, and soon several bottles were uncorked and the wine started flowing more freely. At some point, Alex got up to go to the bathroom, and when he came back, he sat in the big easy chair next to my end of the sofa. He smiled and leaned over to me.

"So how are you liking St. Bede's?"

"It's nice, I guess." I shrugged.

"Nice?" He laughed. "St. Bede's is a lot of things, but nice isn't one of them."

"You don't like it here?"

"Like it? Of course I like it," he said, then took a big easy sip of his wine. "This place is my ticket to the Ivy League. It's just competitive, that's all. But tell me about you."

For a moment I considered telling him the truth, but no one wanted to hear about dead family members and drunken moms. I knew there were certain kinds of girls—damsel-in-distress types—who could expose their family dysfunction and still be attractive to boys, but I wasn't one of those girls. I was more of a Wednesday Addams type, and since my new mission statement was basically just *try not to freak anybody out,* I decided to play it cool.

"There's nothing to tell," I said.

"You have a boyfriend back home?"

"No," I said. "Boyfriends are boring. They always want to, like, hold hands or make out to Coldplay."

"I'm not boring, and I don't listen to Coldplay," he said.

"Good to know."

He nodded, and when he held my eyes for a moment too long, I began to wonder if something was going on between us. But just then Chelsea Vetiver materialized, a thick swamp cloud of effluvium gusting into the room.

51

"Reese, Brody, what's up?" she asked, planting herself firmly on Alex's lap.

He lit up when he saw her, the dumb-puppy-dog look washing over him like so much syrup. She had won the battle, but maybe I could still participate in the war. Though, I had to admit, if she'd won the battle simply by walking into the room, things did not look especially good for me.

"So are you guys *creeching*?" she asked, and rolled her eyes.

"What's creeching?" I asked, sipping the soda water Noel had given me.

"It's when you sneak out of your dorm at night," Helen said. "It's pretty much the worst thing you can do other than cheating."

"Wow," I said. "Next you'll be mainlining battery acid. Kids these days."

"Yeah, pretty wild, right?" Alex said.

"So you walked here?"

"There's a trail through the woods behind school. Lets out basically right here."

"It was scary as hell with just two of us, though," Brody said. "I'm used to meeting up with the whole crowd."

"I was there, man. I had your back."

"You're big, but I bet you'd just lose it if you saw a ghoul or demon or whatever the hell's out there."

"You guys are a couple of weenies," Chelsea said, lighting a cigarette. "There's nothing scary in these woods."

"Like hell there isn't."

"Chelsea, dude," Alex said, adjusting her on his lap so he could look her in the face. "All due respect, but everyone knows these woods are straight-up haunted. We do this walk all the time, and there's always some scary fucking noise that can't be explained. Ask anyone."

"That's such nonsense. I grew up in these woods. You're hearing coyotes."

"We're hearing fucking Bigfoot or the yeti or some shit," Brody said, laughing.

"I'll tell you what we're hearing," Alex said, leaning in, his voice lowering to a moody whisper. "We're hearing the lost girls."

Helen straightened up. "That's not funny, Alex. Don't talk about it."

My chest clenched.

"Oh my God, you guys, Wood doesn't know," Pigeon said, getting all flustered and gesticulating haphazardly. "The woods are haunted. These two little girls were murdered out there."

I coughed, and the cracker I was eating went spewing all over the glass coffee table.

"They weren't murdered," Noel said, color rising in her cheeks. "They died in a fire."

"No." Pigeon shook her head dramatically. "Seriously, you guys. They wandered off into the woods or whatever, but they were totally murdered."

I clenched my teeth and tried to slow my breathing. This was not the turn I'd expected the conversation to take.

Chelsea stood up and circled the group, leonine, in search of something to pour into her empty glass. "Um, why have I never heard this story?"

"Because you don't go to our school," Brody said, pretending to snarl at her. "Why are you even here, Chelsea Vetiver? Aren't you supposed to be at Exeter?"

"The semester hasn't started yet. Anyway, I call bullshit."

"No," Noel sighed, resigned. She poured more wine into Chelsea's glass and then into her own. "It's true. It was before you and your grandparents moved here. One of them was our bio teacher's daughter."

"Yeah," Freddy said, shaking her head with the appropriate level of detached sympathy. "The little girl and her friend died in a fire out here in the woods. It was incredibly tragic."

"So, what," Chelsea sneered, "they just wandered out into the blazing forest and died? And one of them was your bio teacher's kid? What the hell?"

"I know, right?" Pigeon expectorated. "You'd think she'd be, like, all weird, with too many scarves or something, but she's totally normal. Like nothing ever happened. People only act that innocent when they're guilty, am I right?"

Helen raised her eyebrows. "Pigeon, tell me you're not suggesting that Ms. Snow killed her own child."

Noel drew in a sharp breath. "Pigeon."

"I assume she set the fire too?" Helen sneered. "Think before you speak, Pigeon."

"No, it's like . . . suspicious, right? They never found the bodies. How did they just disappear?"

"Whoa, Pidge," Alex said. "Watch it."

"No. She's probably right," Chelsea groaned, draining her glass. "It's always the parent. Hey, Wood, you okay there? You're looking a little peaked."

I tried to get myself together and smile along with the rest of them. *God, what an idiot.* How naïve of me to think they wouldn't know about Clare just because she was before their time. Of course a thing like that lingered. It was, I knew, now or never. I would never be able to go back to this moment and say, *Hey, you know, that was my sister who died in that fire. I guess I just forgot to mention that.* If I kept quiet and someone found out later, it would be a disaster. The smartest thing would be to tell them right then and there. But I couldn't. I just couldn't. Clare was a part of me I didn't share.

I furrowed my brow and cleared my throat. "Doesn't it seem weird to you guys, though? I mean, I just got here, like, five days ago, and this is already the second story of disappearing girls I've heard. So is St. Bede's, like, the Bermuda Triangle of boarding schools or what?"

That got an unexpected laugh from Alex Reese.

"They didn't disappear," Helen said snippily. "They died in a fire."

"Either way," Brody said, his voice suddenly low. "There's something weird going on out in those woods. The Bermuda Triangle is a good way to describe it, actually."

"What do you mean?" I asked.

"This area has a sort of reputation."

"Oh, not this again." Alex rolled his eyes.

"It's true. It's not like I'm into any of that crap, but my sister did a report on it when she was here. Trust me, there's been some freaky stuff over the years."

"Define *freaky*," Chelsea said, leaning in.

Brody shrugged. "According to my sister, there are places

that have something kind of strange about them. It's something about the electromagnetic fields or vortices or something. And these places, these vortices, maybe they attract weird things, or maybe they generate them. Dude, I don't know, but these places—like the Bermuda Triangle—there's something wrong with them."

"The Bermuda Triangle is a fairy tale," Chelsea said dismissively. "Name me one other place."

"Okay." Brody shifted around in his seat. "There's this place back east. The, um, the Bridgewater Triangle. And then in Arizona there's the Sedona Triangle."

"Don't forget about the Fresno Quadrahedron," Chelsea said, laughing.

"Stop being a jerk," he said, and beyond the alcohol flush of his cheeks, I could see real color rising. He was genuinely upset. "I'm serious. You can look it up. There's documented proof. These places, I'm telling you, it's like the land is bad."

"And St. Bede's is one of those places?" Noel asked, her voice almost a whisper.

"No, but the little woods are."

"What are the little woods?" I asked.

"Duh. *Those* are the little woods," Pigeon said, pointing out the window. "What we've been talking about, like, all night."

"So the part you guys just walked through, then. The place where you were hearing noises."

"Yeah," Brody said. "These woods are at the top of a triangle that stretches way out into the wilderness behind us. I'm telling you, there are things out there—weird things, bad things."

"Like what?" Helen asked. "We haven't seen anything."

"It's not like people see stuff all the time, but there have been problems with these woods since the first settlers—before that, even. My sister said the Miwok name for the area was the Woods Where Spirits Walk, and apparently they avoided it like the plague."

"How helpful of us to take it from them, then," Chelsea said, examining her black-polished nails.

"Seriously, though, over the years there have been all kinds of bad stuff," he said, a slight tremor to his voice. "I don't remember the figure, but the number of unexplained disappearances and murders in these woods is like ten times what it should be."

"What do *you* think is going on, Brody?" Helen asked, her voice perfectly even.

"Hell if I know. Some people think the land is cursed."

"I don't believe in curses," Helen said, but everyone else was focused on Brody, and I noticed that I could barely breathe.

"Well, I do," he said. "And I'm telling you, whatever happened to those girls, whatever happened to Iris, I think there's more to it than we can know. Whatever's out there, it's powerful. It's dark."

"Okay, dude," Alex said, placing his hand over Brody's glass. "I think I'm cutting you off. You've had enough."

Brody slumped back in his chair, and after a moment of awkward silence, Freddy shifted the conversation to the upcoming spring play auditions. I tried to seem interested, but I was so shaken I decided I'd better excuse myself early.

* * *

Up in my guest room, I changed into pajamas and stared out into the woods. The trees moved against the darkness like an unquiet sea. *This way,* I could almost hear Clare whisper. *Catch me if you can.*

I read somewhere once about a little boy who'd disappeared, and it turned out nothing really horrible had happened to him. A lonely woman had taken him because she wanted a child. Long ago, I'd decided that was what had happened to Clare. She'd never died in that fire. Like Pigeon had said, she'd disappeared. Someone had taken her because they'd wanted a daughter, and they'd loved her and raised her, and now she was a normal girl. Part of me believed that she was still out there somewhere in those woods, and that all I had to do was look and I would find her.

I climbed into bed, turned out the light, and pulled the covers over my head to muffle the distant wail of the wind through the pines.

I awoke to crisp blue sky and sunshine. I zipped up my jeans and let my hair hang loose. I slipped on my shoes and started downstairs, trying to convince myself that the faint scent of strawberry on the landing didn't remind me of Clare. It had been ten years, and I had been young, but the olfactory system was remarkably pitiless.

Breakfast was catered. Catered. Despite my being disgusted by the very idea of it, the food was kind of amazing. The boys were gone, presumably having *creeched* back to campus during the night, and we were all to head off too after we'd had our fill of quiche and gravlax and crêpes.

Freddy chatted amiably about politics with Richard—everything about her poise and calculation.

"Where do you stand on immigration?" she asked, sipping her coffee with a mildly concerned brow.

Helen and Noel tittered while they picked abstractly at one croissant. They seemed nice enough, especially Noel, but their lives were so different from mine. Their breakfasts were catered, for Christ's sake. Noel noticed me staring and, giving me a big grin, waved me over. Helen looked up and smiled too.

"So, Cally," Noel said, "you went to bed so early last night. You missed everything."

"What did I miss?"

"Just stuff. So"—she smiled—"do you have a boyfriend back home or anything?"

"Me? God, no."

"Do you like anyone here?"

"What? No. I mean, I just got here."

"I saw you hanging out with Jack Deeker."

"Him? Yeah, he's really nice."

"Well, can I give you some advice?" she whispered, leaning in.

"Sure," I said, still trying to decide whether gravlax was delicious or disgusting.

"Jack's totally cute, but he's a train wreck. Helen went out with him for a while freshman year. Now he says he's asexual, whatever that's supposed to mean."

"Yeah," Helen said. "I wouldn't go there if I were you. He's hot and all, but he's a total loser."

"Seriously." Noel nodded. "And sometimes it's better to go for the nice guy who doesn't have any baggage, you know? Like Brody or someone. You know, Brody doesn't have a girlfriend."

"Noel," Helen sighed. "Stop playing Yenta."

"Whatever," Noel said, then took a swig of her coffee. "Gross. Helen, did you put sugar in my coffee?"

"Yeah."

"Oh my God, this is so yummy," Pigeon crooned from her perch on the loggia steps. "It reminds me of the Coeur de Lyon. Have you guys ever been there? My mom's coming in the spring and we're all going to have brunch there."

Freddy rolled her eyes at me and I smiled back. Chelsea slunk in just as breakfast was winding down, and managed to grab a little bit of everything before it was taken away.

"Detective Inspector Wood," she said, laughing and sliding a fistful of gravlax into her mouth. "How goes it today? Did you catch any criminals in your sleep?"

"Yep. I nabbed Jack the Ripper."

"Great," she said, clapping. "I knew you were a talent." Then she headed toward Freddy, but Freddy stopped her.

"Did you have a good time last night, Chelsea?"

Chelsea glanced over her shoulder, then frowned at Freddy.

"Yeah," she drawled. "It was fairly monumental."

I was pretty sure I didn't want to know what she was talking about.

CHAPTER FOUR

I RETURNED TO CAMPUS EXHAUSTED and wary. Despite the school's beauty, it was difficult to feel at ease within its corridors, and I found myself longing for company in a way I never had back home.

I tried to suppress my growing disquiet by focusing on the Cally Wood Social Integration Project, but after the weekend I wasn't sure how close I wanted to get to the Slaters and their friends. They seemed nice enough, but they also seemed a bit like hipster debutantes, and that wasn't really my scene.

I quickly realized, though, that my concerns about my new-found social acceptance had been premature. Come Monday, I found that a fine glass wall had been erected between us, and that while Noel and I shared an afternoon sport, and Helen and I might have some laughs together, when they and the rest of the girls took off to do whatever it was they did, I wasn't usually invited. It was as if I'd failed some test I hadn't known I was taking. If I was being purposely excluded, I would have preferred it be overt, but they were all so terribly friendly that I was never sure where I stood.

"They're creepy, right?" Sophie said. "Everyone thinks they're a coven."

"Really?" I said, a spoonful of Cheerios in my mouth.

Sophie and I had taken to eating breakfast together on the balcony that overlooked the ravine. I hadn't had a lot of female friends growing up, and was quickly finding that girls, especially St. Bede's girls, were much more difficult to impress than the boys back home, who thought it was hilarious when I shoved an entire orange into my mouth or wore my pants on my head. I liked Sophie, and she seemed to tolerate me as one might a perpetually unkempt neighbor's pet.

"No, they're not a coven," she said after taking a tidy sip of her herbal tea. "But it would be great if they were, right? It would make things so much more interesting if they skulked around doing witchcraft instead of talking about pedicures or whatever it is that interests them."

"Actually, they all seem pretty smart. I don't think they talk about pedicures."

"I bet they do. They probably quote Foucault while they do it, but they do."

I set my bowl down and pushed it away. "You don't really think Helen killed that girl Iris, do you?"

Sophie shrugged. "I don't know. I don't have any hard evidence or anything like that, but she's hiding something."

"How did Iris go missing?" I asked as I choked down my cereal.

"No one knows really. The first night of fall break, Iris stayed on campus because we had a math competition the next day. She signed in to dinner that night, and she didn't sign in to breakfast the next morning. Somewhere in between she just disappeared."

"Was Helen on campus too, for this academic thing?"

"No. She had one of her big parties. They always have them the first night of break. Out at that lake house. I hear they're basically bacchanals."

"But if Helen was hosting a party during the time Iris disappeared, doesn't that give her an alibi?"

"Maybe it does, maybe it doesn't. Here, eat my toast. I think I'm developing celiac."

Thursday night was our first advisee dinner. I was vaguely aware of my advisee group because we sat in the same row during our weekly assembly, but I hadn't really spoken to any of them. I usually spent assembly doodling and staring a few rows ahead to where Helen and Alex sat side by side, giggling like schoolgirls. Aside from me, my advisee group consisted of five freshman boys and the Cthulhu boy from the dining hall, who was a sophomore. His name was Carlos, and he seemed always to be doing sudoku puzzles and glaring at me.

Asta lived in a small cottage with a thatched roof and dormer windows at the edge of campus. My heart contracted when the house first came into view, and I couldn't help thinking about Clare. There was a slight mist covering the yard, with its rosebushes and fruit trees, from which were tied strange ribbons and little cloth bags. I stood there a moment, listening to the wind move through the trees, and I had a strange feeling that I was being watched. I turned around and peered into the trees. Twilight was just nestling into the woods, and I thought I could hear the night creatures beginning to creep out of their hollows. It must have been their strigine eyes I felt on my body.

I walked in to find a fire crackling and the boys deep in a game of Risk. The freshmen looked up and smiled shyly. I waved. Carlos refused to make eye contact. Savory aromas drifted from the kitchen—butter and cheese and happiness.

I stood for a moment, unsure where to put myself. For someone so small, I was disproportionately destructive and had found that it was usually best to keep my hands in my pockets.

One of the freshmen whispered something in Carlos's ear. He groaned and looked up at me.

"You want to play?" he asked, clearly pained.

"No," I said, taking a seat on the sofa. "I'm cool."

He sighed, seeming relieved. "So, Calista."

"Yeah?"

"We haven't been formally introduced," he said, standing.

"Yes we have. In assembly."

"Well, I'm Carlos," he said, and somehow it felt like an admonishment.

"Yeah. Yeah, I know."

He shook my hand. "Look, I don't want to be rude, but we have to get a few things straight."

"We do?" He was only an inch or so taller than I was, but he possessed so much gravitas he seemed much larger.

"Yeah. Listen, I know you're supposed to be hot shit, but I pretty much rule this advisee group, okay?"

I nodded, bewildered.

"What I'm trying to say here is don't fuck this up for me. You got that?" He raised his eyebrows at me.

"What?" I laughed, but he wasn't joking.

"I'll take you down," he said. "I'm dead serious."

I couldn't say why exactly, but I suddenly liked Carlos very much.

"Yeah," I said. "We don't have to, like, rumble or whatever."

He nodded, all business, and went back to Risk.

Dinner was delicious, pasta with strange gourmet cheeses, basil, garlic, and succulent diced tomatoes. We ate slowly and lounged a bit too long, and the boys continued their Risk game while Asta and I chatted. She filled me in on some St. Bede's history and told me where the teachers had gone to college or grad school. She said that my dorm head, Ms. Harlow, was only twenty-one and had graduated early from Harvard and come directly to St. Bede's.

"Go easy on her, will you, Cally?"

"What? Why?"

"Some of the girls give her a hard time, and, well, Courtney—Ms. Harlow, I mean—has been having a tough time. We want to keep her."

65

"Yeah." I shrugged, thinking Ms. Harlow would not care one way or the other how I treated her.

"You're a good kid, Cally. I'm so glad you've come to St. Bede's."

I looked away, blushing, wondering how much she knew about me.

Around nine, Asta cut it short and told us it was time to go. The boys groaned and packed up their game. I was gathering my things when Asta touched me lightly on the arm.

"Cally," she said. "Stay a minute, if you don't mind. I want to have a word."

The boys filtered out. Carlos gave me a furrowed brow and a conservative wave.

"What's going on?"

"Tea?" she asked brightly as the kettle whistled on the stove. "Come into the kitchen a minute. Take a seat."

I sat down at the large wooden chopping block, next to a vase of gray-white flowers. I reached out and touched a petal.

"What are these?" I asked.

"Those are asphodels."

"I've never heard of them."

"Really? The word *daffodil* is a derivation of *asphodel*."

"Oh," I said, running my finger along the silky petals. "So these are daffodils?"

"No," she said, laughing. "They're asphodels. They're the flowers of the dead. It's said that when you die, if you've led a drab, unexceptional life, then you spend eternity in a field of asphodels. It's one of the lands of the dead, Tartarus and Elysium being the others, for the villains and the heroes respectively."

She smiled and poured the boiling water into two mugs. "I like to keep them in the house. It reminds me to be exceptional."

Soon I had a cup of tea before me, threads of steam swirling off the top, the scent of chamomile making me a little sleepy. She sat across from me, her eyes wide and gentle.

"So, um, Ms. Snow, you wanted to talk to me?"

"Asta. I want you to call me Asta. Listen, Cally, I think we need to confront the elephant in the room," she said, fixing her cool blue eyes on me. "I've been waiting for you to say something, but it doesn't seem like you're ever going to. You know who I am, don't you? You know I'm Laurel's mom, right?"

I nodded, my stomach contracting in unexpected spasms.

"Not a day goes by that I don't think about your sister. Clare was a lovely girl. You remind me of her." She cocked her head to one side. "Why haven't you said anything?"

"I don't know." I shrugged. "I'm not really telling anyone about, you know, what happened."

"Mmm." She nodded. "I see. But why here? Of all the schools, why here?"

"I don't know. I'm getting a free ride, and I figured why not take advantage of that opportunity?"

If she noticed how finely my statement rode the line between bullshit and sincerity, she didn't let on. She nodded, and then, after a moment of silence, she spoke. "I think that's very wise, Cally. Very mature." Then she reached across the table and took my hand. "You know, in some ways, I think it's fate that's brought you here. And I want you to know that you can come to me with anything. I think you're a very brave girl."

Something about the way she smiled at me and the warmth

of her touch reminded me of my dad teaching me to ride a bike, and how with the warmth of his hand at the small of my back, falling had seemed impossible.

Those first few weeks of school were difficult. I did my best to fit in and be social, but I was finding it somewhat awkward. Cliques had been formed so long before my arrival, and were so firmly demarcated, that I just couldn't seem to squeeze my way in. Helen and her crew seemed always to be off doing their own thing, and while Jack and Sophie were usually better about including me, they were like a long-married couple—straightening each other's clothes and kissing each other's cheeks—and spending too much time with them could make you feel like a third wheel.

Every time I came into the dorm, I checked the message board, just in case Danny had decided to get off his ass and call me back, but my name was never written up there. Then, one Saturday evening, I found a message from Kim.

Her voice cracked when she answered the phone, and I could tell she hadn't been sleeping. Danny had been arrested. He'd been caught with explosives in his backpack and had been sent to one of those boot camps for miscreants where they made you stomp around endlessly in the woods, testing the limits of your humanity. When I hung up the phone, I wanted to cry. Poor Danny. The only thing he hated more than nature was exercise. How was he going to manage? Danny didn't always make the best decisions, but he was a good kid. I knew if I'd been home, I would have been with him, and now I'd probably also be marching around in the middle of nowhere, trying to light fires and survive the elements. Honestly, at the moment that didn't sound too bad.

I needed to talk to someone who'd understand, but telling people my cousin had been arrested didn't seem like the greatest idea from a social-normality standpoint, so I just swallowed down my worry and headed to dinner. If I got up there in time, at least I'd be able to sit and talk with someone, even if it was just about the basketball team. But my social timing seemed to be perpetually off.

I saw Sophie and Jack leaving the dining hall just as I was entering. They were flushed with laughter and linked arm in arm. I thought they were going to stop and talk, but they just waved and passed me by. A moment later, Jack turned and grinned at me.

"I like your shirt," he called.

I stared down at my oversized T-shirt with the logo of a Japanese noise band on the front. I wasn't sure whether he was making fun of me.

"Thanks. Where are you guys going?"

"Town," he said.

"We can go into town?"

"Only on open Saturdays."

"Oh," I said, still not entirely sure what an open Saturday was, despite being in the midst of one.

"We're gonna be late for first bus," Sophie said, and pulled him on.

He blew me a kiss and then they were gone. As usual, I had no idea what was happening. I grabbed a grilled cheese and some chocolate milk and went to sit with Helen, Pigeon, and Freddy. They seemed to be just finishing up.

"Hey there." Helen smiled. "You look cute in that jacket."

"Thanks," I said. I looked at the sleeve of my grungy army jacket I wore pretty much every day.

They were starting to clear their plates away, and with a sinking feeling, I realized I'd be eating alone again.

"Sorry we can't stay and eat with you," Helen said. "We're in a hurry."

"Where are you guys going?" I asked hopefully.

"Town," Helen said, looking around the room. "We have to hurry if we want to get ready and catch the second bus."

Plates clattered and Pigeon giggled excitedly as they gathered up their things.

"Maybe we'll see you down there." Helen smiled and then skipped off with her tray.

I looked down at my sandwich and felt a terrible weight on me. I took a bite and tried to choke down a familiar feeling. It wasn't exactly like I'd been excluded, but I hadn't been invited either. Did everyone need an invitation, or was that just me? Was I socially reticent to the point of phobia? Would a different girl simply have invited herself along?

After dinner, I wandered over to the library and went upstairs to the reading area with the comfy chairs. Carlos was up there reading the *Wall Street Journal*.

"What's up, Carlos?" I asked.

He shrugged. "Just catching up on current events. I hate feeling so isolated here."

"Yeah," I said. "Me too."

I read for a while and then fell asleep in my chair. Carlos woke me just before the library closed, and groggily, I made my way back down to my room.

The next day, I was in my room, trying to keep my books from falling over on the shelf, when the door slammed open and Helen came flouncing in. She tossed her copy of *The Complete Works of Shakespeare* onto the bed and smiled triumphantly.

"Audition go well?"

"Let's just say I tore Miranda a new asshole."

"And that's what they're looking for these days, is it?"

"The part is mine," she said, smiling brilliantly. "Cara Svitt was practically crying when I left. Hey, listen," she went on, placing a hand on her jutted-out hip. "Sorry we kind of ditched you last night. I thought you'd meet us downtown, but you never showed."

"Yeah, I went to the library."

"Next time just come with us, okay? I felt really bad."

A moment or so later, Noel trailed in behind her, a Cheshire grin lighting up her face.

"I just had a really good talk with Asta," she said, and sat on my bed, pulling her legs up into the lotus position.

"God." Helen rolled her eyes. "You are developing a serious case of hero worship."

"I am not. We just have really good talks. She's wise, you know, and it makes me feel better to know that someone has the world figured out."

"I'm sorry," Helen said, shaking her head. "But she does not have the world figured out. No one does."

"What are you up to now, Cally?" Noel smiled.

I shrugged. "Nothing. I don't know. I guess I should go to the library. Do some homework."

A wicked grin spread across Helen's face. "No you shouldn't. Come with me." She grabbed my hand and started pulling me from the room. Noel sprang up to follow.

"Where are we going?" I was resistant at first, but soon we were running down the hill toward the theater, the air around us cold and lit with a kind of moist electricity. My knees felt weak and wobbly as we ran. Helen pulled me harder, smiling back at me over her shoulder, and soon we were laughing, swept downward toward a little rock wall. I stuck my hands out just in time to keep from slamming into it, but Helen simply leapt up and perched on top like a sparrow. A moment later, Noel caught up to us, panting.

"What's going on?" she managed to say. "What are we doing?"

"We're hanging out outside the theater," Helen said, and rolled her eyes at her sister.

Noel shot her a confused look, and then the metal front door swung open and boys started trickling out. Shane Derwitz, Brody, Alex Reese. Now I knew what we were doing here.

I glanced sideways at Helen and she smiled at me. I climbed up to sit beside her.

Alex nodded when he saw me. He came over and leaned up against the wall. Brody followed.

"How'd it go?" Helen asked.

"Okay, I guess," Alex said. "Even if I get the part, I'm not sure I'll be able to do it. The coach is kind of on my ass about it." Then he met my eyes. "Why didn't you try out?"

"For the play?" I laughed. "Are you serious?"

"I bet you'd be good."

"Sorry. I can't act my way out of a paper bag."

"What are you guys up to now?" he asked, and I could feel something tingle and lurch up my spine. I'd never met a boy like Alex before. At my old school, a guy as hot and popular as Alex would have been a dick, and probably kind of an idiot, but Alex was different. He was smart, and kind, and I wanted to hang out with him as much as I could. It was a weird feeling.

"Nothing," Helen said. "What about you guys?"

"Let's do something fun," Brody said, taking my hands to help me jump down from the wall. "Let's go up to the pond and look for salamanders."

"Is that, like, a euphemism or something?" I asked, looking to Alex.

He shook his head. "Brody's really into salamanders."

We walked a short way to the edge of the woods and ducked in through an opening in the chain-link fence. I was pretty sure this was against the rules, but I didn't really want to check with the others. Something fun was finally happening, and I didn't want it to stop. Noel and I walked a few paces ahead of the rest, but I could feel the warmth of Alex's body behind me. Soon we were moving into the foliage, bright green leaves gliding against my face. I tried not to slip on the florescent moss. The air was wet, and magical, and cool.

"How far is the lake?" I whispered to Noel.

She shook her head. "It's not a lake. It's just a little pond out in the woods a ways, but it's really beautiful, and, like, ethereal."

"And we're looking for newts?" I asked, crinkling my nose.

"Salamanders."

"Oh . . . why?"

"Because salamanders are cool," she said as if everyone obviously knew that.

As we walked, I became very conscious that Alex was walking a few paces behind me, and I suddenly wondered if my behind might be weirdly shaped. I'd never really thought about it before, but it suddenly seemed terribly important.

After a short walk through lush green foliage, we emerged into a clearing, and at its center was an enchanting body of water. Like Noel had said, it was just a pond, but what a pond it was. It rested there in a near-perfect circle, mist half shrouding its blue-green waters. Electric-green fiddlehead ferns sprang from the earth, bowing their heads toward it in obeisance. Lily pads and lotus flowers rested on its smooth surface. It was as if we had emerged from the forest path directly into the apse of a magnificent cathedral. My breath caught. I had never seen anything so beautiful in all my life. I felt someone's eyes on me. I turned to see Brody smiling.

"This is the place that's supposed to be haunted?" I said. "It's beautiful."

"Well, it's not haunted during the day, silly," Brody said, smiling like a little boy.

"Okay, so where are these salamanders?" I asked.

Alex gently placed his hand on my shoulder. "They're usually around more after it rains, but it hasn't rained for a few days. It probably would have been better to come tomorrow after it rains tonight."

"You can tell it's going to rain?"

"Yeah, I have Native American blood in me and we can all tell magical stuff like that about the weather."

"Really?"

"No," he said, laughing and crinkling his face into a sneer. "What are you, a crazy racist? I read the weather report in the paper."

"Oh," I sighed, my voice catching in my throat. "I'm sorry. I didn't mean it like that."

"Don't worry. I don't really think you're racist. I was just messing with you."

"Are you really Native American?"

"Nope." He smiled and tousled my hair.

The five of us rustled around in the woods for a bit, looking for salamanders, finding none. I did see violet dragonflies, beetles fat as prunes, and frogs the size of thimbles. All the while mist swirled around me, and I found that it had a near-hallucinatory effect. Maybe these woods really were haunted. If they were, this was the epicenter, this little pond. There was something like a presence here that I found seductive and calming. Was Clare out here somewhere, like everyone said? Was it her presence I felt tugging at me through the mist and the trees, urging me to follow? I could have lost myself forever in that strange call. I could have, but I shook myself out of it. It's lucky when you don't believe in ghosts.

I was sitting by myself, playing in the mud like a child, when

Helen called out, "Let's go swimming!" Before I even realized what was happening, she'd stripped down to her bra and underwear and cannonballed into the pond. Noel shook her head and laughed. The boys were quickly stripping down to their boxers. I tried not to look, simply because I wanted to so badly that it made me feel like kind of a perv.

"You want to go in?" Noel crouched in the mud opposite me. "If you're shy about the boys, we can go in at the same time and I'll do something crazy to distract them if you want."

I thought about it for a minute. "Naw. Too cold," I said, shaking my head.

Noel rolled her eyes. "At least come hang out with us."

Nodding, I brushed the mud from my jeans and followed Noel down to the edge of the water.

"Wood, you better be coming in," Alex said, his grin wonderfully potent.

I shook my head.

"You have to," he said. "You can't sit out there all alone. Come on. The water's not cold."

This I knew to be a lie. He was shaking, and goose bumps were rising on his chest.

"She's not coming in," Noel said firmly, walking into the water in her mismatched bra-and-underwear set as if it were the most natural thing in the world.

They didn't stay in long. Fifteen minutes maybe, and all the while I sat there on the bank talking to them. It looked fun, but cold, and I really didn't need to subject anyone to the full extent of my granny-pantied splendor.

"Do you guys come here often?" I asked.

"Not too often," Alex said. "It's really against the rules, but we risk it sometimes."

"I come out here all the time," Noel said proudly. "But for me it's allowed because it's with Asta. We go looking for herbs and mushrooms and stuff, and we always stop here and dangle our feet in and talk."

"You go hiking with Asta?"

"Wood," Alex said, laughing, "I hate to tell you this, but walking a quarter of a mile through some trees is not considered hiking."

"Herbs and mushrooms and stuff?" I said. "What are you guys, like, witches?"

"Right. No, Asta's an herbalist. It's pretty cool. If you're coming down with a cold or something, she'll make you a tea and you drink it, wrap yourself all up, and sweat it out. It works."

"It tastes like ass, though." Brody laughed and splashed water at Noel. She retaliated, springing at him and climbing up to his shoulders to perch there like a bellicose sprite.

"It works," she said, smacking him on the back. "Now giddyup, horsey."

Brody shook her off and she plummeted into the water, emerging a second later only to scream and tackle him.

"You should come in, Wood," Helen crooned, floating on her back. "Come be a naiad with me."

"Sorry," I said. "I don't think I'm naiad material. And not to be a dick or anything, but you're thinking of Limnades. Naiads are only in running water, and this pond is still, so you're probably not much of a naiad either."

She stood up and shook her fist at me. "Come in here and say that to my face. Alex, make her come in here."

He shook his head. "You don't drink, you don't swim, you don't audition for stupid school plays. How are you ever gonna get to know anyone if you keep to yourself so much?"

"You have to go through me if you want to get to know Wood," Helen declared, winding her saturated hair into a dripping knot atop her head. "And there's a price." She leapt onto him, trying to dunk his head underwater, but he threw her off with ease.

When they emerged a few moments later, I tried not to stare at Alex, but he walked over to me, toweling his chest off with a sweatshirt. I could smell the pond, crisp and alive, on him.

"Are you worried about getting caught off campus?"

"Not really," I said. "I just like to know what I'm getting myself into."

He smiled. "You're wise. Wise is good."

I shrugged.

"Seriously, though," he said, leaning down, meeting my eyes. "If you're ever worried, you know, about, like, what the rules are or whatever, just ask me. I won't steer you wrong and I won't make fun, okay? I was the same way when I got here. I'm an overachieving stress case too."

"That's not really how I see myself."

People were pulling on sneakers, and soon we were heading back into the woods, back to school.

"Maybe that's not how you see yourself, but that's how you are," he said, walking next to me, every once in a while the skin on his arm brushing against mine. "That's why you're going to do great things."

"Yeah. Right."

"No, seriously. You're going places, I can tell."

He was looking at me. I could feel it, and I liked it, so I decided to return the gaze like a girl in a movie would do, but as soon as I lifted my eyes from the path, I tripped over a tree root and plummeted to the ground, scraping my elbow.

"Shit," I spat.

"You okay?" Alex said, reaching down to help me up, but Noel swept in from behind and lifted me to my feet.

"Cally, we're supposed to excel at walking. You're gonna give our sport a bad name." She wrapped an arm around my shoulders, and Alex fell into step with Brody behind us. I tried not to seem disappointed.

"Thanks," I said, watching Helen up ahead, dancing through the trees, unaware that she was rapidly losing the rest of her group.

"Want to know a secret?" Noel whispered in my ear, and for a second I was sure that the secret was going to be about Alex and that I was going to like it, but then she said: "I've seen fairies up here."

I laughed, but she just smiled and nodded.

"Right."

"No. I'm not joking. I did. Back at the pond. Clear as day. Clear as those fiddlehead ferns, I saw fairies. Come on," she said, grabbing my hand, tugging me ahead. "Let's catch my stupid sister."

CHAPTER FIVE

IT WAS DAWN, AND HELEN'S soft breathing made the room seem warm and cozy, like Christmas morning. I was gazing through a slit in the curtains when I saw Freddy on the lawn outside my room. A light rain had dusted her rose slicker, and she walked with a purposeful stride. She slid open the glass door and slipped back her hood.

"Time to get up, ladies."

"What are you doing here?" I asked.

She looked over at Helen, who stirred in her sleep. "Okay," she said, kneeling down beside me. "I've got some very serious pot that needs to be smoked immediately."

"It's like five in the morning."

"All the better. That means we'll be thinking clearly again well before study hours."

"What's going on?" Helen asked, sitting up, chestnut hair

matted to the side of her face. Somehow she still looked unfairly pretty.

"We're gonna go smoke."

"Now?"

"Yeah now. Get dressed. I don't want anyone to see us heading out. Pigeon's coming too. She wanted to do her hair first, so I left her in the dorm."

"What about Noel?"

"She didn't want to get up. She was studying French all night."

Helen rubbed her eyes and tried to focus on Freddy; then, reluctantly, she folded back her comforter and swung her legs off the side of the bed. She stayed there a moment, staring at her ankles, her eyes hazy.

"For Christ's sake, will you get up already?" Freddy whined. "I've got magnificent pot. Harrison told me we're having a surprise white-glove inspection tonight, and I've got to get rid of it before then."

"But it's five in the morning, Freddy. Couldn't we have smoked it last night?"

"I didn't have it then."

"When did you get it?"

"Later. Will you just get dressed?"

"For fuck's sake, Fred, I'm trying." Helen rubbed her eyes again, then pushed herself off the bed and stumbled to her closet.

"You too, Wood." But I'd already pulled on my jacket and was zipping up my jeans.

Helen was pulling a lime-green sweater over her head when Pigeon crashed through the door.

"I don't think I'm going to smoke," she announced.

"Then why are you coming?" Freddy asked, rolling her eyes.

"I want a walk."

When Helen returned from brushing her teeth, she gave me a long-suffering look and indicated that we were ready to set out.

The drizzle had stopped, and the sun had fully risen by the time we took turns squeezing through the opening in the fence, but the sky was a graying pink that hinted at more rain. It seemed to me that we were going a great distance just to smoke pot, but what did I know? We passed the pond and took a right up a trail that lurched into the hills. Eventually the path came to resemble less a path and more a collection of plants most likely to give way when Helen hacked at them. I was beginning to wonder where the hell we were going when Helen stopped abruptly.

"Crap."

"What?"

"There," she said, pointing incredulously. Before her was a dirt hill. "That's where we were going. It must have been those rains over break. There must have been a mudslide." She sat down on a rock. "What are we going to do now?"

"Can't we just smoke here?" I asked, and they all stared at me like I was insane.

"This is a really popular hiking trail. Anyone could come along," Freddy snapped. "This isn't a cigarette, Wood. Helen, can't we just go farther down that way? I'm sure we'll find somewhere else."

"This place was perfect, though," she whined. "It was like this little mini cave. You went behind this rock, and under this bunch of vines, and no one could see you. It was awesome."

"Maybe we should just go home," Pigeon suggested. It was hands down the smartest thing she'd ever said.

We did find another place to smoke. It was only a five-minute walk from where we'd been, and it was remarkably similar to the place Helen had described. As soon as we reached it, Pigeon picked up a switch and started hacking away at the foliage at the mouth of the cave like she was a child playing pirate.

"Quit it, Pidge," Helen said, taking her switch away. "We don't want anyone to know we're in here. We don't want visitors, do we?"

"Sorry," she said, and then we started inside. It turned out to be much larger than I'd expected, with an eerie-looking drop-off from which someone had hung a makeshift rope ladder. Helen wanted to climb down and go exploring, but she was unanimously vetoed. While we were setting up, I thought I noticed a strange odor, but I assumed it must be a dead animal or bat guano or something. I wasn't a nature girl, and satisfied myself with the explanation that nature probably stank most of the time.

"Here's good," Freddy said, pulling a blanket from her bag to throw down onto the dirt and propping a flashlight against the side of her blanket. It spread light around the area. She pulled a dime bag from her pocket and tossed it, along with a lighter, a little purple pipe, and a few more flashlights, onto the blanket.

After a couple of hits, I cut out early, like I always did, and lay back on the blanket, staring up into the darkness. I was kind of paranoid about smoking too much pot. I had this fear I might do something I'd regret, or it would be the only time in my life that someone would ask me to recite Avogadro's number, and I'd suddenly forget it. The others clearly did not share my hesitation. Freddy smoked like it was going out of style, and Helen put on quite a show of it herself. Eventually they gave up and lay down too. That morning turned into afternoon and seemed to last forever, moments blurring and slipping into each other.

Several hours passed. We lolled. We giggled. Pigeon slowly unpacked a sack filled with delicious food, which she passed around, and we ate languidly—fingers or strawberries dipped in Nutella, peaches bursting with juice, french bread smothered with jam. Helen was particularly fond of corn chips. She'd spend what seemed like hours staring at each chip, then gently press her tongue against its salty outcroppings, her eyes growing wide with delight, then going all soft and faraway. As far as I could tell, stoned Freddy was exactly like regular Freddy. Helen coaxed her into singing for us. She was the head of the very exclusive a cappella choir at school, and deservedly so. Her voice rang out clear, cutting through the crisp air and reverberating off the dirt walls. Notes seemed so long I felt like I could climb inside each one and float. Every once in a while she'd stop, claiming she wanted to rest and enjoy herself, but we'd cajole her back into singing.

I was lying on my stomach, tapping my nails against the cold, hard ground, when Helen threw a corn chip at my head.

"So, Wood," Helen said. "Am I a terrible roommate?"

"What?" I asked, looking at her. She was pretending to joke, but there was something in her eyes that betrayed her sincerity.

"No," I said. "You're good."

She nodded to herself. "Good. So you're not going to leave us and go back to Portland and your microbrews or whatever the hell you guys have in Portland."

"I think I'm here to stay," I said, and she smiled.

"You like St. Bede's, then?" Freddy asked.

"I didn't say that," I said, biting into a strawberry, smiling at the sweet tang.

"I gotta take a piss," Helen said, and pushed herself off the ground. She grabbed a flashlight and headed for the rope ladder.

"You are not going down there," Freddy commanded.

"Watch my chiseled ass, Miss Bingham," she said, and descended, the rope from the flashlight between her teeth.

"So how'd you get the name Pigeon?" I asked.

"Helen gave it to me. My real name's Paloma. It means *dove* and Helen said doves are just albino pigeons and so she started calling me Pigeon."

"It stuck?"

"I like it."

"You know"—Freddy smiled, pushing her hair back from her cheeks—"one time in New York, I saw a man catch a pigeon with his bare hands. No joke."

85

Far off down in the darkness, I thought I heard a sound—a horrible kind of scream. My heart stalled. I looked around. Freddy and Pigeon looked pale.

"What was that?" Freddy said. A cold silence surrounded her question. With uncharacteristic haste, she moved to the ladder and called down. "Helen?" Her voice echoed out, strange and strong.

We could hear a rustling below, and then we heard noise as something ascended, the ladder wildly undulating.

"Helen?"

Helen's face emerged into the stream of Freddy's flashlight, and I was struck by her pallor. When Freddy lent her a hand and pulled her up onto the landing, I noticed she was shaking.

"Helen, are you okay?"

Slowly she shook her head and closed her eyes. For a moment I thought she might faint.

"Did you fall? What happened?"

"A body," she said, and stumbled. "There's a dead body down there." A deep retching noise came from her belly. Her hand flew to her mouth, and she choked it back down.

"What?" Freddy gasped, holding a hand to her heart. "No. It can't be a body. Your mind's playing tricks on you."

"It's a person. It's all decayed. Oh my God, we have to get out of here. We have to tell the police."

"No, it's the pot," Freddy said, standing tall, smoothing down her skirt.

Color flushed back into Helen's face in strange patches, and tears came quickly to her eyes. "I know what I saw. You guys don't believe me, go down and look."

So we did, all except Pigeon, who didn't want to look gullible. We followed Helen down the ladder to the bottom of a pit. Nothing, not even the smell that preceded it, could have prepared me for the scene we found below. It was badly decomposed, wet and black in parts, stringy and dry in others. It had hair and teeth, but not much else aside from bones.

"This can't be real," Freddy said, but we all knew it was.

I was numb from my knees down. Helen fought back tears, and Freddy shook her head as if her mere refusal could change the tableau.

"This can't be happening," she said, shaking.

I stifled a scream that threatened to rise.

"Everyone just be cool," Helen said, her voice now low and controlled.

"It really is a person, right? It's a girl," Freddy said, her voice quavering. She was rocking back and forth, clutching her shoulders.

"I think we should leave," Helen said.

"Yeah," I muttered, feeling dizzy.

"Oh my God. Oh holy shit." Freddy was grabbing my arm a little too tightly. And then her eyes widened, and her lips curled back in terror. "There's something on the wall."

"On the wall?" Helen whispered, and moved toward the other side of the cavern, lifting her flashlight. As she neared, we could see chalk drawings emerge.

My brain had nearly as much difficulty interpreting the image as my eyes had extracting it, but soon what appeared to be random blue lines coalesced to form a massive blue creature with swirling blue scales, horrible eyes, and a head like a scythe. I found myself stepping away from it before I realized I was doing so.

"Is that . . . is that a dragon?" Helen gasped.

"Oh God," I heard myself cry.

"Let's get out of here," Helen said calmly. "Let's go right now. Go."

And we did. We climbed back up the ladder as quickly as we could, each of us just barely resisting the urge to push, and when we reached the top, Pigeon was waiting for us with a wry smile.

"While you guys were, like, body hunting or whatever, I ate all the Nutella."

Helen took her firmly by the arm. "Listen, Pidge, there really is a dead body down there. We have to leave right now. No questions, okay? Grab your stuff and go."

Eyes wide, uncertain for a moment, Pigeon slowly nodded and then did as Helen asked. No one spoke until we reached the gap in the chain-link fence and were safely on campus.

"Is someone going to tell me what's going on? You were making that up to freak me out, right?" Pigeon's eyes were red and puffy. I hadn't noticed her crying on the hike down, but she must have been.

"Don't tell her," Freddy said, looking vaguely threatening as she smoothed her apricot hair, her fingers shaking as she grasped at the strands.

"It's all true. We found a dead body," Helen said.

"You're not joking?" Pigeon asked, her voice, for once, relatively quiet.

"I wish I were."

"Oh my God. We have to call the police," Pigeon said, and started off in her pink Uggs to do just that.

"Wait a minute! Wait a minute!" Freddy said, waving her hands in front of her face as if she were being attacked by a swarm of insects. "We can't do that!"

Pigeon wheeled around, her eyes wide and incredulous. "Why can't we do that?"

Freddy was calmer now, more in control. "Listen, we have to wait. It's been up there God knows how long. A few more days won't hurt. We have to figure out a way to make it so we don't get in trouble. I'll call it in anonymously. But we'll wait a week in case someone notices we weren't around today. We don't want to link ourselves to this."

"No," I said, horrified. "We can't just leave her up there. We have to call it in. That girl's got a family. They need to know where she is. We need to report it."

"So you're okay getting arrested, then?" Freddy asked. "Because they'll find out what we did up there, they will. And last time I checked, drugs were illegal. Do you want to get kicked out of school? Do you want to go to jail?"

"No, but smoking pot is a little different from concealing a body," I said. "And I don't want to freak anybody out here, but how do we know that dead body isn't Iris? What if it's her? I mean, think about it. Helen, will you please talk some sense into her?"

But Helen looked strange, faraway, as if she was trying to figure out the solution to an entirely different problem. Then she came back to us and looked at me squarely, soberly.

"It's not Iris," she said. "Trust me. It's not her."

"Okay," I said. "So even if it's not Iris . . . it's still a person, and someone is looking for her. They need to know where she is."

Freddy pulled herself up to her full height and stared down at me. "I don't think you understand. I have early acceptance to Harvard. If I'm linked to any of this, Harvard will rescind. I didn't apply anywhere else. My whole life will be ruined for what? So a body that's been dead for months can be found a few days ahead of when it would be if we followed my plan? That girl is dead. A week's not going to change that."

"What if someone finds her before then?" Helen asked.

"Freddy," I said, stepping away from her as if turpitude were contagious. "I'm going to call it in myself."

"It's not like I don't want her found. I just want some time. Just a few days." She turned to me. "Please, I know you think I'm being a selfish bitch, but I need you to help me. I'm not some monster. I'll make sure they find her, and her family will know as soon as possible. But you have to understand, a few days won't change things for the body up there, but they will change things for me. They could ruin my entire life. Please, I'm begging you. Please don't do anything."

With a slump of my shoulders, I yielded, broken by Freddy's desperate eyes and by that tightness around her mouth, marked there by years of strain and perfection. I knew I couldn't call it in. Keeping silent went against my better moral judgment, but I had no way of knowing whether Freddy was right about the possible repercussions. She was probably just being histrionic, but what if it was true? What if the call really could ruin her life? I couldn't be responsible for destroying Freddy's future.

"Fine," I said. "But I want you to know that I think it's wrong."

She grabbed my hands. "Thank you. I owe you."

I shook her off and started back toward campus. As I walked, I found Clare weighing heavily on me. Drawing instant connections between the body and my sister's disappearance was tempting, but I knew it was also probably the road to madness. I needed to emotionally separate the two events. I knew the body couldn't have been her. She was too old to be my sister. But she was someone, wasn't she? She must have been someone's Clare. A cold wind was kicking up, and the afternoon sky was growing a bluish shade of gray. For a moment I had the distinct sensation that the world was closing in around me.

That night Helen and I did our homework in silence and we passed white glove just fine, but once the lights were out, the silence in the room seemed overwhelming.

"Cally?" she said.

I sat up in my bed, trying to make out her figure in the darkness. It was disconcerting not to be able to see her face as she spoke.

"I told Noel," she said, a defiant note to her voice. "I told Noel about the girl we found. Freddy's going to kill me, I know, but she's my sister. I had to tell her."

"Freddy can piss off," I said, and then Helen laughed.

"Thanks. I knew you'd understand."

"Helen," I said, my breath catching. "What if it's Iris?"

"Iris," she sighed. Her name hung heavy between us.

"Yeah."

"No." She attempted a laugh. "I told you I'm sure. It's not Iris. Iris ran away. Look," she said after a moment, her voice strong and soothing. "That thing up there in the woods is not Iris. It can't be."

"Okay," I said. My eyes were adjusting to the darkness, and I could just make out the pencil smudges of her features. "But then why don't you think anyone's found her yet?"

"I don't know," Helen said, her voice strained. "Honestly, I know I lived with the girl, but I didn't know her. She was erratic. She made stuff up, and you never knew what to believe. I couldn't stand her."

"The night she disappeared, you guys had a party, right?"

"Yeah, but Iris didn't come."

"Were you guys really drunk?"

"Well, I was drunk. Noel had a bad cold, so she went to bed early."

"Yeah, but I just mean, were you too drunk to remember who was there? Like, to remember who stayed there all night?"

"Whoa, Cally, where is this headed? No, never mind. I think I know, and I don't want to go on this little journey with you where you, what, check everyone's alibi? It's not Iris. Iris isn't dead."

"You don't know that."

"Well," she said, laughing, forcing a light tone into her voice. "You'll be pleased to know that Noel and I both have alibis. It was our party, after all, and Pidge was up there, and Brody too, so you don't have to worry about any of us."

"Oh my God." I laughed. "I was not asking you for an alibi."

"Oh shit, Cally, what about your friend Sophie?"

"What?"

"Well, she was on campus. There was a math competition the next day. So by your very excellent methodology, she might be guilty of this murder of yours that was never committed."

"Would you quit it?"

"Gladly," she said, an airy lilt to her voice. "I'm going to have nightmares as it is. New topic: do you want to take a weekend to my house?"

"We have a long weekend coming up?"

"Yeah. It should be a good time."

"Sure," I said. "I didn't know that your parents were gonna be in town again."

"Yeah." She laughed and rolled over to go to sleep.

I closed my eyes and tried to sleep, but I couldn't stop seeing the body, feeling my own scream welling up in my chest once again. I choked it back and tried to take my mind away from the body, out of the cave, through the trees, past the pond with its blue-green water and neon fiddleheads, out through the underbrush and moss, but no matter how hard I tried, I couldn't seem to find my way out of the woods.

CHAPTER SIX

THE WEEK WENT BY QUICKLY. None of us mentioned the body, and sometimes during quiet moments, I could almost pretend none of it had happened. Friday morning at breakfast, I stood in the dining hall, dribbling honey over my Cheerios, trying to make sense of my life, when the hair on the back of my neck stood on end. Alex Reese had just walked in.

"We meet again." He smiled.

"Hey, what's going on?" I said. Seeing him was like breathing deeply next to a eucalyptus tree, and I couldn't keep from grinning.

"Wow. I haven't seen you smile like that before."

"I'm happy to see you, I guess."

"Glad to see you too. Hey, are you headed over to the twins' again this weekend?"

"Yeah. How'd you know that?"

"I'm omnivorous, Wood."

"I think you mean *omniscient*."

"Yeah, thanks. I know what *omniscient* means. I meant *omnivorous*." He winked and then he was gone. I looked down to find that once again I'd ruined my Cheerios.

By the time the afternoon rolled around, I was more than ready to get off campus.

This time there were no parents at the lake house. Noel acted as hostess, indicating the food she had purchased for the weekend, baguettes and various fruits and soft cheeses, apparently the rich man's soda and chips. She said we'd order pizza for dinner, and then we all decided to take a nap. I wasn't really tired, but I did feel like having some quiet time to myself, so I grabbed my detective novel, went up to my room, and sank into my downy blue comforter.

It was dark when I awoke, and I was annoyed to see that it was already eleven-thirty. I hadn't meant to sleep so long. I figured there wasn't much point in getting up again, so I pulled the covers up to my nose and tried to drift off, but then my stomach grumbled, and I realized I'd need to eat something or else I'd have rotten dreams. I was creeping out of bed when I thought I heard something outside. I pulled back the curtain to see light from the kitchen window melting over the lawn and onto the gazebo. The house was silent and still, but someone had to be awake. Then I heard it again. A kind of a bump outside and then something like low voices. Maybe nothing, but I couldn't shake the feeling of being watched.

I opened the door and crept down the stairs. I thought I could hear noise coming from the kitchen, but it was faint. It could be the television, though I didn't think the Slaters had one. I'd just reached the first-floor landing when I caught sight of something out of the corner of my eye. A flash in the dark outside. But then it was gone. I moved into the loggia and crept along the thick houseplant jungle, pressing through the dark foliage toward the window. I put my hands to the glass and tried to see outside, but nothing was there. I turned, and only seconds after noticing a cool breeze on the back of my neck, I felt firm hands clamp around my throat, sharp nails digging into me. I was wrenched back and I landed on the hard, cold tile. Suddenly there were people laughing. I looked up to find Pigeon chortling at her own excellent sense of humor. Tanner stood beside her, and a moment later, Alex Reese, Brody, and Shane Derwitz strode up. As foolish as I felt, the smile Alex gave me more than made up for it.

"You okay?" he asked, and I nodded.

"Wood, you really got scared," Pigeon said with her annoying lisp. "You need to see a therapist or something. Am I right?" she asked of no one in particular, and then she laughed loudly, her pointy chin tilted to the heavens as if to make certain that God had seen her fantastic joke.

Brody pulled me to my feet. "You didn't know everyone was coming, did you?"

"No. Why are you all here?"

"Party," Tanner sneered. "The Slaters' parties are epic."

So that was why Helen had laughed when I'd assumed her parents would be there, and that was why everyone had needed to take naps. Last check in the dorms was 11:00 p.m., so just like Alex and Brody had done on that first weekend, everyone had sneaked out at 11:02 and stolen through the little woods over to Helen's for a raucous night of drinking and discombobulated sex.

More people arrived, and I began to get lost in the crowd of them. Grumbling to myself like an old crank, I started back up to my room, but then I remembered how Alex Reese had smiled at me, and I went to find Helen to ask if she could dress me up to look like a girl. Ten minutes later, I was swimming in a jade peasant dress, and she was applying mascara and lipstick to my flinching face. When she'd finished, I looked like a cat in a tutu, but she seemed pleased.

I didn't think I could reuse the antibiotics excuse, so I grabbed a beer from the cooler, took a few sips so my breath would smell hopsy, spilled some more pretending to stumble on the patio, and then carried it around with me for the rest of the night.

I was talking to Drucy about drosophila when I noticed Alex Reese across the patio talking to Tanner. As I watched him smile, his dimples caving in on either side of his perfectly pouting lips, it became increasingly difficult to pay attention to Drucy. Finally she turned to see what was distracting me.

"Oh, for God's sake," was all she said. She rolled her eyes and walked away. I moved to follow her, hoping she wouldn't think I was an idiot, but then I saw Alex approaching me.

"Wood! What's up?" He smelled faintly of cinnamon. "Wow, you look really beautiful."

"Uh, thanks," I said. "I'm wearing a dress." I held my arms away from my body as if to confirm the veracity of my statement.

"Yeah, I see that." He laughed, and for some reason I started laughing too. Gently, he slipped his hand into mine, and we were walking, the cool night air buoying me up, making me feel invincible.

We were down toward the lake, away from the others, when I looked up at him and grinned. I was too happy to worry about looking stupid.

"You're kind of great," I said.

Abruptly, he stopped walking and stared at me with something approaching surprise.

"You're kind of great too," he said. Then he touched my cheek with the back of his hand and leaned down to kiss me.

We had stood there a good ten minutes just kissing, drowning in cinnamon and oxytocin, when a Nerf football bounced against the side of my head and I looked over to see Tanner, his hands clasped over his mouth. His shirt, the same ugly yellow as his hair, stood out against the night.

"Keep it safe, you guys," he said, snickering, his voice high and nasal.

I straightened my dress and looked up at Alex. He shrugged. I hadn't done much with boys before. I hadn't wanted to. In my experience, the boys who were the cutest were usually also the most annoying, so I tended to bail out before much could happen. But Alex was different. I began to think maybe I did want to fool around with him, but I was too exhausted to know for sure.

"Maybe we should go hang out with those guys," I said.

"Yeah." He smiled. "Rain check?"

"Rain check," I said, and slowly we walked back to the rest of the group, still holding hands.

Without the ersatz energy that alcohol provided my peers, I just didn't have the staying power and soon realized I was in desperate need of sleep. Alex walked me up to my room. We stood there too long, staring at each other, both of us unsure what to do. Awkwardly, he leaned in, and I leaned in at the same time. He ended up kissing the top of my head.

"Good night, Cally," he said.

"Good night," I said, and closed the door.

The party was still going strong when I turned out the light. I fell asleep to the discordant sounds of Pigeon singing "Stairway to Heaven" beneath my window.

CHAPTER SEVEN

I WAS AWAKENED TO HARSH morning light by pounding on the front door. Loud, vigorous blows that seemed like they'd never stop. Presumably, I was the only person in the house who wasn't hungover, so I figured I should see who it was.

All the bedroom doors were closed, and there were a few bodies nestled into couches or curled up in corners. The whole place reeked of old beer and fancy cheese. People began stirring as the pounding grew more insistent. I opened the door and, to my horror, found Mr. Reilly, looking haggard and worried.

"Wood, listen, I know there are a lot of people here who shouldn't be, but the administration will turn a blind eye if you all get in the van here with me now and head back up to school."

"But my weekend was approved. I'm supposed to be here."

"Well, good for you," he said, clearly unable to keep that bitchy tone from his voice. Apparently my distaste for him was reciprocal. "But I'm still going to need everyone back on campus stat. There's been an incident, and Dr. Harrison's going to call an emergency assembly. Anyone within a reasonable distance from the school needs to come back, and that means you, Wood, so gather everyone up. I'll wait in the van."

He snapped around on his heel, in danger of twisting an ankle in his requisite Birkenstocks, and I was left to round up the troops. It wasn't easy. At first, no one would believe me. I had to drag Drucy to the window and show her the van with the St. Bede's insignia on it to create a stir.

Exhausted and disoriented, we straggled out the door. Helen looked wrecked, her feline eyes circumscribed with swollen red skin. With a twist and a clip, she affixed her tangled hair so that she looked like a glamorous drug addict.

"Do you think they know?" she asked as we climbed into the van.

It hadn't occurred to me until then, but surely there was no way. Maybe someone else had found the body, but there was no way that person could know about us. On the short ride back to campus, Reilly put some Grateful Dead on the stereo. Noel promptly fell asleep on Freddy's lap and Freddy stuck her head out the window, her pale skin variegated with splotches of bluish green.

"Freddy got busy last night," Helen whispered to me. I looked at her wide mischievous eyes, suddenly the eyes of a child. "With Tanner."

"Why would I possibly want to know something like that?" I grimaced.

"Because he's been going out with Cara Svitt for years," she whispered, raising her eyebrows. "It's craziness, I tell you—utter craziness."

I decided it was best to ignore her, so I leaned my head against the window and tried to block out "Casey Jones."

School was a madhouse. We arrived just as assembly was starting, and the whole room was infused with a violent energy. Everyone was talking too loudly and too quickly and no one was in his or her assigned seat. Freshman boys ran up and down the aisles, and senior girls looked intensely put out. I took a seat in my usual row next to Carlos, who was asking Asta if he could go up front to sign up for an announcement. She looked out of sorts, her hair held back by barrettes, her face pale and drawn.

"No. No announcements this morning. Carlos, just sit down, okay, this is serious. Cally," she said, pointing in my direction but barely seeing me, "keep track of the boys, will you? I need to talk to Dr. Harrison."

I watched as she waded through the confusion up to the front. Dr. Harrison looked horrible. If I hadn't known better, I would have said he'd been crying. He leaned down to hear what Asta had to say, and I could tell it wasn't pleasant.

From across the auditorium, I saw Sophie looking at me. I raised my eyebrows at her as if to ask if she knew what was up, but she just shook her head and mouthed, "No idea."

And then I noticed the cops. They were plainclothes, but they were definitely cops. They hung back by the doors of the east entrance, which no one ever used. Something horrible was happening, and I was pretty sure I knew what it was. I put my head in my hands, massaging my temples to try to stave off the incipient headache. How could I have let this happen, me of all people? I'd never met the girl, but somehow I'd known it was her out in those woods, and I'd just left her there.

Dr. Harrison broke off from Asta, looked at his watch, and approached the microphone.

"I apologize for calling you all back here this morning, but I'm afraid a terrible incident has occurred. I'm sorry to inform you that your classmate Iris Liang has been found dead. Her body was located in the woods behind school by some passing hikers."

A wave of crazy swept through the auditorium. It moved like wildfire, hitting each person at a different time. The awful thing was that despite the genuine horror in the auditorium that morning, an overwhelming atmosphere of excitement accompanied it. A few girls started crying, but it was immediately clear that they were not supposed to, and they worked to staunch the flow. There was danger in such unrestrained outbursts of emotion. If some people started crying, then everyone would cry, and we couldn't let that happen, so the girls swallowed their tears, and their friends kept their distance.

Dr. Harrison patted the air with his hands, indicating that we needed to calm down. He cleared his throat. "Obviously this is horrible news. I know that many of you were friends with Iris. We will make grief counselors available to those of you who need them. Just talk to Nurse Raben and we can set something up. In the meantime, we're going to need a lot of cooperation from you guys. Things may be kind of strange here for the next few days while we try to get our bearings, and I'm asking that you be extra vigilant about following the rules. Obviously, I don't need to tell you that the little woods are now, and always have been, strictly off-limits." His eyes grew wide, and he opened his mouth as if to say something, but then a wave of sorrow seemed to engulf him, and shaking his head, he changed tack. "We're going to need a lot of help from you to find out what happened to Iris. I'm going to turn the assembly over to Detectives Cryker and Levy now."

The cops I'd seen earlier moved up to the front of the room and took the podium. The one who started speaking was small and hirsute. He had a goatee and a disconcerting twinkle to his eye. He smoothed his hands. The woman who stood beside him was tall and blond with an unfortunate jaw. She fiddled with her sleeve as the small man spoke into the microphone.

"I'm Detective Cryker," he said, a not-unpleasant crackle to his voice. He had that kind of extreme toughness that is often found in tiny men. You could picture him killing a man twice his size with his bare hands and then casually eating a jelly doughnut. "Some of you may remember me from October when I spoke with a number of you regarding Iris Liang's disappearance.

"Let me begin by saying that I'm sorry for your loss. I know this is tough, but we're gonna need to ask you guys to remember anything you can about the last time you saw Iris Liang. Right now we have her last sighting at six p.m. on October third. That was the first night of your fall break. We spoke with a lot of you back in October, but the case has taken on a different light. We're going to speak to each and every one of you, but if you think you have valuable information, please come forward right away. Try your best to remember what you can. We're going to start with people who were the closest to her. The rest of you are temporarily excused. Go eat breakfast and then come back here. And once we've talked to you, Dr. Harrison wants you to proceed to your normal afternoon sport. There will be impromptu practices. Okay, right." He cleared his throat. "Drucilla Keller. Let's go."

Drucy looked completely bewildered, and I was fairly certain from her reaction that she had not, in fact, been friends with Iris. I watched her disappear into a back area with Cryker as the rest of us stood up and started milling about like misplaced cattle.

Helen, Noel, Freddy, and I found each other in the crowd and started up to breakfast in silence. Helen looked as if her mind was trying to unravel a puzzle far beyond her capabilities, and Noel looked ill. We had sequestered ourselves, taking a circuitous route along a brick path through the poplars and avoiding the rest of the students, who were bubbling and buzzing in a herd up to the dining hall.

The rhythm of patent leather Mary Janes slapping against the brick caused me to bristle at the sound of impending Pigeon. Her cheeks were red, her dark eyes were sparkling, and she was slightly out of breath when she caught up with us.

"Oh my God, you guys, can you even believe it?"

"Mmm," Helen mumbled.

"I cannot believe it. Like, she was in my advisor group. It could have been any of us. It could have been me. Oh my God,

Helen, what if she was kidnapped from your room and then she was killed? What if you hadn't been away already? I bet he would have taken you instead. I mean, you are way prettier."

"Pigeon," Freddy gasped.

"She was not murdered," Helen spat. "Obviously this was an accident."

"No, she was totally kidnapped and murdered. That's why the police are being so aggro. Oh my God, this is so scary, you guys."

I noticed that Noel's huge charcoal-lined eyes looked wild, terrified, and she was gripping her short blond locks. Helen wrapped an arm around her sister, knit her brow, and glared at Pigeon.

"Pidge," she snapped, "we're all feeling kind of upset right now. Maybe we could drop it until after breakfast, okay?"

"Um, hello, like we're not going to talk about last weekend. We're gonna tell that we found her now, right?"

"Pigeon," Helen sighed. "Why would we do that? They don't need to know. And she was not killed, for God's sake. She had an accident. It must have been an accident."

"They're questioning the whole school," I said. "They don't think she had an accident."

"Look," Helen said lightly, regaining composure. "Okay, it was either an accident or it wasn't. Either way, it no longer involves us, so I suggest we stop talking about it. It has nothing to do with us. This is where we walk away."

Pigeon shook her head. "They'll know we were up there."

"How?" Helen put her hand on her hip and tilted her head to the side, a clear indication she was ready to fight.

"I don't know." Pigeon shrugged. "DNA?"

"This isn't some lame TV show, Pidge. It's not like the government keeps everyone's DNA in a giant database. And I don't know about you, but I didn't go around licking the floor up there. None of us touched the body. None of us touched the wall with the creepy drawing. If they get half a fingerprint off something, so what? It's not like our prints are on file. None of us has a criminal record. The only way we could screw this up is if we act crazy and draw attention to ourselves. They have no reason to suspect that we were there, so unless they come around scraping our cheek cells, I suggest we fucking drop it. Are we clear?"

Pigeon opened her mouth to speak, but Freddy placed a hand on her arm, and she stopped.

"Are we clear?" Helen said again, unable to keep the venom from her voice.

Silently, Pigeon nodded, all the frenetic Pigeon energy drained from her black eyes.

After a quick breakfast, we gathered our things and headed back to the auditorium, where I muddled through my weekend problem set. They called Helen in around one-thirty, and immediately after she emerged, looking a little frazzled, they called me. She gave me an encouraging, complicitous smile that drained me of what little energy I had.

Cryker looked askance at me as I mounted the stairs. They were conducting the interviews in the theater's greenroom, which, I was pleased to find, had been painted a soft shade of lime. It smelled acrid and musty, hinting at the diva break-downs and late-night hookups to which it was privy. Cryker pulled up a chair while the blond female detective gave me a bored look. I didn't like the police. They'd never done anything for me but harass my family and not find my sister.

"You're new here," he said, his voice scratchy.

"Yeah," I said, looking at the far corner of the room.

"Well," he said, tapping his pen against his yellow tablet. "Are you liking it here, Miss Wood?"

"Um. It's okay, I guess."

"No problems so far?"

"Nope."

"Is there anything you'd like to tell us?"

I noticed my hands were starting to sweat, and my head was getting hot.

"I really don't think so," I said.

"Hmmm." He stroked his beard. "Well, I'm just going to lay my cards on the table, Miss Wood. I know who you are. I know that your sister disappeared here ten years ago."

I shrugged and looked away. Why did adults always force me to act like a drug-addled teen in some crappy TV movie?

"Listen, Miss Wood. I take it you don't want your loss to be general knowledge, and I'm happy to keep things on a need-to-know basis, but we've got to have a conversation. I need to ask you some questions about your sister."

I looked into his eyes and asked the question I only half wanted him to answer. "Why? You think Iris's death is con-nected to Clare or something? Clare died in a fire."

He tapped the desk. "In the file it says you were with your mom in Portland, and your dad was in Sacramento when Clare and Laurel disappeared. Is that correct?"

I nodded.

"And no one in your family had any knowledge of anyone who would have wanted to harm Clare? No strange family friends. No bizarre relatives."

"Yeah. No bizarre relatives unless you count my mom. Why are you asking all these questions? Clare died in a fire," I said, my voice threatening to break. "Didn't she?"

He sighed. "You were very young at the time. Six years old, it says here, but maybe you remember something—something you didn't tell the police at the time—something you were too scared to say? Maybe even something you tried to block out."

"Sorry," I said, my heart beating too quickly. "But what the hell are you getting at?"

"Calm down, Miss Wood." He cleared his throat. "Sometimes an event is so traumatic our brain tries to shield us from it, but sometimes it creeps back in. Has to do with the breakdown of the neurons or the myelin sheaths or what is it?" He looked to his partner, who nodded.

"Yeah. Neurons," she said.

"So do you remember anything—anything at all?"

"Why are you doing this?" I asked, my voice breaking, the tears starting to come.

"Doing what, Miss Wood?"

"You're trying to make me think Clare was murdered. Is that what you think happened?"

109

"That's not what I said."

"But that's what you're suggesting," I said, suddenly on my feet, unsure where I was going.

"I'm not suggesting anything."

"Iris, she was murdered, wasn't she?"

He nodded. "We have reason to suspect so, yes."

"And you think my sister was murdered too. That's what you're saying."

"I'm simply asking you some questions, and I'd appreciate it if you would sit down."

"I will not fucking sit down," I screamed, tears suddenly cascading down my face. "My sister died in a fire. That's what they told me. You can't just untell me that. Not after all these years. Not now."

"Let me ask you something, Miss Wood," he said, his voice smooth. "Do *you* believe she died in a fire?"

"Yes," I said, stumbling over the word.

"Then why are you here?" He arched his eyebrows at me, his eyes discordantly kind beneath them. I wiped away my tears and glared at him. Who was he, anyway? Who was he to come into my life and speak my fears aloud as if they were the text on the back of a cereal box, as if they didn't completely change the world?

"Miss Wood," he said, smiling. "I can see that you're upset. I can assure you that wasn't my intention."

I said nothing.

Cryker sighed and looked to his partner, who rolled her eyes. "Well," he said, scratching his beard. "If you remember anything, please come and talk to us."

"I'll be sure to do that," I said. "Is that it?"

"For now," he said, tapping his fingers.

I stormed out of the auditorium, wiping away my tears. I walked quickly, my legs shaking. Clare hadn't been murdered. She'd died in a fire. Cryker couldn't just come into my world all of a sudden and change that. No matter what I believed in my heart, no matter what I believed when the lights were out, there was an objective truth that existed outside of me, and that truth was that my sister had died in a fire. It wasn't his right to question that truth. Only I could do that. A sharp wind kicked up and helped shock me out of my choler. Maybe sports weren't such a bad idea. At least they would keep our bodies occupied so we couldn't think too much. I headed down to the gym to sign in with Ms. Sjursen. She was engaged in some kind of bizarre craft involving knitting needles, a glue gun, and Lego blocks. She looked up at me with those distant eyes.

"Oh," she whispered. "I've got something for you."

"You do?"

"Mmm-hmmm. Now let me see here. Where is that?" She rummaged around beneath her desk and extracted a bulky manila envelope.

"This is for me?" I asked.

"Yes, dear. They said to give it to you. Said you'd understand what it meant. There was a Post-it note on top with your name on it. Oh, where is that?"

"Who left it for me?" I asked, my heart suddenly surging. Alex? Had Alex left it for me?

Ms. Sjursen squinted her eyes, and her cheeks flushed. "I don't remember, dear."

I didn't want to push her too hard, but I needed to know. "Was he tall and African American?"

She stared at me, her smile dropping, that devastating windowless gaze sinking back into her eyes. "I don't know," she said, shaking her head, her voice filled with shame. I didn't want to upset her, so I took the package and smiled brightly.

"Thanks for the package, Ms. Sjursen."

She smiled again and changed the setting on her glue gun. I walked out into the cold afternoon, staring at the package, a lump in my throat.

I ripped it open and shook out a small present wrapped in thick pink paper. Unwrapping it, I found a wooden box, sculpted from lush mahogany and riddled with carvings. The top was composed of eight delicately engraved tiles, though there were clearly meant to be nine, and where the missing tile ought to have been, there was a flat, hollow space.

Examining the sides of the box, I saw that they had been crosshatched with intricate detail. My fingers searched the lines for an opening, but I could find no hinge, no apparent aperture. Turning it over, I found that the bottom was a cubist mélange of geometric shapes and patterns. At the bottom left corner, two small circles stood side by side, each containing two letters, an upside-down Y and an O, and a backward E and an I respectively. They were separated by a T. It looked almost like a factory logo, one I felt I'd seen somewhere before, and yet I was fairly certain the box was handmade. Gingerly, I shook it, and a faint rattling replied from within. There was something inside.

My eyes scanned the top. The tiles were smooth and stood

in contrast to the rest of the box. Each tile contained a different symbol: a flower floating on water, a chalice, a skull, a whirlpool, a musical note, a lock, an eye. And then one of the pieces contained a disturbing scene: twelve female bodies strung up by their necks. It was a gruesome image, one I vaguely recognized but couldn't place. I wondered what symbol the missing tile might have held. I wondered why it had been removed.

It didn't seem right. I was missing something. Despite my supposed academic prowess, I was about as mechanically inclined as a pile of dead mice. I needed Sophie. I'd heard that Alvarado had canceled softball practice despite Harrison's mandate, so I headed over to Prexy to see if she was in her room.

I'd yet to be invited to Sophie's room. We usually spent time with Jack, which mostly necessitated hanging out in open spaces. I also got the sense that Sophie's room was an intensely private space, and when I knocked on her door, I noticed that I was slightly nervous about doing so. It was the ideal of a girl's room. Her pale yellow comforter was feminine but not cloyingly so. A Georgia O'Keeffe print hung above the head of her bed, and a light perfume lingered in the air. The only thing out of the ordinary was a quote from Linus Pauling that she'd tacked up on her wooden door. She sat on her soft yellow rug, reading *Lolita*. She gave me a sad smile.

"Aren't you glad you transferred here?"

I sat down on the floor opposite her.

"So I guess you were right," I sighed. "About her being murdered, I mean."

"I feel terrible about saying that now," she said, closing her book. "I was just trying to be dramatic, trying to make life less dull. But Jesus, the poor girl. How awful."

"What was she like?" I asked.

Sophie sighed. "I wasn't really in her field of vision. I mean, she was into art and fashion. She wore designer clothes and paraded around claiming she was going to be a model. Not really my thing, you know? But she was good at math and physics, so we ended up together sometimes because she and Freddy and I would be the only girls sent to the Math Bowl or whatever. She seemed nice enough, but we didn't have much to talk about, and she didn't seem interested in being friends. I only ever really saw her with boys."

"Her poor parents," I said, unable to suppress the image of a man and woman just biting into their morning toast, staring in horror as the phone rang. "Is this what it was like when the police were here in October?"

"Not even remotely. They talked to some of the kids who knew her best, but God, it was nothing like this. I can't believe she was out there all this time. But the little woods are scary as hell. That's why they make such a fuss about us not wandering in there. A few years back they found this guy living out there, and it turned out he'd murdered an entire family in their beds over in Sonoma. He'd taken their prescription drugs and nothing else. Just murdered them, and was hiding out here, back in those woods."

"God." I shivered. "I had no idea."

"Well, it's not exactly the kind of thing they put in the viewbook. Yeesh. I'm getting creeped out. You want to go for a walk?"

"Actually, I was wondering if you could help me with something," I said, pulling the manila envelope out of my backpack. I shook out the box and handed it to Sophie. "I can't get this open, and I've got a suspicion I'm missing something."

She examined it and a silly grin spread over her face. "Oh man. This is awesome. It's a puzzle box."

"A what?"

"A puzzle box. Like, to open it is a puzzle. I love these. But this one's handmade. Look at the tiles. Cool."

"What are you talking about?"

"Look at all these tiles on the top. See the empty space?"

"Yeah. One of the tiles is missing."

"It's not missing. It was never there. This is a classic slide puzzle. We need to arrange the pieces into a specific order, and that's the free space so we can maneuver them." She slid the flower tile over into the empty space and then pulled the skeleton down into the space the flower had previously occupied. "Now we just need to arrange them into sequential order, and we'll see what happens."

"How do we know what the sequence is?"

She raised an eyebrow at me. "Don't tell me you haven't noticed the theme. Look at the images again. Look at them closely. What do you see?"

I leaned in, my mind straining for a moment, and then I saw it.

"Oh God," I said, smiling. "It's *The Odyssey*, isn't it?" I scanned the tiles again, realizing that each represented a different station on Odysseus's journey. It was the grotesque image of the twelve hanging women that had clenched it for me. They were Odysseus's supposedly disloyal maids who were hanged upon his return. I shivered when I thought about it. Then there was the whirlpool. That had to represent the Charybdis; the eye represented the Cyclops, and the lock represented Odysseus's imprisonment by Calypso; the musical note stood in for the Sirens; the skeleton meant the Land of the Dead; the flower represented the Lotus Eaters. That left us with only the chalice.

"I'm not getting the chalice," I said. "What does it represent?"

"Circe," Sophie said, rolling her eyes. "The Enchantress. Remember, she offered Odysseus wine laced with magical herbs. Whoever drank it was trapped with her."

"Oh right. With the pigs and all that."

"Exactly."

"God," I said, feeling proud. "I'm glad I just read it. . . ."

"We all just read it, Cally. It's on the syllabus."

"Whatever," I said, pointing to the box. "Let's put them in sequence. First we'd have Odysseus imprisoned by Calypso, that's the lock. It needs to be moved to the top left space. Then going across, we have the Lotus Eaters, then the Cyclops. On the next row we need to have Circe, followed by the Land of the Dead, followed by the Sirens. The last line should be the Charybdis, and finally the hanging of the maids."

Sophie nodded, her hands slipping quietly over the pieces, sliding them into place. When she slid the final tile into position, it seemed to trigger something. We heard a click, and the top opened. Inside was a folded white piece of paper.

"Oh my God," I gasped, stunned that it had actually worked.

"Maybe it's a treasure map." She giggled and started to open it but then handed it to me. "Where did you get this, anyway?"

"Someone left it with Ms. Sjursen for me. I guess I have a secret admirer."

"Well, open it. Let's see who it is."

When I hesitated, she understood and slapped my knee. "You shit. You're not going to read it in front of me, are you?"

"Not right now, okay?" I said, gripping the paper tightly in my fist. "And don't tell Jack."

"Get out of here," she said, laughing. "Go read your stupid secret love letter."

Outside Sophie's dorm, I sat between two poplar trees to read what I hoped was going to be a fantastic love letter. I was sorely disappointed by what I found.

15 36 9 2 3 22 24 , 5 12 7 4 17 36 30 128 77 46 44
18 39 31 23 40 75 54 87 95 82 43 99 84 25 72 42
104 74 ? 127 105 1 42 124 134 100 45 70 153 141
49 J 133 147 53 54 55 56 57 173 171 174 5 106 175
140 172 107 48 143 165 32 7 111 190 . 64 122 133
174 145 184 86 128 80 158 39 94 173 47 42 138
103 69 131 189 140 155 48 82 117 75 99 178 190
153 170 169 121 135 186 189 188 82 43 146 . 107
126 151 141 71 86 138 13 133 129 182 124 147 149
113 162 22 8 174 137 15 , 173 83 175 92 .

I had no idea what to make of it. Unzipping my backpack, I pulled out the manila envelope and examined the blank cover.

I reached inside and pulled out the pink wrapping paper. And that was when I saw it. Lurching across the inside of the wrapping in manic black Sharpie scrawl were the words *THERE IS ONLY ONE WAY OUT.*

I leaned against a tree and tried to swallow, but something was blocking my throat. Okay, what the hell was that supposed to mean? If there had been any doubt before then, I was now certain that it wasn't from Alex. I had no idea whom it could be from or what it could possibly mean, but I didn't like it.

I shoved the note into my pocket, hid the box in my room, and headed down to Ms. Sjursen, determined to see what she could remember. I found her underneath her desk, cursing at an outlet. I bent down and shoved the plug in for her. She smiled up at me, then looked triumphantly at her glue gun.

"Oh, thank you, dear. This thing can be a real bastard sometimes."

"Ms. Sjursen, do you think you could try to remember who left that package for me?"

"What package, dear?"

"It was a manila envelope with a Post-it note on top with my name on it. Can you remember anything about the person who left it?"

She smiled and shook her head. "I can't say that I remember any package. You say I gave it to you? When?"

I stared at her a moment. If she didn't remember giving me the package, there was no way she would remember who had given it to her. This was a lost cause. She looked worried, so I did my best to redirect her attention back to her crafts. After she showed me how to glue a button onto a piece of cardboard, I ducked out and started on my walk.

The air was crisp, and walking did wonders to clear my head, though the heaviness of Iris and Clare held fast to my heart. When I was confident I was out of view of the lacrosse field, I pulled the note from my pocket and examined it again. It looked like a series of random numbers, but maybe it was something. Maybe it was a kind of code.

I leaned against a tree and did my best to understand what I had in my hands. Reading "The Gold-Bug" in ninth grade had led me into a super-geeky cryptanalysis phase. I'd gotten Danny into it too. We used to leave notes in cipher for each other. We still did if it was something we didn't want Kim to understand. My heart sank when I thought about him. Kim hadn't returned any of my calls. I knew she was having a hard time, but it didn't seem fair for her not to at least let me know he was okay.

I tried to focus on the note and fight back the sadness. I'd had enough emotions for one day.

"The Gold-Bug" dealt with a specific type of cryptanalysis called frequency analysis—a system based on the idea that within a given piece of text, certain letters in the English language were bound to come up more often than others. By analyzing the frequency at which each letter appeared and then consulting a table, one could plug letters in based on the percentage rates at which each given symbol appeared in the cipher text. I had been hoping that if the note was indeed an encryption, it would be one that I could solve using frequency analysis, but I could already see that whatever this was, I didn't know how to solve it. An encryption that could be solved using frequency analysis wouldn't contain any numbers greater than twenty-six, and there would necessarily be repetitions, but the numbers in my note went all the way up to 190, and there were way too few repetitions.

Another oddity was the run of consecutive numbers: 53, 54, 55, 56, 57. I hadn't seen anything like it during my (admittedly brief) foray into cryptanalysis. I couldn't help thinking that it might be important, but I had no idea how. And then there was the inclusion of the letter J, which made no sense at all. Why shove a letter in there?

Crumpling the note, I shoved it into my pocket and started walking back to campus. Maybe it was just a random string of nonsense. *There is only one way out.* Maybe that was the real message. It didn't sound like code, though. It sounded like plain English. It sounded like a threat.

I headed over to the dining hall to get a drink, the verdant splendor of the campus rising before me. Scenic view or not, I couldn't help wishing I had somewhere else to go. I missed my dad, and I wanted to be somewhere like home. I wanted to go somewhere safe—to feel warm and loved. But home was not that. Home was my mom, and the constant fear that the worst possible thing could happen at any second without the slightest warning. Now, with Iris, it looked like school was heading in the same direction, but, I told myself, no matter how bad St. Bede's was, there was no way it could hurt the same way home did.

Just as I was climbing the steps up to the dining hall, I saw that Alex was leaving. He smiled at me, and suddenly I remembered everything that had happened at Helen's.

"Hey, you," he said. "Drink machines are off if that's where you're headed."

"Damn it," I said, and kicked a step.

"That was a little dramatic, Wood. You know there are vending machines out behind the kitchen, right?"

"No."

"Come on," he said, gently taking my hand. "I'll show you."

We wandered through the dining hall, then out the french doors and into the back patio courtyard. Soon we were behind the dining hall at the soda machine. He put seventy-five cents into the machine, then looked down at me.

"Orange or peach?"

"Peach." I smiled.

"Me too," he said.

"So this is all crazy, right?" he said, his voice crackly and kind. He handed me my drink. I took a sip, then set it down on the wall.

"It's really sad," I said.

"Yeah. I just can't believe she'd go out into the woods like that by herself."

I squinted at him. "Maybe she didn't."

"What?" he said, then took a swig of his drink. "What do you mean?"

"What if she didn't go out there by herself? What if someone took her out there, or, like, lured her out there?"

He shook his head. "No, they're saying she went out there

to do drugs or something, and some sick vagrant found her and killed her. I heard she was raped."

"Really?" I choked. "God. That's horrible."

"I know. It makes me sick. I heard there was this weird painting up on the wall of the cave where she was found. They're calling the bastard the Dragon Killer."

"God," I groaned. "So what's going to happen now? Do you think school will keep going on like normal, or do we all go home?"

"It's tricky," he said. "I talked to Dr. Harrison, and he told me that all the parents are being called, and he's telling everyone not to worry. Some people might leave, though. You never know. Nothing like this has ever happened before. There was a suicide back when I was a freshman, and school just went on as normal. I think that's best. Not to dwell. This is different, though."

"Yeah," I said, my head starting to hurt.

"But I wanted to talk to you," he said, setting down his soda, gently taking my hands in his. "So I know this is weird to talk about right now, but what did you think about last night? About what happened?"

It was a swift change of subject, but I decided to go with it. The last thing I wanted to do was think about that poor girl getting raped. He put his arm around me.

"Well, what do you think?" he asked. "Do you want to, like, be together?"

A tingling warmth rushed through me. Maybe he could be a kind of home, I thought, but I couldn't say something like that, so I just nodded.

He bent down and kissed me softly on the cheek, but then he pulled back. "Crap," he said. "I forgot. I have to catch Brody before dinner. Do you want to hang out with us after study hours?"

"Sure." I smiled. "You get to stay out during study hours because you're a cool senior, huh?"

"Yeah," he said, laughing.

"So what do you guys do when we're in our rooms studying?"

"Honestly? The truth?"

"Yeah."

"We go to the library and study."

I laughed and he touched the back of his hand to my cheek.

"Come by my dorm later?" he asked.

I nodded and took a breath. He kissed me, slowly sliding his hand around my waist.

After saying goodbye to Alex, I didn't quite know what to do with myself. I tried to block out the image of Iris, this girl I'd never even known, being brutalized out there in the woods. What must her last moments have been like? How much had she understood about what was happening to her? How terrified she must have been.

A wind was picking up, and I was starting to shiver, but for some reason, instead of going back to my dorm, I headed to Jack's room. He was sitting in his balcony hammock and shredding a napkin with short, irritated bursts of movement.

"Are you okay?" I asked as I climbed over the railing. I took a seat next to him, and the hammock buckled beneath me, half throwing me onto his lap.

"No," he said. "How could they not have known she was dead? They told us she ran away. How could they tell us that?"

"I'm sorry," I said. "I didn't know you were friends."

"We weren't. I thought she was a jerk, but she was a person, for God's sake. She was just a girl. How could they give up on her so soon? You weren't here, but the administration clearly didn't give two shits about her. They just wanted to write her off and move on, lest things get too public and affect our rankings. And the cops were hardly here. I know we were on fall break for the first week, but everyone shouldn't have given up on her so soon. If she had been white and blond, she would have been on the cover of *People* magazine for months. She would have been the top story until she was found. It makes me sick."

"What *did* happen back in October? Why did they tell you guys they stopped looking?"

"I don't know. They said some bullshit about her being troubled, about her being a classic runaway, whatever that means, and then someone up in Olympia thought they saw her at a bus station, and that was enough. Case closed. It was bullshit. It was racist bullshit. It's always the same. A white girl is worth our attention, but how many Mexican girls have to be mutilated for us to pay attention to what's going on in Ciudad Juárez? How many black kids had to die before we gave a shit about the Atlanta Child Murders?"

"I feel like a serious jerk, but I don't even know what those things are."

"Of course you don't. Most people don't. Look them up sometime and you'll get so angry you'll feel like your head is exploding." He looked at me, something soft settling over his eyes, and then he wrapped an arm around me and leaned his head into my shoulder. "Sometimes it's all too much, Wood. You know what I mean?"

"Yeah," I said, closing my eyes. "I do."

CHAPTER EIGHT

THAT NIGHT I SAT OUT on the lawn with Alex and Brody. The pall of Iris's death hung heavy on the school, but no one was talking about it. There was such a rampant fervor to carry on with life as usual that it was almost like talking about her was taboo. So I did my best to laugh at their jokes and to seem like I wasn't upset.

I was just beginning to get comfortable when the in-dorm bell sounded. Police were everywhere, and it was difficult not to be a little unnerved by it. But nothing freaked me out as much as the teachers, all acting like they were newly deputized and St. Bede's was the Old West. Teachers like Reilly and Ms. Harlow weren't supposed to have real power. Power in the hands of teachers like them was more disconcerting than the idea that we were in any actual danger.

I made it to breakfast the next morning, but it was complicated. I'd slept like a corpse and barely been able to wake up. My head was fuzzy, and my eyes felt like they were covered in a wispy film. As a result, I hadn't dressed properly; I'd thrown a skirt on top of the moose pajamas, and a bra under the T-shirt I'd slept in. There were too many breakfast choices. Strawberries and cereal, toast and bacon. I'd forgotten what I liked to eat.

"You look like shit," Jack breathed down my neck.

"That is a blatant falsehood." I yawned, grabbed some cinnamon raisin bread, and wandered over to a table, where I slumped down.

"God," I heard Sophie say. "Cally, you look terrible. What's wrong?" She sat down next to Jack and started eating his toast.

"Sophie." He beamed and gave her a peck on the cheek. "Don't you look pretty?"

"Why, thank you," she said, pretending to preen. "Cally, I was looking for you after dinner. Where were you?"

"With my boyfriend," I said. "How ridiculous is that?"

"No," Jack said, turning to me, all bursting red lips and sparkling eyes. "You don't have a boyfriend. Who would date *you*? You're a little troll."

"It's not Alex Reese, is it?" Sophie asked, and I thought I detected a slight tension in her smile.

"Ding! Ding! Ding!" I said, raising a finger in the air.

"God, Wood," Jack said. "Show some originality."

"As long as she's happy."

Jack surveyed my dress with a fey smile. "How shocking

to learn he's into the sartorially challenged. I guess he gets points for being an equal-opportunity hottie."

In English, I tried to concentrate, but I couldn't help wondering what was going on with Ms. Harlow. Throughout class, she was watchful, her eyes heavy and red-rimmed. As usual, she insisted on linking everything back to Homer. We were supposed to be talking about *The Oresteia,* but off she rambled on some Homeric theme like he was the only author she'd ever read. I occupied myself with doodles while she blathered and wrote various ancient Greek words on the board.

"What is this word? Anyone? Cally?"

I looked up from my doodles.

"I don't remember."

"You would if you'd done the assignment and completed *The Odyssey* like the rest of the class. Just because you entered midyear does not mean you're exempted from the yearlong syllabus."

I made a face at Jack, but he looked away.

"I did read it. I'm just drawing a blank." I sighed. "*Outis?*"

"And what does *outis* mean?"

"Oh yeah, it's the name Odysseus gives to the Cyclops. It means *nobody.*"

"That's right," she said with distaste. "But it's more than that. Throughout the years it has been used as a nom de plume—as an artistic pseudonym. Now why would someone need to write under a pseudonym? Someone else . . . Miss Taye?"

"Religious or political persecution?"

"Definitely. But there are also some cases where an artist uses a pseudonym just for fun. One example I can think of is

Edgar Allan Poe. There was a famous case where he publicly attacked Longfellow and then someone who called himself Outis defended Longfellow, but it's theorized that it was probably Poe himself. Can you think of any reason why someone would do that?"

"Because he was an opium addict," Shane said, chuckling.

Ms. Harlow raised her eyebrows and continued. I did my best to ignore her. I was feeling very thrown by Jack's weirdness. I kept trying to get his attention, but he wouldn't respond, and as soon as class was over, he took off.

Alex was sitting in Helen's seat when I walked into bio.

"Hey there," I said, taking the seat next to him.

"You're turning me into a stalker. I came by during second period to see if you had it free, but you were in class."

"Yeah, I hear the administration likes that kind of thing."

He leaned back in his chair and put a chiseled leg on the table.

"Um, I was gonna eat off of that."

"I'll come by after study hours tonight," he said, and tousled my hair.

I'll come by, not *Brody and I'll come by.* So we were going to hang out alone, then. I hadn't thought about it much, but I was beginning to notice that public displays of affection were basically taboo at St. Bede's. The thinking being that we all had to live together twenty-four hours a day, and no one wanted their sense of space any more invaded than it already was. So during the day it was best to keep things platonic. But at night, there were places you were supposed to go—anywhere that was out of the way, or that had a lock on the door. Preferably both. I had yet to frequent any of these places, but I had a feeling that I'd end up in one that night.

Helen came in and smirked at Alex. "Oh my God. I got really fat and ugly."

"No, Helen." Alex laughed, standing up and heading back to his seat. "You've always been fat and ugly."

She stuck her tongue out at him. Then she smoothed my hair and gave me a maternal kiss on the forehead. "Jealous, Alex?"

He stuck his middle finger out and laughed.

"I get her all night," she crooned, sitting down.

"Girl, you gotta stop. You're giving me strange ideas."

"Please shut up," Drucy sighed. "I need quiet right now. Iris is dead. Do any of you understand what that means? Can we just have some quiet?" She was slipping her glasses on and off her nose like she always did when she was upset. Everyone brought their conversations down to a lower level.

"So," Helen whispered. "Are you guys going out now, or what?"

I looked at him, sitting with his arm around Drucy, comforting her.

"I think so."

Helen wrung her hands like an excited child. "Oh my God. That is so cute. Do you even know what a catch he is? He always dates older girls. Everyone's been trying to hit that since forever. He's, like, *the* main conquest, and my little roommate just stumbles into this as soon as she gets here. You make me so proud."

That night, as soon as the nine-thirty bell sounded, there was a gentle knock at the window.

"Um, Rapunzel," Helen said, not lifting her gaze from her homework. "I think you have a visitor."

"Shit," I said, looking around the room wildly. I'd been busy studying and had no idea he'd be so punctual.

"Wood, stop acting crazy. He's watching you. You don't want to Sylvia Plath it on the first date."

"This is a date?"

"You know what I mean," she said, smiling and waving out the window. "Would you get out of here?"

"But I look like crap."

"No you don't. You look cute."

"Helen, I'm wearing moose pajamas and a plaid flannel. I need to put jeans on at least."

"No, seriously, the moose pajamas are better. They slip off."

He slid the door open just as I was wiggling my toes into my electric-blue flip-flops.

"What's up, *chicas*?"

"Ms. Harlow," Helen called lightly. "There's a boy in the dorm."

He was wearing an ivory sweater and jeans. He smiled at me, and his cheeks dimpled.

"Shall we?" he asked, extending his hand. I took it, and soon we were trudging up the hill, wet grass sneaking in through the straps of my flip-flops and licking my toes. We held hands. It felt awkward, like his was too big or mine was too small. He held on like I might try to escape.

"So, how's bio going for you?" he asked.

"Good. I, um, always like science."

"Me too."

"But," I went on, trying not to think about where we were headed, "we're having trouble isolating the virgins." Oh my God, had I just said *virgins*? What was happening? Where was I going? "I mean the flies. The fly virgins. We're having trouble isolating them so we can count them. You know, for the separate generations."

"Wood," he said, laughing. "I'm doing the same experiment, remember? We had trouble at first too. But the lab is always open. Shane checks ours last thing at night, and I check them again at five-thirty in the morning."

"You're up at five-thirty in the morning?" I gasped.

"Yeah. I like to get a run in. I like to read the paper, chill out a bit before the day starts."

"You go running, check the flies, and read the paper before I even wake up? God, this place. It's like no matter what you do, you're still lazy."

"What time do you wake up?" he asked, eyeing me sideways.

"Like two minutes before class starts. Eight minutes if I want breakfast."

"I'm usually sitting in my desk eight minutes before class starts."

"Jesus."

"You snooze, you lose, Wood."

"Obviously not. I am pretty amazing."

"I have to say, for a complete lazy ass, you always look really cute, but you don't use what you've got."

"What do you mean?"

"I mean, you're one of the cutest girls in school, but you dress like a little goth boy."

I flushed, suddenly uncomfortable. "I like how I dress."

"I wasn't trying to be mean. You're low maintenance. That's good."

"It is?"

"I think so. You're different from the girls I've gone out with before."

"Were they high maintenance? I mean, like, compared to me?"

"Compared to you I think Brody is high maintenance. You're lucky if you brush your hair, huh?" He laughed.

"Brush my what, now?"

We stopped outside one of the humanities classrooms. He held open the door for me, and I sort of skipped in and turned on the light. He quickly turned it off.

"We should probably lock the door. Is that cool with you?"

"Um. I think so."

I wasn't sure exactly what I meant to do with Alex Reese, but he was a safe person. I was sure of that much. He slipped his hands around my waist and kissed me softly, sweetly. I gave in to the kiss, trying not to think about where I was going. I wanted to relinquish a tiny bit of control, but it was difficult. My mind kept narrating everything that was happening, analyzing and decoding it. I had to relax. He knelt down and gently pulled me on top of him. I was straddling him now and wondering what the hell I was supposed to do, when I was distracted by his unfastening my bra. Oh my God. Soon my bra was completely off, resting on my knee, and he was lifting up my shirt, delicately kissing my belly, my torso, and then my breasts. Before I realized what was happening, I let out a loud belly laugh.

"Is this okay?" he asked gently.

I nodded, but I couldn't stop laughing. I covered my mouth, but when he put his lips back on my breast, I let out a little scream. I hadn't meant to. I'd never been in this situation before, and it turned out my body was unexpectedly connected to my vocal cords.

Just then there was a loud bang at the door. Alex pulled back. Someone tried the door. It thudded back and forth.

"Who's in there! Come out immediately!"

I was shaking, freezing. Every inch of my body was confused and terrified. Alex grabbed my hand.

"Shit," he breathed. "The window."

He opened it swiftly, deftly, and motioned for me to go first. I made my best attempt at an action-hero dive roll through the window, landing on a thorny plant a few feet below. I didn't even hear Alex come through. He grabbed my hand, and laughing, nearly hysterical, we ran across the lawn into the cover of the pine trees outside the dining hall. Smiling, Alex handed me my bra.

"You left this behind."

"Oh shit," I said, covering my mouth and laughing. "That would have been kind of bad, huh?"

"It would have been like Cinderella, them coming around trying the bra on every girl."

Cinderella. I looked down and noticed I was wearing only one flip-flop.

"Crap, Alex, my shoe."

He looked down.

"Oh no. When did it come off?"

"I think it hit the window when I went through."

"Well, here, take the other one off and give it to me."

"And what, I just pretend I decided to go barefoot?"

"You're eccentric, Wood. Play it up. But look," he said, his brow furrowed. "We should separate now."

"Okay, um, I'll go to the library."

"No, we should go to our dorms. We can get kicked out."

"I thought you did this all the time."

"I do," he said, laughing. "I mean, I've done it before, but I've never come so close to getting caught. It's the increased security; everyone's on patrol. We'd better split up." He kissed my forehead. "I'll see you tomorrow, okay?"

My heart was still racing when I got back to the dorm. Helen was gone, and with the adrenaline still pumping through my system, I didn't quite know what to do with myself. Of course I would almost get caught and risk getting kicked out of school the very first time I really hooked up with a guy. What would happen when I decided to have sex? I'd probably get attacked by sharks.

I thought about doing some extra homework, but instead I pulled out the note and stared at it. I opened my notebook and started futzing around with the numbers, but I had no idea what I was doing.

I tapped the note with the back of my hand. There had to be something there. If only I knew where to look. I had a double free period the next morning, so I decided to spend it in the library. There had to be methods of cryptanalysis besides the one I'd read about in a Poe story. It was a ridiculous mixture of hubris and puerility that had kept me from looking further into the possibility of a different kind of encryption. I needed to roll up my sleeves. The next day I would get to work.

CHAPTER NINE

I FELT SELF-CONSCIOUS THE NEXT morning as I pulled on my Dickies and perfunctory black T-shirt. I surveyed my situation in the mirror. I didn't know what Alex was talking about. I thought I looked fine. I'd cut the shirt myself so that the neck hole displayed my clavicle. That was sexy, wasn't it? Uncharacteristically panicked about my appearance, I searched through my desk drawer for my tube of brick-red lipstick. I swept it across my lips and wondered if it made me look more or less like a little goth boy. After a bit of grueling self-consideration, I traded the black shirt for a plain white one, and my Dickies for a short plaid skirt Kim had given me, which a girl at my old school had once called slutty, and I pulled my hair back into a high ponytail like I'd seen Helen do.

In the library, I set myself up with a couple of cryptanalysis books and started reading. It was heavy work and required more brain cells than I was comfortable using first thing in the morning, but slowly, things started to come into view, and before long, I had an idea of what I might be dealing with.

I was almost certain that decrypting the note would require what was called a key text. When working with a key text, the sender and recipient would agree on a piece of text to use as an alphabet. The text itself didn't matter; you could use any book. What mattered were the predetermined edition and starting points within the text. So say you wanted to use the first line of *Anna Karenina*:

> *Happy families are all alike; every unhappy family is unhappy in its own way.*

If you wanted to communicate *Hello,* using that line as the alphabet, the encryption would work out to: 1 12 10 18 57.

But while such an encryption would be ridiculously easy to decode if I had knowledge of the key text, without that piece of information, the message would be next to impossible for me to penetrate. But I had to give it a try. Since I'd needed to solve an *Odyssey*-themed puzzle to get the note, I figured it was also the obvious choice for the key text. I pulled out the Fagles translation we used in class and gave it a go. The first few lines were:

> *Sing to me of the man, Muse, the man of twists and turns*
> *driven time and again off course, once he had plundered*
> *the hallowed heights of Troy.*

Many cities of men he saw and learned their minds,
many pains he suffered, heartsick on the open sea,
fighting to save his life and bring his comrades home.

Next I consulted the first line of the encrypted note: 15 36 9 2 3 22 24 , 5 12 7 4 17 36 30 128 77 46 44 18 39.

I set about decoding but was quickly disappointed when the line read *Anoinhm, thmgmnwsavruu.*

Not exactly what I was looking for, but I tried not to get too down about it. I tried a few different editions, but I had a deepening sense that I was on a fool's errand. I bit down on the end of my pen. It was possible that the key text was the *Odyssey*, and that the starting point was not the beginning. The string of consecutive numbers, which I now realized was a word lifted straight from the text, perhaps for emphasis, could be an indicator that a particularly meaningful passage had been chosen to use as a key text. This also explained the addition of the letter *J.* If the sender intended for the passage itself to have a clear significance, it might be a passage that happened not to include the letter *J.* Either way, there was just no way I could solve it without more information.

I was chewing my eraser and staring out the window when I saw Freddy emerge from the stacks. Clearly agitated, she looked at me as though I'd caught her doing something. I waved, but she pretended not to see me. Weird, I thought, but then, I didn't exactly have Freddy figured out yet. I decided to ignore it and tried to focus back on the note.

There had to be another way. Maybe I was going about this

all wrong. In essence, I didn't really care what the note said. What I wanted was the identity of the sender. Because of the timing, I couldn't help but connect the box with Iris. What if someone I knew had found the body and was trying to bait me? It occurred to me that maybe I should be thinking about who would have the skill and the time to make something as complicated as the puzzle box. It seemed to me you'd have to have a bit of the artist and the engineer about you to be able to make something like that.

What struck me was that from what I knew of Iris, that described her rather well. Maybe it was someone close to her, someone who liked the same things she did. My stomach soured when I thought about what that could mean. Maybe that was the link. But then why send it to me?

I looked out the window and noticed the sky was growing dark. As much as I fought it, I knew I had to examine the very real possibility that the box might be from the killer. I also knew there was another step I needed to take—to Clare, and the possibility that she hadn't died in the fire—but I couldn't go there quite yet. That was a chamber of my heart I needed to keep closed a while longer.

Someone opened the library door, and a cold breeze rushed in. I looked up to see Carlos. He nodded at me, then headed up the stairs. There was something I was missing, some avenue I wasn't exploring. I wrote the words *puzzle box* in my notebook and then circled the word *puzzle*. I knew Iris had been a math kid, and sometimes math people liked puzzles. I knew Carlos did. He was always playing sudoku and doing crossword puzzles. Maybe someone else had the same interests as Iris. Maybe they'd gotten obsessed with her. Maybe they'd let their obsession get out of control. It was worth checking into, but I didn't know where to start. It wasn't like they had a puzzle club at St. Bede's.

And who would be able to make something so intricate? I figured I could talk to the art teacher and ask him about the woodworking shop, see if there were any students who were particularly skilled. And then there was the dragon. I had to figure out why the killer had drawn the dragon on the wall of that cave. If I could figure out his reasoning, I would be one step closer to him. From history class, I knew that in some cultures dragons could be a good luck symbol, but mostly they were perceived as symbols of evil. In the Bible, they stood in for the devil himself.

I bit my lip and tapped my pencil against the desk. I knew that if I kept my head straight, I could manage to turn something up.

The bell rang and I started gathering my things. I felt a sense of accomplishment as I slung my bag over my shoulders and headed down the stairs, but something else weighed on me. At some point I was going to need to have a little chat with Carlos.

Later that day, I returned from the bathroom to find Jack splayed out on my bed, reading Jean Genet. His face erupted into a sybaritic grin, the kind that made something catch in my throat and sent a surplus of oxygen to my brain.

"Hi," he said, pushing himself up to stand. "You look weird. Why are you dressed like that?"

"I don't know," I groaned. "I feel kind of ridiculous. Are you even allowed to be in here?"

"No. Can we talk outside?"

"I was just going to see Alex," I said, grabbing my sweatshirt. "Do you want to walk me?"

"Don't go. Hang out with me." His huge brown eyes were shameless, pleading. He extended his hand, his hips jutting forward. "Puhleeez?"

"Walk with me," I said. "Is Sophie busy? Is that why you're here?"

"Yeah," he said, falling into step alongside me. "She's got this math thing, so I thought I'd go slumming and drag you over to the side of the hill for a smoke and a cuddle."

"Sorry. I promised Alex. And since when do we cuddle?"

"I don't know. We could start."

"God, you really can't handle Sophie being occupied."

"It's true. Also, you're my chemistry partner, doesn't that get me some rights? You can recite the elements of the periodic table to me and tell me I've been a naughty boy."

When we reached the trail that led down to the side of the hill, he stopped. "Come on. Boyfriends are lame. Come watch me smoke cigarettes."

"Well, lung cancer *is* cool, but I think I'll pass."

He shook his finger at me. "Someday I'll be famous and then you'll beg to watch me smoke cigarettes."

"I'll see you later, okay?" But just as I waved and turned to go, he got a strange look in his eye. "What? What is it?"

"Nothing," he said, shaking his head. "It's just . . . Don't sleep with him."

"What?" I gasped, blood rushing to my face. "Are you out of your mind?"

"So then you haven't yet," he said, and for some reason, I found myself staring at his hips, the smooth lift of his abdomen, the curve of his torso. I looked away, but not before he noticed.

"That is seriously none of your business," I said.

"It kind of is, though," he said, curiosity giving way to theatrical sanctimony. "Sex leads to babies, and babies lead to overpopulation, and the next thing you know you've basically destroyed the planet. Why do you want to destroy the planet, Cally?"

"Oh my God."

"Plus it's a sin," he said with childish delight. "It says so in one of those religious books. I can't remember which one."

I didn't know why I did it, but for a moment, I let myself again admire his silhouette, lithe and angular, set against the evening sky, and then I shrugged and headed over to see Alex.

"Don't make the baby Jesus cry!" he called after me.

On the walk to Alex's, I found Iris weighing heavily on me again. I knew there couldn't be a connection between her and Clare, yet the two were beginning to fuse together in a way I found disconcerting. I needed to separate them. I needed to find out more about Iris—the girl no one seemed to know.

Alex sat on his bed, reading Proust.

"You look really nice."

"Thanks," I said, taking a seat next to him. "But I'm feeling kind of creeped out."

"I can't say that's the usual reaction when someone starts dating me."

"It's about Iris. It's just really disturbing, you know?"

"Of course," he said, delicately placing a bookmark in *Swann's Way* and setting it beside him. "Everyone is a little on edge, but I can imagine that it must be worse for you."

"Why for me?"

"Because you're sleeping in her bed. That has to be really weird."

"Yeah, I guess. You know, I was kind of wondering if I could ask you about her."

"Me?" he asked, raising his eyebrows. "Can't you ask Helen?"

"I know they were roommates, but Helen says she didn't know her at all."

Alex shook his head. "Helen's being a drama queen. Iris used to go to the lake house with all of us. At some point last year she stopped coming. I think she and Helen had a fight or something, because I never saw them together again after that."

"Really?" I asked. "How random that they ended up roommates."

"There's nothing random about it," he said, shaking his head.

"What do you mean?"

"Room assignments aren't random."

"They're not?"

"Nope. One of those ladies put a request in for the other."

"That is so weird. Why would they do that if they hated each other? And the way Helen tells it, living together didn't make them any friendlier."

"Dude, I have no idea."

"So what was the deal with Iris? Why didn't people like her? If she was so pretty, why was she unpopular?"

He laughed. "She wasn't unpopular. She was just kind of different, you know? Like there was something a little off about her. She was cool and everything. We hung out sometimes, but some of the guys sort of thought that she might be, like, sick."

"Sick how?"

"It's embarrassing."

"Tell me."

"She was just . . . she wasn't promiscuous, but everything for her was about sex. I can't explain it exactly. It's just that it was like the language she spoke."

"So she slept around a lot?"

"No. I don't think she slept with anyone. But every interaction was about sex. I totally fell for it. Everything she said was a double entendre. Everything was loaded and sexual, and obviously she was hot, so I was pretty much putty in her hands. For about a week, I just followed her around and did what she said, sort of endured her sexual hegemony. . . ."

"Sexual hegemony? Nice."

He rolled his eyes. "Anyway, I hung around for a while until I figured out I wasn't going to get anywhere, then I took off."

"And she just kept doing that?"

"Yeah. She even flirted with faculty members. Some were even into it, I think."

"I bet I can guess who," I said, my mind returning to Reilly leaning over Shelly Cates in chemistry lab.

"It was weird," he said. "And when she left—or I guess now I should say 'when she was murdered'—I thought she checked out and went to be a model or something. But I should have known something was up."

"What do you mean?"

"I sort of wondered if she was mixed up in something. Like maybe she was dealing drugs to the local kids or something. She seemed to have money all of a sudden, and it was kind of weird. I just wonder if she got herself mixed up with some bad people."

"Did she have any friends?"

He shrugged. "Friends? No. I don't think so."

"Really? How could she not have any friends?"

"She'd always pick one boy to string along and that's who she'd spend time with. Then he'd get sick of her and she'd move on to somebody else," he said, shifting around. "Last spring she got sick and spent a couple of days in the infirmary. Turned out she wasn't sick like in the traditional sense. It turned out she had some kind of emotional breakdown. I haven't really told anybody, so keep it on the DL. I only found out because I tore my meniscus and ended up in there at the same time. Anyway, whatever she was going through, whatever happened to her last spring, I think it must have really messed her up, because she changed after that."

"How'd she change?"

"I don't know. I mean, she always had problems relating to other people, but she got really cold after that. And she always seemed to be focused on something a million miles from here. She was involved with something. I don't know if it was drugs or what, but she went from an A student to a C student really fast. Rumor had it she was failing marine bio. If that happened, she wasn't going to get asked back."

"Asked back? What does that mean?"

He crossed his arms in front of his chest. "Every summer we all get evaluated, and the administration decides whether or not we'll be asked to return in the fall. With Cs, Iris might have managed it, but not with an F. With an F she was going back home to Queens."

"Maybe she was trying to get sent home," I thought aloud. "Maybe whatever happened to her in the spring was so traumatic that she was failing on purpose so she could leave. God." I sighed, suddenly overwhelmed with sadness for the girl. "If only she had been kicked out, she'd be alive today."

He looked at me strangely. "Why are you so interested in this, anyway? You didn't even know the girl."

I shrugged. "That's probably why. I just want to understand who she was. I just want to know what happened to her."

"Cally, it's no big mystery. She went out to meet her dealer. Either he killed her or some vagrant killed her."

"Or maybe a vagrant drug dealer killed her," I snorted. "Anyway, how can you be so sure?"

"Because I saw her get the call."

"What?" I asked. "What are you talking about?"

"The day she disappeared, I was in the bio lab working on our cellular respiration lab before dinner. Iris was in there too—she was Asta's lab assistant, so she was in there a lot, but that day she was super edgy. She even yelled at Asta about some grade. She was really hostile, raising her voice, even. I mean, no one talks to Asta like that, you know? They were arguing. It seemed like it was about something Iris had found in the display case or something. It was super weird, and then someone came and got her, told her she had a call back on the dorm phones. She never came back. The next day she was dead."

"Have you told anyone else about this?"

"Of course I told the police back in October, but no one thought she was dead back then. It takes on more importance now that they've found her."

"Do they know who it was?" I asked, running my hand across my forehead. "Do they know who called her?"

He shook his head. "No. The person who came and got her can't remember who called."

"What? Really?"

"Yeah," he said, rolling his eyes. "She doesn't even remember taking the call."

"Really? You'd think you'd remember something like that."

"Yeah. You would. Especially if you were someone with early acceptance to Harvard."

"Freddy?"

"President Bingham to you," he said, and wrapped his arm around me.

* * *

I was reading *Don Quixote,* wondering if I was Dulcinea or Quixote and deciding that I was probably just Sancho Panza, when Helen asked me if I wanted to come to her house for spring break.

"We have a spring break?"

"I think that's kind of implicit in my invitation. Don't tell me you haven't started studying for midterms."

"Why would I study for midterms?"

"I thought you were supposed to be this wunderkind. Don't you ever study?"

"Don't have to. That's why I'm a wunderkind." I smiled.

"You're lazy is what you are."

"Yeah, well, I know you are but what am I? Hey, though, I wanted to ask you something. It's about Iris."

"Oh God, not this again."

"Do you know if she was into puzzles?"

"Puzzles? How would I know that? I told you, I didn't know her." She shook her head.

"Yeah, but you were roommates. Did you ever see her doing a crossword puzzle or anything?"

"Dude, no. You are so weird sometimes."

"What about art? Was Iris an artist?"

"I don't know. Can we drop this already? You are seriously creeping me out."

"Fine," I sighed. "Is everyone going to your house? Pigeon and Freddy?"

"We're only inviting *you,* silly," she said, and knit her brow as if anything else would be absurd. "The others are wonderful, don't get me wrong, but we just want to chill and not think about things." She stretched her arms up over her head and then fell back onto her bed. "It should be really relaxing. Really earthy."

I didn't know what *really earthy* meant, but I figured I'd put in my request form anyway. That night I slept fitfully, drifting into and out of fever dreams. At one point I was convinced Helen was gone for what seemed like several hours, but when I forced myself awake to get up and go wash my face, I saw that she was sleeping soundly, and when I took my temperature in the morning, it was normal.

Midterms were mildly unpleasant, but I survived them, and before I knew it, it was the night before spring break. After study hours, I packed my things and headed up to the library to check in with Carlos before he left. I found him reading in his usual spot. I slumped into the chair beside him.

"What's up, chickadee?" he said without looking up from his paper.

"You're into puzzles, right?"

He shook his head. "Into puzzles? No."

"Come on. You're always playing weird little games."

"I'll have a go at Settlers of Catan now and again. I enjoy a good RPG session, and I've been known to dabble in a brainteaser or two, but that does not make me *into puzzles*. That sounds like I'm ten."

"Sorry. I just wanted to ask you something."

"What?"

"Well, this is totally random, and you're gonna think I'm weird."

"I already think you're weird. Go ahead. Speak your mind."

"Okay, well, Iris Liang, do you know if she was into puzzles or games or anything?"

He nodded. "Sure, she was in puzzle club."

"No way," I gasped. "There really is a puzzle club?"

He groaned and put his head in his hands. "God, no, Wood. I'm messing with you. Why do you want to know this?"

"It's complicated," I said, opening my novel. "Never mind. I shouldn't have bothered you. It's stupid."

"No it's not," he sighed. "Listen, I'll come clean with you. I think I might be able to help you."

"You're not still messing with me?"

"No. Listen. Iris Liang wouldn't have given me the time of day, but she used to come by Tanner's room pretty often. I live next door to Tanner and spend a lot of time on the hammock on my balcony, so I am, as you might imagine, privy to a lot of pretty intense stuff that goes on at this school."

"Okay, but does any of it involve puzzles?"

"It does, in fact." He raised his eyebrows.

"Oh my God, really?"

"I think so. It might be nothing, but I did see her with something like a puzzle once—at least, I think it was a puzzle."

"Seriously?" I said, turning to face him, hands on my knees.

"Yeah. One night when she was waiting for Tanner, she leaned over his balcony and a bunch of papers fell out of her notebook. I, of course, sprang to her assistance. She wasn't the least bit grateful, I assure you, but one thing I can tell you is that the pages, at least the glimpse that I got, seemed to involve a really complicated crossword or something."

"A crossword?"

"That's what it looked like. And I remember thinking that was kind of weird, but then, Iris was a weird girl. Does that help?"

"Yeah," I said. "I think it does. Thanks. What about anyone else? Is there anyone you think of as being into puzzles? Or someone you saw working with Iris on something that might have been a puzzle."

He shook his head. "Now we are reaching into the realm of total speculation."

"Hmm." I tapped my finger against my lip. "Well, let me know if you hear anything."

"Sure thing." He nodded. "And if you ever want some truly juicy gossip on Tanner, I am your man."

"Yeah, thanks," I groaned as I thought about Freddy. "I think I'll pass on that."

"Suit yourself." He snapped open his newspaper and resumed reading.

"Wait," I said. "One more thing. You know much about the art teacher? What's his story?"

"John? He's a good guy, a really good guy. Don't you take art?"

"No. I hate it."

"You're missing out. He's the best teacher here. You should sit in on one of his classes. He lets me do that during my free periods."

"Carlos," I said, impressed. "I didn't know you were an artist."

He shook his head. "I've got no natural talent, but I love it."

"Hmm, maybe I will go talk to him. Is he down at the art barn, do you think?"

"No. You've missed him, I'm afraid. Left early for break."

"Like I said, I'll talk to him when we get back from spring break. Have a good one, my friend."

"You too," he said, saluting. "See you back here a week from Sunday."

I saluted him back and headed out.

CHAPTER TEN

IT WAS DURING THE CAR ride over to the Slaters' that I first noticed that Noel had lost an alarming amount of weight. Bony concavities were visible on her wrists, and her fingers looked frail and gray as she gripped the steering wheel. I was almost sure she hadn't been that thin a week earlier. Was she sick? Should I say something? But when I thought about it, I realized that I hadn't seen her eat anything for quite a while. Suddenly, I felt ill.

We'd been at the house fewer than ten minutes and had barely unloaded the car when Chelsea Vetiver appeared, lank and dissolute, spindly digits crisscrossed over a white unfiltered cigarette. She wore a slip the color of mayonnaise and an alarming number of silver bangle bracelets. Her eyes were heavy with charcoal liner.

"What's for dinner?" she asked Helen, sweeping her eyes over me once, letting them linger just long enough to make an appraisal, then moving on to Helen. "You need a new look, Helen. This whole classic beauty thing is getting old. I'm thinking massive body mods, transdermal implants, the works."

"Thanks," Helen said, rolling her eyes at me. "I'll take it under advisement."

Chelsea's gaze slipped back to me, a smile playing on her lips.

"Columbo," she croaked, falling into a low chair and tossing her legs over the rattan arm. "I heard about Alex Reese. Good on you. He was a little, um—how should I put this?—short-lived for my tastes, but I'm glad you're making it work."

"How's truancy treating you, Chelsea?" Noel asked, poking her head out of the kitchen.

"Holy Christ, Noel, what the hell happened to you?" Chelsea asked, her lips curled into a snarl.

"What do you mean?" Noel asked, looking away.

"What do you think I mean? Are you auditioning for *Dachau: The Musical,* or what?"

Helen choked on a piece of bread and scowled at Chelsea. "Chelsea, do you think you can try not to be offensive for just a few minutes? Why don't we talk about subjects you can manage, like, say, your art? How's the big project going?" She turned to me. "Chelsea decided not to go back to Exeter this semester. A mental-health break. She's using it to work on some amazing art project that's going to transform all of us, society as a whole, in fact. Am I right, Chelsea?"

"See, Wood, I told you I was an art star." She cackled and blew little rings with her smoke.

"Hey, Chelsea, do you know how to French inhale?" Helen asked.

"No," she drawled. "Because it's disgusting. And it makes you look like a fucking whore."

"I think it's sexy," Noel said, laughing.

"Yeah, well, I think eating is sexy." Chelsea laughed, then popped up from the chair into perfect yoga posture. "What's for fucking dinner? Don't you guys have a fucking cook?" And with that she was gone. I expected her to show up as soon as Noel finished with the chicken curry, but it was just the three of us eating—well, two, really, though I did see Noel suck on a few strands of red pepper.

"Where's Chelsea?" I asked during a quiet moment. "I thought she wanted dinner."

"Who cares?" Helen said. "Pass me the wine. Oooh, Margaux. Nummy choice, Miss Slater."

"Why, thank you, Miss Slater. Here, Wood, you want some?"

I shook my head. "No. No thank you."

The next morning, Chelsea Vetiver came bearing doughnuts. I was immediately suspicious, and rightly so, because as soon as I bit into my first maple bar, she explained that she wanted me to model for her . . . out in the woods . . . immediately after finishing my maple bar. Weakened by my sugar daze, I acquiesced, and she led me out a fair way from the Slaters' place to a spot where the leaves were an otherworldly kind of green.

Chelsea's monstrous black Nikon hung pendulous from her neck.

I wondered if it was safe, walking in those woods, but I couldn't bring myself to ask Chelsea what she thought. I was sure she'd laugh at me, so I tried to forget about Iris. I tried to act cool.

"Um, can you hang upside down in a tree for me?" she asked, genuflecting before a giant oak and fiddling with her camera lens.

I wrapped my sweatshirt around my waist. "You want me to hang from a tree?"

She looked up and squinted at me. "Yeah," she said in that languorous monotone.

So I climbed trees, hung upside down, performed a few impromptu cherry drops, and finally, after about three-quarters of an hour, Chelsea shook her head.

"Come on, we need to change location. The pond, I think."

"We're close to the pond?"

"Yeah, it's right through those trees a bit. I like it there. I like to think there. My thoughts are clearer. If you want, I'll even let you watch me think while we're shooting."

"Um, thanks."

"No problem. Come on."

After a short walk, we emerged into the clearing, the pond sparkling with early-morning sun. It was strange to see it there. Conceptually, Helen and Noel's place seemed a million miles from school, and it was a vaguely unpleasant reminder to see how close we actually were, separated only by these haunted little woods, and that fey pond.

157

"Okay," she said, rummaging around in her bag. "So you're gonna be pissed, but I need you to put on this dress and wade out into the water."

"No."

"Come on," she groaned. "Don't be a pussy. Do you hate art or something?"

"Chelsea, you're serious?"

She nodded and tossed me the dress, a gossamer white thing.

"Here, take your hair down. There, I want it to be kind of wild. Good. Right, now, get your ass out there. Waist deep."

I pulled off my jeans and T-shirt and slipped the dress over my head. It made me feel strange, like a doomed fairy princess. I walked to the pond and paused at the edge of the water. My breath caught, and I found myself inexplicably excited and frightened. It was just a pond, so why did it feel like something else? I had the distinct impression that once I stepped in, in a way, there would be no turning back.

I set a toe in. Crisp, cold, nipping at the base of my spine.

"For fuck's sake, get in there, Inspector Wood. I don't have all day."

I stepped in and began wading—the water rising, my skin tingling—and something inside me changed. A shot of electricity bolted up my spine to the base of my skull and suddenly my vision seemed more lucid. I started to laugh.

"No laughter," she called. "This is serious business."

I turned to see that she had the camera trained on me and was already taking pictures.

"So you really just didn't go back to school this semester?"

"No. I'm right here. I can't be in two places at once, now can I?"

"I don't know," I said, sinking my hips in, the water licking at my waist. "Quantum mechanics might say different."

"Oh, shut up, wondergeek. Now turn around."

"So why didn't you go back?"

"I told you. Psychological problems. I'm taking some personal time."

"And your parents don't care?"

"I don't have parents; I have guardians."

"Guardians?"

"Yeah. My grandparents. Lift your hair up above your head and then drop it. There you go. Good."

"My dad died too," I said, then bit down on my lip.

"Christ, Wood, my parents aren't dead. They're just not here. Turn around. Dip your head over and spread out your arms. Sorry about your dad, though. That blows."

"Yeah. Sorry about your craziness. I hope you get better."

"Yeah, thanks. Turn around and start walking away from me."

I did, the trees rising before me, the water drifting through my fingers. High in nests, birds rustled and peeped.

"Hey, Wood. What would you say if I told you I was fucking Richard Slater?"

My heart jolted and I spun to face her, unable to keep the disgust and horror from my face.

"There we go. That's the shot I wanted. You can come out now."

I waded toward the shore, watching Chelsea pack up her

gear. Had that been just a stunt? Something to shock me? When I got to the shore, she grinned at me.

"That was brilliant."

"You were joking, right?" I said, changing out of the wet dress.

"God, Wood, you're unbelievable."

"You *were*, right?"

She sighed. "Yes, Wood. I was joking." But then she laughed, and something in my gut told me she was lying.

She let the camera fall from her neck and gathered her things. We were weaving our way through a shining sea of yellow sour grass flowers when she brought up Iris.

"Pretty creepy," she said, eyeing me to watch for my reaction.

"It's horrible," I sighed. "Did you know her at all?"

She shook her head. "Not really, no. I knew *of* her."

"Yeah, I guess she and Helen weren't exactly friends."

She raised an eyebrow. "Or so Helen would have us believe."

"What do you mean?" I asked, trying to seem nonchalant.

"Oh, you know," she drawled, sweeping her arm down to pick a flower without breaking stride. She bit into the stem. "Mmm. So good. When I was little, I thought the stems were sour because dogs peed on them. I ate them anyway, though. Want one?" Again, she raised an eyebrow at me.

I shook my head.

"You should just know that Helen doesn't always tell the truth."

"What are you saying?" I asked, trying to keep my voice steady.

She stopped and rolled her eyes at me. "For fuck's sake, I'm not saying *that*. It's not like I think Helen killed her or anything. Christ, Detective Wood, get a hold of yourself. I'm just saying that there was something going on between them."

"What makes you think that?"

"I saw Iris here more than once."

"Yeah, I heard they used to be friends a long time ago."

"No," she said. "I saw Iris up here last spring, which seemed sort of strange, since Helen was always saying, 'Iris is such a liar, she's such a stalker, requesting me for a roommate,' that kind of thing, but I think she's covering her tracks or something."

"Last spring?"

She nodded, pleased with herself. "Mmmhmm. How you like them apples?"

We were at the path to the Slaters' place now, and it was clear she was dropping me off.

"Thanks," she said, patting me on the head. "And shhh. Don't tell Helen you heard it from me, 'kay?"

I nodded.

"See you around, Columbo." She laughed. And then she turned and headed back out into the woods, the verdant morning light seeming to close in around her and swallow her up.

Inside, the house was empty. I had no idea when the twins would be back from wherever they'd gone, so I grabbed my notebook and climbed into a lake-view window seat. From my perch, the water looked still as glass. If only I could stay in that seat, staring at that lake forever. But I would need to go back eventually, and when I did, I would need a plan. I opened my notebook and got to work. I decided to devise a two-pronged attack. First I would talk to John, the art instructor. I hadn't tried to grill a teacher yet, and I thought it best to be prepared. I even went so far as to write out a list of questions to ask him. It made me feel a bit like Lois Lane.

Next—and I felt this was a particularly ingenious plan—I would go to the library and make a list of anyone who had checked out books pertaining to woodworking, in case our killer happened to be an autodidact. I would then narrow down that list and continue my investigation. I closed my notebook and stared out across the lake, satisfied I'd done all I could for the time being. Now, I decided, I would enjoy my vacation.

The break turned out to be phenomenally pleasant. Mornings were spent lounging at the lake, afternoons reading in the woods, evenings eating, talking, watching movies or listening to music. Noel had a tremendous jazz collection on vinyl, and she did her best to fill in what she deemed the formidable holes in my music vocabulary. Helen was more relaxed than she ever was at school, and that in turn chilled me out. Chelsea would show up every once in a while to cadge a meal, standing over Noel while she cooked, picking bits and pieces out of the saucepan, or to coerce the twins into ordering pizza. She liked it with pineapple, she would remind them. And sometimes we'd see her down at the lake, stretched out on a rock in an uncharacteristically modest navy one-piece. I wondered if she was being completely honest with me about Iris and Helen. I didn't see why she would lie, but then, she was Chelsea Vetiver, and I never really knew what to make of her. The last night of break, she showed up in a faux-fur coat, demanding that Helen go into town with her to see a movie.

"It's about scorpions, Helen. *Scorpions.* You know how I feel about scorpions."

I couldn't disguise my disappointment when Helen went with her.

"Don't worry, Droopy Dog," Noel said. "We don't need my stupid sister to have fun."

It was still early, so we grabbed a bottle of red wine and went out to the gazebo. It was a beautiful night—clear and light, warm enough that we didn't have to wear sweaters, but with a slight crispness to the air that paired nicely with the cherrywood warmth of the wine. We drank out of her mother's crystal goblets, though I noticed that Noel barely touched the cup to her lips. Since I didn't really drink either, the whole thing seemed like a bizarre but necessary custom.

We talked for a while about school, about boys, about whether we were going to fail the eleventh grade because we'd basically made up a sport, and then Noel looked sick and exhausted, and I felt I finally needed to say something.

"I know you don't want to talk about it," I said. "But are you okay? I mean, about the eating thing."

She smiled and looked at my hairline. "I'm fine, silly. Don't worry. I just lose weight when I'm stressed, and things lately have been a little stressful."

"Are you sure? I just want you to be okay."

She took an actual sip of her wine and closed her eyes. She smiled, and for the first time since we'd found the body, Noel looked at peace.

"Do you know who Kuan Yin is?" she asked.

"No. Does she go to St. Bede's?"

"No," she said, laughing. "No, not at all. She's a goddess. She protects women and children. You can call on her and ask for her protection, and when you die, she comes and holds you, and she takes away all your karmic debt. She just holds you, and you're free. I'm not sure it would be too bad, being held like that."

"I guess not," I said, trying to keep the skepticism from my voice.

"Cally, do you ever think about it?"

"About what?"

"About suicide."

"Whoa," I said, nearly spilling my wine. "Where the hell did that come from?"

"I don't know," she said, her voice soft and quiet. "I don't think I'd ever do it, but in a way it does seem kind of noble, or beautiful, or something."

"Noel, listen to yourself. Suicide is terrible. It's not beautiful. It's horrible. And not every culture thinks it's noble or whatever. Catholics think suicides go to hell."

"Lucky I'm not Catholic, then."

"Well, whatever, it seems pretty stupid to me."

"So if you do something horrible, you don't think you should make amends for it?"

"Noel, what could you possibly have to make amends for?"

"Nothing, I guess." She shrugged.

"You talk about this goddess coming to hold you, but what if there aren't any goddesses to hold you? What if there's just a cold black nothing?"

She opened her eyes and gave me a brilliant smile. "But there are goddesses. I know for a fact."

"How do you know that?" I laughed.

"I'm serious," she said. "I know someone who saw one."

"Seriously?" I said, and took a sip of wine, the bitter warmth running through my veins. "Someone told you they saw a goddess?"

"Yes," she said, laughing. "I swear."

"Who?"

"I can't say."

"Oh my God, you have to tell me. I promise I won't tell."

She leveled her gaze at me. "Asta."

"No. She must have been kidding."

"She was serious. I was at her place borrowing a book and we got to talking and she was drinking, like, a lot of wine, and she told me that I was her favorite student and that she wanted to tell me a secret. See, I tell her lots of secrets."

"You do?"

"Oh yeah. I've told her stuff I'll never tell another living soul. I've told her terrible things. She's like my father confessor. Anyway, I guess since I tell her all my secrets, she decided to tell me one. She said she'd never told anyone else."

"Okay, so what was it?"

"Well, she said that the night that her daughter disappeared, she went out to the pond in the woods. It was midnight, and there was a storm coming and the sky was strange and filled with magic, and she had to go and be out in it. Asta's like that. She's a nature person. So she lay there looking at the stars, and then a goddess came to her and whispered in her ear that there was an afterlife, and that she and her daughter would meet there when the time came to pass. It didn't make any sense to her at the time, but when she went back to her house and the girls were missing, it was like, oh my God. She said whenever she gets upset about her daughter, she remembers what the goddess told her, and she feels better."

I couldn't speak. I felt like I'd been kicked in the teeth, my gums numb with shock. I needed to say something. I needed to get the knot out of my chest. I shook my head.

"That doesn't make sense."

"Sure it does. Just because you don't believe in something doesn't mean it's not real."

"No," I said. "That's not what I mean. The night Asta's daughter disappeared, she couldn't have gone out to the pond."

"Why not?"

"Because the whole forest was on fire."

"Oh," Noel said. "This was earlier, then, before the fire started."

"It couldn't have been. The fire started when it was still light out."

"How do you know so much about the fire?" Noel asked, looking confused.

I froze for a moment, certain I'd revealed too much, but then I saw a way out. "I got curious. I read about it in some old papers in the library."

If Helen had been there, she would have grilled me, but Noel accepted my explanation without question.

She took a large swig of her wine. "Oh," she said. "Maybe you're right. I guess I misunderstood. Sometimes Asta says some weird stuff. She gets things wrong when she's drinking."

"It's kind of weird that she drinks around you. Isn't that, like, not kosher?"

"I don't know. Don't judge her just because you don't drink. She's had a really tough life, you know," she said, nodding to herself. "Even before her daughter died. She told me once that she was supposed to get a PhD. She was halfway through her dissertation when she got pregnant. The guy left her for her best friend, and she had to drop out of school to raise the baby. She never finished. Her whole life got derailed."

"Wow," I said, distracted. "That sucks."

Noel nodded and started saying something about Freddy, but I couldn't concentrate. Why would Asta make a mistake like that? Hadn't that night been etched into her memory? Had she really gone out to the pond, like she'd said? If so, which night had it been, and while she was out there, had she left my sister and Laurel alone in the house?

I knew these were questions I couldn't ask Asta, but if Asta had left them alone in the cottage, it really did change things. Maybe there was another reason the girls weren't in their room the night they disappeared. Maybe they hadn't left the house that night. Maybe they'd been taken.

CHAPTER ELEVEN

I COULDN'T BELIEVE HOW REFRESHED I felt after the break. Who knew that people needed to eat and sleep? Soon after I got back to my dorm, I looked over my notes and then started down to the art barn to talk to John.

I'd never spoken to him before, though I'd seen him around a lot—the curly-haired brunette with the kind eyes. But he seemed to know who I was as soon as I walked in. He was slicking a streak of black onto a canvas, and when he looked up, he smiled.

"Hey there," he said. "You're the new kid."

"Yeah," I said. "I'm Cally."

He put down his brush and nodded. "I heard you specifically petitioned to get out of my class."

"Yeah," I said, leaning my back into the side of a tall work-table. "I don't like art."

"Really?" he said, laughing. "Not even when you were little? Not even finger paints?"

"I don't know. Maybe I kind of liked watercolors. I just didn't want to take art as a class, so I petitioned. Sorry."

"Don't be sorry," he said, wiping his hands on his smock. "I thought it was funny. So what's up? Did you change your mind?"

"Um, no. I was wondering if I could ask you something."

"Sure. Ask away."

"Well, I'm wondering about Iris Liang."

"Okay," he said, sadness flooding his eyes. "If I can help with something, I will, though I don't know that I'll be able to. I didn't really know her well."

"I heard she was down here a lot."

"Yeah," he said, nodding. "All the time. There are a lot of kids like Iris, kids who find art calming. I think it helps relieve the stress of the more academic stuff, and it helps with the emotional strain of being away from home. That's why I like to keep an open-door policy down here."

"Did she ever do any woodworking?"

"Sure," he said. "She did everything. Sometimes she'd have several projects going at once."

"Were there ever any boys down here with her?"

"Yeah." He nodded. "I'd say there was usually a boy down here with her."

"Do you remember which ones?"

He frowned for a moment, as if attempting to retrieve a stubborn memory. "I don't know. Last year she mostly brought Kyle Lily down here, but he graduated. This year, you know, I don't know that I can say for sure. I had a death in my family this fall. I usually sit out here and work on my own stuff and make myself available in case anyone needs help, but that was a rough time for me. I shut myself up in my office a lot," he said, indicating a door at the back of the room. "I don't know that I can say with any certainty who was down here and when. I'm not even sure Iris was down here as much as she was last year." He paused and looked at me, concern in his eyes. "Why are you asking?"

I had a lie prepared about a school project, a kind of homage to Iris, but he'd been so open with me that I couldn't bring myself to tell it.

"It's complicated," was all I said.

He nodded, satisfied and unprying, two qualities I'd never before observed at St. Bede's.

"Do you remember anything she might have been working on during the fall semester?"

"Sure." He nodded. "She did several oil paintings that were really good. She also made a bowl. Do you want to see it?"

He was so enthusiastic that I couldn't say no. I was just being polite, but when he returned a moment later with a shallow bowl the color of sea grass, my heart felt like it might break. It was beautiful, but there was something else to it, a sense of despair.

"It's beautiful, isn't it?"

"It's sad," I said without meaning to. "Or maybe that's dumb. Bowls aren't sad, are they?"

"No," he said. "You're right. It is sad. Everything Iris made was sad."

"Did you . . . ," I said, shifting uncomfortably. "Did you think she was in trouble?"

He sighed. "I don't know. In retrospect I think maybe she was and that I should have seen it. Someone should have seen it, and if not the teachers, then who?"

"What do you mean?"

"It's our job to take care of you guys, but obviously we didn't take care of her. I just . . . I don't know."

A couple of students showed up at the door, regulars back from vacation, and quickly he pulled himself together and waved them in. I decided it was time to go.

"Thanks for your help," I said, making my way to the door.

"Sure thing," he said, smiling at me with genuine kindness. "I hope you find what you're looking for. And if not, the door's usually open, and the watercolors are on that shelf over there."

I smiled at him and headed back out into the night.

On my way back up to the heart of campus, I ran into Alex.

"Hey," he said, his voice soft. "I've been looking all over for you. Can we talk for a minute?"

"Sure," I said, falling into step alongside him. I slipped my hand into his. We walked to an alcove near the science buildings, and then we stopped. I hopped up onto the wall and smiled at him, and only then did I see the wariness in his eyes.

"What's going on?"

"Wood, listen. I just want you to know I really like you. Like, I really, really like you. I don't know that I've ever liked anyone this much so early in a relationship."

Cold swept over me.

He put his head in his hands. "I don't know how to say this, so I'm just gonna say it. I took some ecstasy, which I know was stupid, and I hooked up with someone else." He breathed out a sigh, seemingly relieved. "I'm sorry, Cally. Really I am."

It took me a minute to understand what he was saying.

"I really wanted things to work out between us, but . . ."

But what? I wasn't pretty enough, smart enough, worth it? I didn't want to hear the end of that sentence, so I slipped down off the wall and walked quickly away. When I did, I went numb. I didn't feel a thing. I started back to my dorm, trying to remember how to walk, the world teetering.

"Wood," he said, grabbing my arm. And I turned on him, and whatever look was in my eyes must have been enough, because he didn't follow. The bell rang. I was walking, oblivious to everything around me, when someone caught hold of my arm.

"Whoa, are you okay?" Jack asked. We were right outside his dorm and about twenty feet from mine, but there was no time to talk.

"Alex cheated on me."

"With someone from home?"

I nodded.

"That dick," he said, and then pulled me close to him, up tight against his body, and for a moment I was sure he was going to kiss me. It was in his eyes. And for the first time, the obvious dawned on me. Jack's whole asexual thing was a total pose.

He didn't kiss me. He stopped just short, but my body got all hot and flustered in all the wrong ways just the same. He put his lips to my ear. "Meet me on the north side of the far gym. Three a.m."

I had nothing smart-ass to say. I just nodded and ran to the dorm, making it right before the second bell sounded. The lights were already out. I slipped into bed. I didn't need to set an alarm clock. I knew I would be up until I met Jack. There was no way I could sleep.

The dorm was silent when I pulled on my jeans and slid open the glass door as quietly as possible. I tried my best to keep thoughts of the Dragon Killer from my mind, though I noticed my breathing was more uneven than it should have been. Campus was dark and still as I crept across it, but my eyes had adjusted by the time I reached the gym. Jack was sitting up against the wall, his navy hoodie pulled over his eyes.

He reached into his backpack and tossed a flashlight to me.

"Where are we going that we need flashlights?"

He pointed to the ground below him and I noticed for the first time that he was sitting on top of a metal grate.

"What the hell's that?"

"What's it look like, Wood? It's a grate."

"Yeah, but why did you bring me out here to look at a grate?"

"To cheer you up. Listen, this grate is no ordinary grate. It leads to a tunnel, which leads to a storeroom, which has the most ridiculous St. Bede's reject paraphernalia you can possibly imagine. It'll be an adventure."

"No one else knows about it?"

"Sure people know about it, but normally it's locked up. Every once in a while it isn't. I don't know who the hell unlocks it. I sort of think it's one of the custodians who feels like we're too repressed, but I don't know. Anyway, tonight I noticed it's open. Then I ran into you. Perfect timing. You ready?"

I nodded and he lifted the grate, sat down, and dropped deep into the darkness. A moment later he reappeared with his flashlight. "Come down, I'll catch you."

I let myself fall and Jack caught me by my waist. I could feel the warmth of his fingers sinking through to my belly. Then he dropped me to the hard earth floor. He crouched and indicated that I should follow him. At first I just needed to hunch and the tunnel was fine, but the farther we went, the more I felt like Alice in Wonderland, kneeling, then crawling on hands and knees, trying to avoid thick black wires, random metal spiky things, and of course the multitude of rats and spiders that apparently lurked beneath the school.

"I think this is it. Just a few more feet. Okay. Hold on. Here we are. There's a drop-off here, so you stay there and I'm going to drop down and try to find the light."

I did as he said. Something small and light with spindly legs moved quickly across my hand. I stifled a scream and shook it off. And then, with a heavy thunk and a blinding flash, light flooded the little crawl space. I had to close my eyes for a moment, and when I opened them, I found below me a storeroom of some kind, littered with boxes and sprinkled with dust.

"Where are we?"

"Part of the old gym basement."

I hopped down, and Jack caught me, sliding his hands along my hips, my waist. He unzipped his backpack and pulled out a fluffy pink-and-green-checked blanket.

"Jack." I laughed. "Is that yours?"

He smiled and bit his lip. "I borrowed it," he said, spreading it out and lying down on his side. He kept reaching into his backpack, pulling out things that didn't make any sense. Water bottles, a stuffed animal, Pixy Stix, a deck of cards, some flowers. I just kept laughing.

"Um, Jack? What are we doing?"

"Well," he said, reaching into his pocket. "I was planning on coming out here tonight and taking it all myself, because I really really hate sharing."

"Jack, what are you talking about?"

"But . . . *but* as luck would have it, before in-dorm time, I ran into the one person in the world I'd want to share it with." He opened his delicate fist to display two little white pills.

"Oh my God. What are those?"

"Ecstasy. It's going around campus right now."

"So I heard," I sighed, sitting down on the blanket.

The smile fell from his face. "What's wrong?"

"I don't know," I said, hanging my head.

"I don't want to pressure you."

I shook my head. "I can't take it, Jack."

Suddenly, I wanted to cry.

"Oh man," he said, wrapping his arms around me. "You are so hard to figure." He kissed my forehead and pulled back to look me in the eyes. "We don't have to do it. I'll save it for another time. We can just hang out. I didn't realize you were so upset about Alex. We can talk and play double solitaire or something."

"I'm sorry." I shook my head, trying to get myself together. "I'm just a mess. You can take it if you want. I don't want to ruin your night."

He looked at me and squinted, then bit his bottom lip again and shook his head. "Not a good idea. I'll save it for another time. Take the whole dose myself. Let's play cards."

He hopped up and started walking swiftly around the room. He unzipped his sweatshirt to reveal his usual off-white button-down shirt. How did he manage to make something like that look so suggestive?

"What are you doing?" I asked.

"I don't know," he said. "I'm really confused right now." He stopped near a tall box and started drumming on it, his eyes closed. And for the first time in my life, I shocked myself. Something about his hips, the way they crept up above his belt. Something about his torso, his eyes, his mouth maybe. Whatever it was, it drew me to him, and with uncharacteristic force I took his face in my hands and I kissed him. His lips were receptive, and I felt the first inklings of his desire as his hip crushed against my belly. He had been wanting this as much as I had. But then his body tensed and he backed away from me. I stared up at him, suddenly ashamed. Had I done something wrong?

"Cally, I can't."

"Why not?"

"It's difficult to explain."

"Jack, aren't you attracted to me?"

He pushed his hair out of his face and leaned against the wall.

"Wood, you know that I am. Don't make me do this."

"Then why won't you kiss me?"

"It's complicated. I just can't," he said, avoiding eye contact.

I spoke slowly, afraid of an answer. "Jack, are you seeing someone?"

His face flushed pink, and he laughed but didn't deny it.

"Someone in secret, maybe?"

"Leave it alone, Wood, you wouldn't understand."

Despite what he said, he moved closer to me, a strange sort of electricity seeming to flit between us. He ran a hand through his hair and bit his lip, and then suddenly he pulled me to him, kissing me hard on the mouth. He held me close, and my body warmed to him, his hips flush against mine. I tried to catch my breath. He looked at me, holding my face in his hands, his cheeks flushed, his lips full and welcoming. And then it was my turn to back away. I crossed my arms in front of my chest and tried to steady myself.

"Oh my God, Jack. What the hell was that?"

"Too much?" he asked, his eyes wide.

I shook my head. "No. No. Definitely not."

"Um," he said, smiling and shrugging, "then should we continue?"

I nodded.

And we did until it was light outside.

CHAPTER TWELVE

I WAS STILL FLUSHED AND dizzy when we straggled back to the dorms.

"We are so dead if someone sees us," he said, laughing, clearly delighted.

"Couldn't we say we were out jogging?"

"Look at us, Wood. We do not look like we've been jogging. We look like we've been up to our eyes in the dirty dirtiness."

"Then why aren't you scared?" We were passing the swimming pool now, about a hundred yards from our respective dorms.

"I don't know," he said, smiling, his eyes bright and clear. "I think we're lucky."

When we reached the fork in the path, it was clear we didn't know what to do, so I held my hand up for him to slap.

"A high five, Wood?"

I shrugged. It seemed as good as anything else.

"Fine," he said, joyfully slapping my palm. And then he ran off, and I slipped into my room. Helen cracked her eyes open and smiled at me.

"Where the hell were you?" she muttered, and then turned over and went back to sleep.

I showered quickly and wrapped myself in a towel. While I combed my hair and brushed my teeth, I noticed that I felt lighter than I'd felt in a decade. I hadn't slept with Jack—it was nothing like that—but I'd done more with him than I'd ever considered doing with a boy, and somehow it had changed something fundamental in me. It was as if a layer of grief had been peeled from my aching shoulders.

When I got back to the room, Helen's alarm was going off and she was stirring.

"You want to get breakfast?" she asked, staring up at me with one blue cat eye.

"Sure."

"You look weird," she said, but left it at that.

I had a hot breakfast for the first time since coming to St. Bede's: warm chocolate chip pancakes smothered in butter and maple syrup. I ate with abandon while Helen looked at me funny.

"So what happened with Alex last night?" Helen asked, a strange glint in her eye.

"Nothing. I don't really want to talk about it right now," I said, smooshing half of a pancake into my mouth.

"Okay," she said, holding up her hands. "When you're ready." Then she cocked her head to one side. "You're, like, really hungry, aren't you?"

Despite the many pancakes I'd eaten at breakfast, I walked to English class with a joyful pit in my stomach. I had no idea how to act when I saw Jack. I'd just seen him vulnerable and in compromising positions, but the thought of him sitting fully clothed discussing Aeschylus seemed absurd to me.

He and Sophie were chatting when I walked in. I greeted them both like nothing was out of the ordinary, and he looked up at me and burst out laughing. That was exactly how I felt, but I didn't want to be suspicious, so I choked back my laughter and took a seat next to Sophie.

"What was that about?" she asked Jack.

"Nothing," he said. "I'll tell you later."

I tried not to make eye contact for the rest of class, but once or twice I couldn't help looking over to find him grinning at me.

He walked us to Spanish class, and the entire time I was painfully aware of the distance between us. I couldn't stop questioning myself. Were we walking too close together? Were we suspiciously far apart? And all the while, my head was drunk and spinning, swimming in a lusty happiness I found totally unfamiliar.

In between periods, I headed up to the library to compile my list of people who had checked out woodworking books. Unfortunately, the library's woodworking collection consisted of one book, last checked out in 1993 by someone named A. Schumacher. Apparently I would need to devise an alternative second prong for my two-pronged attack.

The rest of the day went well until I got to bio lab. Staying up all night was making me woozy, and I had second lunch, which meant I'd have to wait until after bio to eat. Alex was waiting for me when I came in.

"Can we talk?" he whispered, his eyes deeply serious. "Outside on the stoop. We can pretend we're emptying the morgues."

And for some reason I felt guilty. He had cheated on me, and here I was feeling guilty. I nodded and grabbed one of the jars of oil we used to dispose of the flies, and we met on the step. We closed the door behind us.

"Wood, I feel sick. I know you're pissed, but I am so so sorry. I swear, it didn't mean anything. Please don't break up with me. It was the drugs. I didn't know what I was doing. And it was nothing serious. It wasn't sex or anything." He blushed. And then, to my horror, he wiped a tear from his eye.

Oh my God. I wasn't prepared for this. I had been under the impression that he'd broken up with me, but apparently, he, um, hadn't. I wondered what he would think if he knew even half of the things I'd done with Jack while he was sleeping peacefully in his bed.

I should have broken up with him right then and there, but there were a few things holding me back. First, he was hot. He was gorgeous and brilliant, and I liked hanging out with him. I'd miss him if we broke up. Second, if I broke up with him, it would be a big deal with Helen and her lot. I knew they'd all simultaneously pity me and think I was a killjoy for dumping him. There would be tension in the group, and even though it would be his fault, I knew I was the one who would be on the outs. They'd all known each other for years. I was the new girl. If someone suddenly wasn't going to be invited to the lake house, it was going to be me, not Alex. Then, of course, there was Jack. I really liked him, but it wasn't like we were going to start dating or something. If I broke up with Alex, he'd keep feeling awful and guilty, and then I'd have to feel awful and guilty too, because technically, I'd cheated on him too. So I decided to do the most reasonable thing I could think of. I decided just to pretend none of it had ever happened.

"Okay." I nodded.

"What?" He looked shocked, totally confused.

"It's okay, let's, um, just forget it, okay?" I dumped out my jar and twisted the cap back on.

"You're not mad?" he asked, slack-jawed.

"Does anyone else know?"

"Brody."

"Well, let's just pretend it never happened," I said, and opened the door and walked back inside.

This decision to keep going out with Alex was totally antithetical to my ideology. It had been born of intense guilt, sleeplessness, and a voluptuous kind of exhilaration, and I figured it was best not to think too much about it. I wandered up to lunch in a daze.

I hadn't had a chance to talk to Freddy since Alex had told

me about the phone call, so when I saw her sitting alone at lunch, I figured it couldn't hurt. I'm not sure what I expected, but it certainly wasn't what I got.

"What did you just ask me?" she said, her voice calm and cold. She set down her fork.

"Nothing," I said, a little stunned. "Alex told me you took the call, so I thought maybe you might remember something about it."

Her eyes narrowed. "Don't you think that if I remembered anything, I would have told the police?"

"Yeah," I said, suddenly uncomfortable. "I was just thinking maybe there was something you didn't want to tell them, or I don't know. . . ."

"You think that I would purposely deceive the police in a murder investigation?" Her voice was measured, her tone so crisp and cool that I had trouble matching it with the anger evidenced in her eyes. She picked up her fork again, and gripping it with bloodless fingers, she pushed her food around the plate.

"No," I said, trying to think of some way to backpedal out of the conversation.

"You think . . . ," she whispered, color rising in her cheeks. "You think that I could have information that leads to the person who killed Iris and that I would lie about it? What do you think I am?"

I was frozen, unable to speak. A strange kind of intensity radiated from her, and I was thankful I would never have to face her in a competitive debate. I could see how with Freddy involved a debate could quickly resemble something involving Christians and lions. Standing up, she dropped her fork onto her plate with a resounding crash. It bounced off and landed on the floor with an understated clink.

"Watch it, Cally," she said, pulling down her crisp white sleeves, arranging the cuffs just so. "Don't get too big for your britches, okay?"

She leveled her eyes at me, and I stared right back at her. Then she nodded to herself, mistaking my silence for acquiescence. She turned and clicked away in her oxfords, leaving her plate on the table, her fork where it lay on the ground.

I hovered somewhere between amusement and shock as I watched her go. I knew Freddy was tightly wound, but her reaction was crazy. I picked up her fork and put it on my tray. The only question was whether she was acting like a psycho because she was psycho, or she was acting like a psycho because she had something to hide.

That afternoon, Noel and I got back from independent walking even earlier than we usually did. We signed in with Ms. Sjursen, who seemed to be in the process of making a birdhouse out of a boot.

"Did you have a nice break, Ms. Sjursen?" Noel asked.

Ms. Sjursen peered up at Noel and smiled. "Why, yes, Calista, I did. Thank you so much for asking."

Noel grabbed my arm as we headed out of the gym.

"I can't believe she thinks I'm you," she whispered.

"What?" I laughed. "What's so bad about being me?"

"No offense, but sometimes you look like Robert Smith mated with a mouse. Like, a construction-worker mouse."

"That's very specific, Noel. Thank you."

Back in my room, I decided it was maybe time to clean my closet. I'd unpacked so hastily that I hadn't noticed at the time just how dirty it was in there. The last time I'd pulled something out, one of the sleeves had been covered in dust. A bit of spring-cleaning would be good for me; it would keep my mind occupied. I put on a Dead Kennedys album and got to work. I pulled all the clothes out and set them on my bed, then grabbed some of Helen's cleaning products and climbed inside. I was momentarily overwhelmed by the scent of cedar. As I adjusted to the darkness, my eyes focused on the back wall, and I froze. I found myself face to face with the blue dragon. It was drawn in hatched blue ballpoint, but it was the same wretched thing, with its terrible eyes and its sickle head. Had that been there when I'd moved in? The walls had been completely marked up, and it had been too dark to see much. What did it mean? Had he, whoever he was, been in my room? My breath caught, and for a second, I thought I might puke, but instead I let out a single bleat of a scream and clutched my hands to my chest. After pulling myself out of the closet and bumping my head in the process, I grabbed my messenger bag. I opened the door and slowly backed onto the lawn.

I stood outside staring into the chasm of my room for a moment or two before I gave in to the overwhelming urge to run to the library. I was barely able to choke back my scream as I raced, the sweat dripping from my forehead. When I reached the front entrance, I leaned against the wall and tried to catch my breath. I had to try to shake it off and get my bearings so I could think like a rational human being. I headed inside and up to my usual seat. I took the steps two at a time and was relieved to find Carlos wearing his bifocals and playing sudoku.

"You look kind of bad. Are you okay?"

"Yeah," I said, sinking into my chair. "Totally fine. I just need to read."

"Maybe you should get a book, then."

"I mean think. I just need to think."

He shook his head and turned away. I pulled my knees up to my chest. Next to Carlos lay a stack of manga and a large black book called *Mysteries of the Unknown*. I picked it up and began leafing through the pages.

"Help yourself there, Wood," Carlos said without looking up from his sudoku.

I sat staring at Goya's horrific *Saturn Devouring His Son*, and I noticed that I was shaking. I slammed the book. What if Brody was right? What if there really was something wrong with this place? What if it really was cursed? I shook my head. No, that was ridiculous. There had to be some reasonable explanation for what was happening, and whoever had drawn that thing in my closet was just a person—a person with a real-life connection to Iris.

I pushed myself up out of my chair and wandered over to the yearbooks.

"Iris," I whispered. "What were you hiding?" I pulled out the previous year's and there she was, right on the second page, laughing, her arms slung around two boys, presumably lame-duck seniors. She was radiant, incandescent. Joy seemed to spill forth from her, and the two boys looked at her like she was magic.

Despite everything I'd heard about her, I found myself thinking that I would have liked her, that I would have thought she was fun. What had she been mixed up in? It couldn't have been just drugs. Lots of people took drugs. They weren't all being brutally murdered.

"Who were you, Iris?" I heard myself say aloud again.

"Cally," Carlos called from his chair. "They're gonna send you to the counselor if you start talking to dead girls in the stacks."

And then I looked more closely at the picture, and suddenly it dawned on me. Her fingers, perched like spider legs on the boys' shoulders, were stained with ink. And I knew. No monster, human or otherwise, had crept into my room and drawn that horrible thing. It would have taken far too long. The only person who'd had the time and the opportunity to draw the dragon was Iris.

I knew with every fiber of my being that Iris had put that thing there. But if Iris had drawn the dragon in my closet, then that meant that Iris had also drawn the dragon up in the cave. She hadn't been lured there. She hadn't been dragged there and murdered. She'd gone of her own volition and had been comfortable enough up there that she'd had the time and inclination to draw a massive version of her dragon.

What was it about those woods that seemed to draw people to them? Iris, my sister, Laurel—why had they gone out there? Hadn't they known there was something rotten out there, something spoiled? I had to admit, though, that as much as the woods frightened me, as much as I wanted to stay away from them, I found myself thinking about them when I didn't mean to, waking from unremembered dreams to catch a hint of pine, a whisper of wind through the needles.

I didn't believe those woods were haunted—I couldn't believe that—but there was something strange about them, something dark. Sometimes it seemed to me that a fine curtain hung between St. Bede's and those woods, and that if I could only find a way through it, if I could pull aside the veil, I could find the truth. I could find Clare.

CHAPTER THIRTEEN

"WHY ARE YOU HIDING IN your closet?" Helen asked.

My muscles tensed, and I banged my head stumbling out. I had been having another look at Iris's handiwork, trying to figure out what it could mean. I shut the closet door.

"You know, we have a whole LGBT society here, Wood. People are very open-minded."

"Good morning to you too," I said, feeling like I'd been caught trying to blow up a mailbox. Adrenaline surged through my veins. "You were up early."

"I went running."

A gentle knock on the glass drew our attention. Alex, dressed in a french-blue sweater, waved from the other side.

"You should probably tell him you're bi-curious," Helen said, batting her lashes. "It's me, isn't it? I'm always making people gay."

Ignoring Helen, I grabbed my things and went out to meet him.

"You're gonna get kicked out for wearing that," he said, eyeing my Sex Pistols shirt. "You couldn't find any ones with pictures of dead puppies on them?"

"Those were all sold out."

"You were wearing normal girl clothes for a while," he said, wrapping an arm around my shoulders. "What happened?"

"Didn't take."

"I thought I was having a positive influence on you."

"I think I'm immune to good influences."

Just before we reached the classroom, he slipped his arm around my waist, and beneath the arch of the door, he gave me a kiss. I didn't have to look to know that Jack was watching. I could feel his gaze running up and down my spine. After I waved goodbye to Alex, I walked over to Jack and Sophie. He was laughing.

"So you guys worked out your little, um, problem, then?" he asked.

Sophie raised an eyebrow at me.

"Yeah. No, everything's fine now, Jack. Thanks for asking."

"I'm here for all your needs, Wood."

"Jack, don't be disgusting. You okay?" Sophie asked, turning to me, concerned.

"Yeah. I am totally fine, thanks."

I tried not to look at Jack during class, but his lure was overwhelming, and I found myself constantly distracted. Eventually I had to give in and take a peek across Sophie. He was staring

at me, just staring. When he saw me look over, he gave me
a smile with something like admiration in his eyes and then
laughed as he shook his head.

I was both dreading and looking forward to chemistry. We
had a lab, which meant my time would be largely unsupervised
with Jack. He was leaning against the table, already hard at
work, when I came in.

"Eager much?"

"I had third period free. I thought I'd get us out of here a
little early."

"Jack, that thing with Alex . . ."

"Pumpkin," he said, looking wounded. "You can do whatever you want with your boyfriend. I really don't care."

"You don't?"

"No. I have my own situation to attend to, remember?"

"You mean your secret girlfriend?" I teased, but he tensed
up and looked upset, so I dropped it. "Okay, so we'll just be
friends, then?"

He smiled at me, slow and vulpine, and I felt a little dizzy, a
little like I might attack him right there in chemistry lab. "BFF,
Wood. BFF."

We did finish half an hour early, and Reilly let us go. We
walked in a strange sort of silence, the air between us thick
and charged.

"Wood, um, I think we need to talk," he said.

"Sounds good," I said, tripping over my tongue, trying not
to choke.

And just as we were passing the boys' bathroom, Jack

slammed the door open and pulled me inside. He kissed me, heavily, eagerly. I melted at first but then pulled away.

"Jack, I'm with Alex now."

"So?" he said, leaning against one of the stalls.

"So? So? I'm going out with him again."

"So what do I care?"

"So I'm not going to cheat on him."

"Why not?"

"Because it's wrong."

"He cheated on you," he said, moving closer.

"So? Two wrongs and all that."

"Are you trying to tell me that you didn't enjoy our little activities, because it seemed to me that you did . . . like, a lot."

"Obviously," I said, unable to keep the grin from my face.

"So?" he said, moving closer, taking my wrist gently in his hand. "Why not keep on doing it, then? It's not like we're having sex or anything. We're just fooling around."

"I can't go out with Alex and fool around with you."

"Sure you can. You haven't taken any vows."

"No. It's dishonest. Besides, what we did the other night was kind of intense. I can't keep doing those things with you if I don't do stuff like that with Alex."

"And you don't want to do those things with him?"

"No."

"Well, that's great news." He beamed. "I don't want you to either. See, we have totally the same priorities."

"But do you want to keep hooking up with someone else's girlfriend?"

He nodded and smiled. "Yes. Yes I do. I absolutely do. Alex

cheated on you." He moved closer to me, and I could feel his breath hot on my neck. I backed up against the wall, and slowly, softly he pressed into me. "You have carte blanche right now." He leaned in and kissed me. "I think you should use it."

It happened again, strange and electric, and in the boys' bathroom, of all places. We clung to each other like frightened children, our hands seeming to move of their own volition. This was not my personality, not my typical behavior. When we'd exhausted ourselves, he held me close against his chest like he didn't want to let me go. I knew that what Jack had said to convince me didn't make a ton of sense. I wasn't a moron. But my time with Jack was in some ways the only honest time in my life. With him I simply was. There was no narrating every detail: *Now Alex's hand slides up my waist. Now he is kissing me. Kiss him back.* With Jack it was more of a deranged psychosis, and I loved it. But there was something I needed to know.

"Jack," I said, trying to get my clothes back in order. I could see him in the mirror, leaning against a stall watching me, his eyes soft and gentle.

"Mmm?"

"I need to know one thing if we're going to keep doing this."

"Anything."

"I need to know who you're seeing in secret—I mean, besides me. I need to know who the other person is."

He shook his head.

"I really can't tell you. I'm sorry. I don't want to keep things from you, but this is beyond my control."

He started to approach me, but I stopped him.

"I need to know that it's not Sophie."

He frowned incredulously. "Sophie? Like our Sophie? You think I'm seeing Sophie?"

"Obviously, or I wouldn't have asked."

He shook his head, a strange set to his eye. "Of course not. She's my best friend. No. Not Sophie. God, I can't even think about Sophie messing around with anyone, let alone someone like me. I'd kill anyone who touched her."

"Okay," I said, feeling kind of jealous about his protectiveness. "Enough. So it's not Sophie, then? You promise?"

"I absolutely promise you. I swear on my life."

That was all I needed. And finally, at last, the true charm of boarding school became overtly, achingly obvious to me.

I sat with Noel at dinner, but she didn't say much, and she ate even less. I wanted to help her, but I felt powerless.

"You're sure you're okay?" I asked, watching her push food around on her plate.

She gave me a weak smile. "I'm fine. Would you stop worrying about me?"

I gritted my teeth, not knowing what to say. "Remember over spring break when you were talking about suicide?"

"Yeah."

"That was all theoretical, right?"

She rolled her eyes. "Don't be naïve."

"What do you mean? Why am I naïve?"

"It's not like I'm obsessed with suicide or anything. It's just that we talk about it sometimes, so I've been, like, relating stuff back to it lately. You know when that happens? When you're studying, like, owls or something, and then you start seeing owl symbolism everywhere?"

"Not really," I said, laughing.

Noel shrugged. "Well, that happens to me."

"Wait," I said. "Who's *we*? You and Asta?"

"No," she said, her cheeks flushing.

"Who, then? You and Helen?"

"No one," she said, her voice weak. "I don't want to talk about it."

She stood abruptly, leaving her plate on the table. "I gotta go. I'll see you later, Wood."

That night when Alex came to get me after study hours, I didn't know what to say to him. *It's no big deal, but I've accidentally hooked up with Jack Deeker twice in the last two days?* I didn't think that would go over too well, so I decided to omit it.

Walking with Alex, I could almost forget what had happened with Jack. Alex had an easy kind of charm about him. There wasn't the strange, muddled electricity that I felt whenever Jack was near, but that just meant I could relax around him. He slipped his hand into mine and stared down at me with almond eyes, a faint smile playing on his lips.

"How was your day?" I asked.

"Kind of intense, actually," he said. "We had an unscheduled prefect meeting tonight, and it's just been a really tough time. You have to keep this on the DL, but Harrison told us the police found a bag in Iris's pocket that had trace amounts of psilocybin."

"What?"

"Psychedelic mushrooms. That girl was tripping balls when she died. Harrison's really upset," he sighed. "You can see how this looks for the school. He wanted to know if we'd heard of anyone in possession of something like that, and wants us to be on the lookout from now on. Pretty intense."

"What? Why is it your job to inform on your classmates?"

"We're prefects. That's one of our responsibilities."

"So you guys are like narcs?"

"We have responsibilities, that's all."

"You've never done it, though, right? You've never turned anyone in."

"Yeah I have." He smiled. "This kid back in November. I caught him smoking pot in his closet under my watch. Not cool. I got his ass thrown out."

"But *you* do drugs," I said, my gut telling me that something was off.

Quickly he looked around, then lowered his voice. "Cally, that was different. God, I can't believe you'd say something like that out in the open. What is wrong with you?"

"Nothing," I said, shaking my head. "I just can't believe you got that kid kicked out."

"You wouldn't understand," he said, clearly disappointed.

We continued on, an uncomfortable silence between us. As we walked through the grass, my thoughts fell to Iris and the mushrooms. Had they been her decision, or had someone manipulated her into taking them? Had her killer drugged her before taking her life, and if so, why use mushrooms? I shook my head and tried to put it from my mind. It seemed that every time I got closer to understanding what might have happened that night, something else crept in to complicate it.

The next day, sitting alone on the balcony, I found I barely had the will to finish my lunch. For the billionth time, I wished I had my dad to talk to. Back home I had Danny, but he wasn't much for emotions. He would have suggested we find whoever had sent me the puzzle box and beat the shit out of them. The main thing that got under my skin was that I felt like a victim—like I'd been chosen because of Clare's death—and it felt like someone gouging my wounds with stinging nettles.

I took a bite of my sandwich, something slowly settling onto me. If Clare was the reason I'd been contacted, then was it possible that Asta had been contacted as well? I noticed that at the thought of Asta, my blood pressure dropped to a nice, easy level. She had said to talk to her if I had a hard time at St. Bede's, and I was pretty sure that was what I was having. She seemed kind, and she seemed to really like me. Maybe it was okay to reach out to her, to trust her.

I left lunch early and headed down to the bio lab, thinking I could catch her alone between periods, but when I walked in, I found her with Noel. They sat across a lab table from each other, and Noel flinched when she saw me.

"Sorry," I said. "I'll come back later."

"No, Cally." Asta smiled. "Please stay. In fact, you might be exactly what this discussion needs."

"I'll finish up the display cases," Noel said, not making eye contact.

"Perfect," Asta said. "You keep an eye to your work and an ear to the conversation, and we can kill two birds with one stone."

"What's up?" I asked, still unable to place the vibe in the room. I felt like I'd just walked into the middle of an uncomfortable situation, but Asta seemed perfectly at ease.

"Well." She smiled and slid one of the jars of oil and dead flies across the table toward me. "We were just discussing the morality of killing all these flies. Of course we all know that releasing them outside would be potentially harmful to the ecosystem, but Noel here was saying that by killing them, we might be doing something wrong."

I shrugged. "Yeah. I feel kind of bad killing them too."

"That's good." Asta nodded. "Illogical on some level, but good. Tell me, why do you feel bad about it?"

"I don't know. They're living things. It doesn't seem right for me to decide whether they should live or die."

"Are you religious, Cally? Do you think that taking a life is a sin?"

Images of Clare flashed before my eyes. Was that what she was talking about? This felt strange, inappropriate.

"No, I'm not religious," I said slowly, holding her eye contact. "But I know that as far as humans are concerned, no one has the right to take anyone else's life away. If they do, they should pay for it. Whether that extends to insects, I can't say. I hope not. I'd hate to think we're all going to hell or whatever for taking AP bio."

Asta laughed, her gaze warm. "I'd hope not too. Think how many times I've taught AP bio. I'd probably end up down in the seventh circle with Pol Pot. But there's more to what Noel and I were discussing. We were wondering if, hypothetically, killing fruit flies was a sin if we would be able to atone for it, either in this life or the next. Noel thinks not. I say absolutely. I feel that no matter how grave the crime, when we leave this earth, whether we go on to Elysium, or we return here for another life, our soul is cleansed, that the very act of dying cleanses us."

"No," I said, shaking my head. "I don't think that's true. I think if you do something really bad, like if you kill a person, there's nothing you can do to take that back."

Asta scratched her chin and nodded. "But what if you did something, committed an act of attrition, some kind of sacrifice to show you were truly repentant?" she asked, her voice calm and sweet, and I wondered what she could possibly be trying to tell me. It was as if the content of her speech and her tone bore no relation to each other. How on earth could she say these things to me? Anger began to well inside me.

"So," I said, my voice breaking. "Whoever killed Iris, they're just going to go to heaven if they're sorry enough?"

"Cally," Asta said, her eyes wide. "I've upset you. I'm so sorry. Clearly you're not comfortable with this conversation. Let's forget it, shall we? Why was it you came by before I dragged you into our silly epistemological debate?"

"Nothing," I said, backing away, trying to staunch the un-comprehending tears that were choking my esophagus. "I was looking for Alex."

I didn't wait for her to say goodbye. I hurried out of the room and ran across the lawn, staving off the tears until I reached the safety of my bed. I sat sobbing into my hands. I felt so alone. I hated that there was never anyone there to hold me when I felt like I might shatter. Every time I put my faith in someone, they betrayed it. Asta of all people should have known how I felt. How could she say those things to me, and in front of Noel? Why would she do something like that, and do it all with a smile and a tender note to her voice? It was like she was carrying on two entirely different conversations.

I sat there feeling next to empty, my face stretched and aching from crying. Maybe some of us were different, I thought. Maybe some of us just didn't have guardians. Maybe some of us never would. Maybe we needed to learn to be our own guardians, to take care of ourselves.

I found Jack outside the dining hall. He was talking to Drucy and Cara, but when he saw me, he came right over.

"Are you okay?" he asked, reaching out for me but then stopping himself. There were too many people around.

"Jack," I said, the world seeming to spin around me, pressing in. "Do you have any condoms?"

His eyes grew wide, and slowly he nodded.

"Okay," I said, my hand shaking as I brushed my hair behind my ear. "Meet me behind the theater in five minutes."

"Cally," he said, breathless. "Are you sure?"

I wasn't, but I nodded anyway. I took the slow route to the theater, and when I got there, Jack was already sitting on the grass, looking up at me with a little boy's eyes. He looked frightened and beautiful.

"You're sure about this?" he asked again.

"Jack, I don't want to talk, okay?" I said, and led him into the woods, just out of view.

I didn't know what to do, so I undressed and lay down, the forest floor rough against my back, my legs shaking.

It was slow and strange, and not at all what I'd expected. He told me I was beautiful, but I didn't want to hear that. I wanted everything to go away, to disappear, and for a little while it did.

When it was over, we dressed in silence, and then Jack sat back down on the ground. He reached out for me, but I didn't take his hand. Instead I knelt down, picked up the empty condom wrapper, and shoved it into the pocket of my jacket. I figured I could bear half the responsibility for hiding what we'd done.

"Are you okay?" he asked.

I wanted to tell him the truth, that I wasn't okay, that I hadn't been okay for a very long time, and that nothing, not even sex with a beautiful boy, could fix that thing inside me that was broken. But I couldn't say that. I could see from the look in his eyes that somehow what we'd done had just broken his heart a little.

"I gotta go," I said.

"You don't have class yet," he said, forcing a smile. "Can't we hang out for a bit?"

He held out his hands again, reaching up for me, but I couldn't take them. I backed away.

"I have something to do," I said.

"Oh," he said, his voice quiet, his smile falling. "Okay."

I left him there. I didn't look back. I don't know how long he stayed. I didn't see him for the rest of the day, but when I got back to my room that night, I found a single white flower on my pillow.

CHAPTER FOURTEEN

I WOKE UP THE NEXT morning to Helen peering down at me.

"Yes?"

"I don't know," she said, clearly upset. "Your hair. I just don't like it."

She'd said that the night before when I'd come back to the dorm with what she called my Sex Pistols hair. It wasn't a big deal. It was just something I needed to do. After dinner, I'd borrowed bleach and clippers from Cara Svitt, and I'd shaved most of my head, leaving only a spiky patch up front, which I'd bleached a shocking blond.

It was allowed. There were other kids at St. Bede's with weird hair, but for some reason, Helen couldn't handle it on me. I didn't know why anyone would care, but people tended to freak out when you did something drastic to your appearance.

They thought you'd gone crazy, but really maybe you'd been crazy all along, and doing something like that made you feel less crazy, giddy even, in control and out of control all at the same time.

I didn't feel like dealing with her comments, so I waited until she'd gone to the bathroom, and then I slipped on my shoes, grabbed my books, and headed out the door.

Jack was outside the dining hall, sitting on the little brick wall, reading his Genet. When he saw me, he gave me a big thumbs-up and smiled.

"You've gone completely mad," he said, laughing. "I love it."

I gripped my gritty blond tendrils. "Thanks. I'm glad you like it."

"Of course I like it. You look like a pint-sized Sid Vicious," he said, taking my hand and pulling me down to sit next to him on the wall. "Did you get the flower?" he asked, and I nodded.

"Are we okay?"

"Yeah," I said. "I was just in a weird mood yesterday."

"Clearly," he said, indicating my hair. "I really do like it, Cally. It brings out your eyes."

"Thanks," I said, trying not to blush.

"You're sure everything's okay, though? You seem like something's going on with you that you're not telling me. Not just yesterday. Sometimes you get all quiet and look like you're trying to figure something out. What are you thinking about when you do that?"

"Deeker," I said, shaking my head. "Has television taught you nothing? I'm a teenage girl. I'm probably just thinking about shoes."

"You can tell me things, you know," he said, and I could tell from his eyes, the liquid emotion of them, that he was serious.

This was what he wanted. He wanted me to tell him how I felt, to include him in parts of me that I wasn't comfortable sharing even with myself. Standing there, staring into his eyes, I wanted to cry. I wanted to cry, and then I wanted to kiss him. But I didn't do either of those things. Instead I laughed.

"Let's get some juice," I said, and his smile seemed to drop just a little. We went into the dining hall after that and were filling up our beveled red cups with apple juice when I felt a familiar hand on my waist. I turned to find Alex, with something like disgust on his face.

"What the hell happened to your hair?" he asked, looking at me like I was some kind of complicated joke.

"Hey," I said. "I like it."

Alex didn't smile. He looked disappointed. He didn't say anything—he just stared—and then I noticed Jack was staring back at him, standing maybe a little too close.

"Do you have a problem with me, Deeker?" Alex said, squaring himself on him.

Jack straightened up, craning his neck to face Alex, and the two of them looked like Japanese fighting fish all set to rumble, but then Jack eased up and laughed. "Why would I have a problem with you, man?"

Just then Brody walked over and placed his hands on Alex's shoulders.

"Hey, buddy," he said, his voice hypnotically calm. "You got a second?"

Alex's shoulders relaxed, and with one last look at Jack, he allowed himself to be led away.

Without missing a beat, Jack took my hand.

"Last one to class has ugly hair." He laughed, then took off running.

Our race to class ran into a few detours, and we ended up being late to first period. Jack let go of my hand and put a bit of space between us before we walked in. Ms. Harlow was already lecturing on A Midsummer Night's Dream. She came to a full stop when we entered, her hand pressed against the hip of her bell-bottom jeans.

"Cally!" she exclaimed, her voice cracking with spurious joy. "It is so awesome of you to come to class today. And oh, great, you brought your excellent new hair."

I ignored her as Jack and I took our usual seats on either side of Sophie.

"You look insane," Sophie whispered, gripping my hand. "I think I love you."

After sports, I went down to see Alex. He was on his bed, reading Proust. He looked up and smiled, hesitant. He was dressed for hiking and had a pack leaning against his bed.

"Running away?" I asked. "Did my hair scare you off? And you're still reading Proust? I blew through that whole thing in, like, a weekend."

"I'm glad you came by."

I smiled. "Seriously, though, where are you going?"

"Going on an overnight into the woods with Reilly and Brody."

"Is that safe?" I said, trying not to sound as shocked as I felt. "I mean, considering."

"Reilly got it okayed. We're big guys, and we'll have Tinker with us."

"What are you going to do out in the woods?"

"There's a sweat lodge back there. We're going to work out some of our demons, then spend the night under the stars and head back at dawn. We'll be back in time for class."

"That sounds pretty cool, except for the Reilly part."

"You're delusional. Reilly's solid." He sighed. "Cally, we need to talk."

"Yeah?"

"Seriously, what's up with the hair?"

"What?" I could feel my cheeks start to burn.

"You had gorgeous hair. Why maim yourself?" He grabbed his guitar and began picking idly at the strings.

"I like it. What's the big deal?"

"It's just weird is all."

I didn't stay long after that, and as I walked back to my room, I realized I had to break up with him. He was everything a perfect guy was supposed to be, but he wasn't my perfect guy, and I sure as hell wasn't his perfect girl.

I'd do it the next day. I had to. It didn't matter how beautiful he was or how much everyone loved him. It didn't matter that when I nestled my head into the crook of his neck, he smelled like fresh lime and mint. None of those things mattered anymore.

The next morning Helen and I got up early to quiz each other for our bio test. We went to the dining hall at six-forty-five, and in my memory I heard someone screaming, but I don't know that it happened that way. There were people everywhere, milling around. Too many people. I was confused, trying to figure out what the strange flashing light was. It was pulsating against the side of the dining hall.

"Oh my God," Helen gasped, and then I took in the whole scene. The flashing light was from a police car. There were cops everywhere. Something bad was happening again.

And then Freddy was there, standing right in front of me like a splotch of ruddy marmalade.

"They found something," she said, her eyes wide. "I don't know what it is. Maybe it's another body. Oh God, do you think someone else was killed?"

I opened my mouth but nothing came out.

"Who found it?" Helen asked, her voice shaking.

"Alex did. He and Reilly and Brody were hiking back, and Alex was way ahead of them with Tinker, and apparently Tinker darted off the trail. Alex followed and found him digging like crazy. He found something—Tinker did. It must have been a body. What else could it have been?"

That was when I noticed Alex. He was wrapped in a blanket, talking to a police officer, who was taking notes and nodding.

The officer closed his tablet and walked away just as the nurse handed Alex a steaming drink. He was shaking. I ran over to him, and he looked up at me distantly. The nurse held me back a little.

"What happened?" I almost whispered.

Helen was yelling somewhere, demanding to know what was going on. Why was she doing that?

Alex just shook his head.

"He's had a shock," the nurse cautioned. "I think you'd better leave."

"No," he said, his voice wavering. "No. I want her to stay."

I sat down and put my arm around him. Helen was still yelling at Cryker, expletives flowing freely.

"I'm so glad I have you, Cally. Oh God," he said, putting his head in his hands.

"Are you okay? You're not hurt, are you?"

He shook his head, then wiped his eyes and tried to get himself together.

"They were out there," he said, his voice breaking. "In the woods. Buried. I found them."

"What was?"

"They were buried. In a gym bag. All these little bones. Tiny bones." He bit hard into his lower lip, trying to fight back tears. "They think it's them—the girls."

I was cold and tingly, suddenly aware I couldn't feel my fingertips. "What girls?" I demanded.

"The lost girls," he said. "The ones who disappeared. Asta's daughter, Laurel, and her friend. They said her name was Clare."

After that everything went black.

PART TWO

*Yo sé quien soy, y quien puedo ser.**
—Miguel de Cervantes, *Don Quixote*

*(I know who I am, and I know what I can be.)

CHAPTER FIFTEEN

"WHY DIDN'T YOU TELL ME?" I heard Sophie say as my eyes strained to bring her into focus.

I looked around me, trying to understand where I was. White walls, paper cups, cots.

"The infirmary," she said. "The nurse asked me to keep an eye on you while she deals with the boys."

"Oh God," I groaned. "I fainted, didn't I? How embarrassing."

"Why didn't you tell me, Cally?" she said, and sitting on the side of the cot, she put her hand on my arm. I noticed tears were welling in her eyes.

"Tell you what?"

"About your sister. About Clare."

It came back to me in a strange flood—Clare, the bag, the

bones—and for a second I thought I might faint again, but I shook myself out of it.

"How did you know?"

She exhaled and shook her head. "I've been wondering what was up with you for a while. I knew there was something you were hiding, but God, I didn't think for a second it was that. I saw you when Alex told you. I saw the look on your face, saw you go down like a load of bricks, and I just knew. I asked one of the policemen if Clare's last name was Wood, and that settled it. God, Cally, I can't even comprehend. I don't even know what to say. I am so sorry."

She squeezed my arm, and before I knew it, I was crying, and she held me there, my snotty, weeping face smashed against her like a child's, and I thought this must be what it was like to have a sister. I told her everything after that. Well, not everything. I didn't tell her about Jack, but I told her about finding the body, about the encryption, about the dragon. We went back to my room and I curled up on my bed, cold and too tired to cry.

"Poor thing," she said, patting my leg. "I wish I could give you some brandy. That's what they always do in the movies. Sucks being seventeen."

She had a look at the dragon in my closet and shuddered.

"That can't be good," she said.

"Dragons are good luck in some cultures," I muttered.

"Yeah, but still. This is disturbing."

I shrugged and asked her if she was absolutely positive she couldn't procure that brandy.

I had her take another look at the puzzle box and the note,

and humming to herself, eyebrows furrowed, she examined it while I closed my eyes, drifting into and out of sleep.

It took Sophie about five minutes to cover the cryptographic ground it had taken me weeks to attain, and I felt like an ass for not giving her the note in the first place. Sometimes the smartest people don't make a big deal about how smart they are. Sophie was one of those people.

She tapped her finger against the paper. "This doesn't look good."

"You mean you can't decipher it?"

"Not without knowing the starting point of the key text, no, but that's not what I meant. I mean why did someone send this to you, the sister of one of the missing girls, right after the body of another girl was found?"

I rubbed the bridge of my nose. "I've thought about this. I realize the person who killed Iris could be the same person who took my sister, and I know the person who left me the box could be the same person, but it also could be someone else, someone who knows something and is trying to communicate with me. I just need to figure out what they're trying to say."

"Cally," she said, fastening her eyes on me. "This isn't a game."

"I know it's not a game."

"The thing that worries me is if someone knows something about your sister, why come to you? Why not go to the police? Leaving this for you, it just seems really bad. Really creepy. You said someone left it for you?"

"With Ms. Sjursen."

"Great. I'm sure that wasn't an accident."

"What do you mean?"

"I mean that her memory is notoriously bad. Even if she did remember someone, no one would believe her. That was planned. Whoever left this for you is smart. They're thinking several steps ahead."

"More than that, considering I don't even know what the hell's happening."

"What do the police say?"

She looked at me with such guilelessness that I almost couldn't bear to disappoint her. I shook my head, and her mouth fell open.

"You didn't tell the police?"

"What are the police going to do?" I whined. "They'll just take it all away from me and then I'll never know what happened to her. I know there has to be more to solve with the box. I just have to figure it out. Whatever this person has to say to me, whether it's the killer, or someone else, I know it has to do with my sister, and I can't risk losing that chance."

Sophie shook her head. "No. You have to hand it over. You might be in danger."

"They're not going to be able to protect me. They couldn't protect Iris. They couldn't protect Clare. They couldn't even find her."

"Cally," she said, her voice low and soft, the kind of voice you'd use to talk to kittens. "This isn't negotiable. You have to tell them. It's not just about you. Other people might be in danger."

I opened my mouth to protest, but how could I?

"Fine," I sighed. "But let me make a copy of the note before I hand it away."

When I'd finished, we walked up to the top of campus in search of Cryker.

"It'll be okay," she said, her arm around my shoulder. "Everything will be okay. And I'll go in with you."

But when we got to the teachers' lounge, an officer told Sophie to head to her room, and he ushered me inside. She tried to protest, but he closed the door in her face.

The teachers' lounge had been turned into a kind of impromptu police headquarters. Cryker sat at a desk, examining an array of plastic bags. There was a strange energy to the room, a sense that something was about to happen.

"Good. You're here. I just sent someone to find you. Nice hair, by the way."

"Thanks."

"Please, take a seat."

"I'm fine standing," I said. "It's her, isn't it?"

He looked up at me with a lifetime of sadness in his eyes. "We have reason to believe it is."

"How can you know?"

"Please sit down," he said, and I did as he asked.

He cleared his throat, and then, with a pair of tweezers, he held up a plastic bag. I leaned in close and saw that it was Clare's pink charm necklace. If someone had asked me about it the day before, I wouldn't have remembered, but seeing it there like that, I suddenly felt blind, eclipsed by Clare's presence, her strawberry smell, her crisscrossed teeth as she leaned down, her face level with mine, offering her hand. God, how I missed her. I still missed her.

"Miss Wood, do you recognize this?"

I choked.

"Yeah," I managed to say. "It's Clare's."

He nodded. "We're checking with dental records, but it's looking like these bones belong to your sister and Laurel Snow."

I tried to keep it together. "That necklace . . . it was just in the bag with the bones?"

"Yes." He nodded. "I know this must be extremely difficult for you."

"I'm okay." I shrugged. "It's not like I had some fantasy she was alive. I'm not stupid."

"I can't tell you how sorry I am for your loss. There are no words."

He shifted around in his seat and cleared his throat. I looked at him, and for the first time, I saw a real person, the forehead inscribed with worry lines, the eyes possessed by the devotion to finding the person who had murdered my sister. That pain was his job, and for a moment I was overwhelmed with gratitude to him. I cleared my throat as if in solidarity with him and nodded.

"It's the same person, isn't it?" I asked. "The same person who killed Iris did this to my sister and Laurel, right?"

He sighed and massaged his pencil with yellow-tipped fingers. He looked at me for a second as if trying to decide how

218

much to tell me, then grimaced, showing finely demarcated canines. "This is confidential. I can't have you spreading this around. This information doesn't leave this office, *capisce*?"

I nodded.

"Iris was strangled, and it's looking like at least one of the girls might have been strangled as well."

"Strangled?" I managed to say. "So you're sure, then. You're sure they didn't . . . they didn't die in the fire?"

He shook his head. "I'm sorry. It's looking like murder."

"You're sure they were strangled?"

"We can't know for sure, but"—he cleared his throat—"but there's evidence to suggest as much. I'm sorry."

"You're telling me my sister was strangled?" I said, my head spinning. "You can't know that. How can you know that?"

"It's not conclusive, but one of the hyoid bones is broken. That's a flag for strangulation. It's possible it could have happened postmortem, but it got our attention because of Iris."

"And you're sure Iris was strangled?" I asked, trying to keep my breath as even as possible. "Someone just strangled her with his bare hands?"

He shook his head. "The killer probably used an implement of some kind—a cord."

"Okay, um, okay," I said, stumbling over myself, trying not to make eye contact. "People are saying Iris was raped. I have to know."

"Iris wasn't raped," he said, his gaze suddenly much sharper. "Who told you that?"

"I . . . I can't remember," I lied.

He shook his head. "Well, that's not true. Listen, you're going to hear all kinds of things. They're rumors. If you don't hear it from me, then it's not true. You got it?"

"Yeah, okay."

He leaned back and scratched his eyebrow. "Along those lines, there is something I want you to hear from me." He looked for my consent to go on. "The bones. We don't understand the significance, but it looks like the bones were bleached," he said, his voice faltering.

"Bleached?"

"Bleached. Boiled, cleaned, and bleached."

A rip cord of tension shot up my back, and I sat up to try to ease it.

"What? Why would someone do that?"

"I wish I knew. It's possible someone was looking to preserve them. Sometimes . . . sometimes these people like to keep trophies."

"Okay, so someone killed my sister ten years ago and buried her in that bag out there. . . ."

"Actually, they were recently buried."

For a moment, I saw the impossible flit before my eyes: Clare grown, wild in the forest, having run feral for ten years, a silk dress of ruby red trailing behind her. I saw her standing behind me the day we hunted for salamanders, her feet caked with mud, her hair falling to her waist in thick black waves. I saw her perched in a tree, her scarlet lips swept into a smile as she watched me pose for Chelsea Vetiver.

"No," he said, alarmed at the look I must have worn. "The bones are old. The burial is new. The killer must have had them at a different location and buried them, well, we're thinking he buried them after he killed Iris."

"What?" I said, trying to get myself together. "Why would he do that?"

"My guess is the bones were somewhere close to him, and after he killed Iris, he wanted to distance himself from his past crimes."

"No," I said, shifting in my seat. "This is crazy. It doesn't make sense. Did you . . . Does my mom know?"

He shook his head. "I can't reach her. I spoke with your aunt. She said your mom goes off sometimes and no one knows where she is."

"Yeah," I said, avoiding eye contact.

"Do you know where she is?"

I fought the urge to laugh. "No. She never tells me anything."

He nodded. "Your aunt wants you to come home. I gotta tell you, I'm of a similar mind. What about you? Do you want to go home?"

I thought for a moment and then shook my head. There had been a time when I might have wanted to leave, but that was before I knew for sure that my sister had been murdered, before I knew that her killer was so close I could almost feel it. I wanted to stay. I wanted to stay and finish this thing.

"Listen," he said. "You probably want to talk to someone. A counselor. You want me to set that up for you?"

"No," I started to say, but just then, the door swung open and an officer entered. Cryker practically jumped up from his desk when he saw him. The man's eyes connected with Cryker's, and a strange energy bounced between them. He handed

Cryker a note. Cryker's eyes scanned the page, and color rose in his cheeks.

"Miss Wood," he said, not bothering to look at me. "That's all for now. I'll contact you if we need anything else."

He moved across the room quickly and handed the page to his partner, her blond curls bouncing as she nodded. I looked down into my bag and saw the puzzle box staring up at me like an abandoned child. I knew there had to be more to it. There was something about that logo that wasn't right, but I couldn't figure out what it was.

"Detective," I said, and he looked over, already lost in whatever he was reading.

He held up a hand. "Can it wait?"

"Yeah," I said. "Yeah it can."

"Good," he said. "We'll talk later, then."

He went back to whatever he was doing, and I walked out into the crisp air, my shoulders somehow a little lighter. Somewhere at the end of a very long thread was the answer to the question of what had happened to my sister, and I was certain that thread was somehow connected to the puzzle box. I couldn't let it go. Not yet.

When I got back to my room, the air felt heavy, and everything looked gray, but I had a spark inside my chest, lifting me up, pushing me forward. I would need to let go of my fantasy now. There was no fairy-tale cottage in the woods. No more kindly stranger, but now, at least, I had the truth.

I was just returning from the shower when Helen came in.

"Whoa, right?" she said when she sat on her bed. "How's Alex doing?"

"I don't know. I haven't seen him since early this morning."

I'd forgotten about Alex. The day before, I'd been so sure that I needed to break up with him, but now I wasn't. Now he seemed solid and good in a grotesque world.

"Really?" She looked at me, puzzled. "He had kind of a shock. You should really be supporting him through this. He hurt his leg too, tripping over a log on the way to tell the others."

"Yeah, I'll go see him in a bit."

Helen nodded. "And Asta, oh my God. Can you imagine? It was her daughter. Noel's over there comforting her. I heard her tell Harrison she needed a few days off to process or something, but that ultimately it was good to have closure. I mean, I can see what she means."

"Yeah," I sighed. "Closure."

"They're saying whoever did this probably also killed Iris," she said, twisting her hair. "I mean, like, duh, right?"

"What's going to happen?" I asked, trying to keep my voice from shaking.

"What do you mean? We're all going to be under crazy watch again."

"What's going to happen to the school? Aren't people going to pull their kids out, like, left and right?"

She bit her nails. "Huh. I hadn't thought of that. I don't know. Hardly anyone left after they found Iris."

"But this is different," I said.

"Seniors hear from colleges next week. The school has the

letters mailed to us, because we live in the seventeenth century. No one's gonna want to wait for them to be forwarded. And besides, I heard they have some hot lead—some kind of forensic evidence. They're gonna catch whoever did this and then there won't be anything to worry about."

I felt cold as I watched Helen pull out her gym bag and start packing it.

"What are you doing?"

"State championships."

"Today?"

"Tomorrow morning. We're leaving tonight."

"They're letting you go?"

She shrugged. "It's state. We're probably gonna win. You don't want to miss something like that."

"But with what's going on here, they're still letting you guys go?"

"It's not like the psycho dragon killer or whoever is going to follow us and, like, attack the bus."

"So you're not going to be here tonight?"

She paused a moment and then seemed to understand. "Oh, my poor Woodsy," she cried, and immediately wrapped me up in her arms. "You're scared, aren't you?"

"I'm not scared," I said, pulling away from her.

"Talk to Ms. Harlow. I bet you could sleep on the floor in someone's room. Ask Drucy. Or Cara. I bet either one would let you."

"Naw," I said, watching her zip up her bag. "I think I'll be fine."

I didn't go see Alex. I needed some time to figure out how

I felt before I saw him again. I spent the rest of the night in my room, reading. I knew everyone would think it was weird, but I just couldn't stomach comforting him through the trauma of finding my sister's bones. I also couldn't talk to him about it. I just couldn't.

Like Helen had predicted, security was heavy again. They even kept the hall lights on, and most people slept with their desk lamps on, but I turned mine off and went to bed early. The bastard wasn't worth losing a night's sleep over. I settled into my bed and tried to let go of the day. My thoughts muddled together as I sank further into sleep, slipping into gray, charcoal, black.

I awoke with a jolt in the middle of the night, as if I'd been pushed. I was disoriented and sweating, trying to catch my breath. I'd been dreaming about something. A monster, maybe? A dragon? I rubbed my eyes and tried to recall. Yes, it had been a dragon guarding a treasure. No, it wasn't guarding a treasure; it was guarding a secret.

I switched on the light and stared at the closet. What had that dragon meant to Iris? Was it a good luck symbol to her? Why had she drawn it up in that cave? Why had she drawn it in my closet? I was close. I could feel it.

I found Helen's flashlight in her desk and set about emptying my closet and confronting the great blue dragon. I stepped into the closet. In the dark, with the dragon illuminated only by the flashlight, it was now clear why I'd missed the beast when I'd first moved in. Each of its scales was filled in with graffiti, and its body seemed to sink back deep into the years of semiprivate inscriptions. Only its horrible eyes peered out at me, like great gashes of disbelief. As if it were shocked that someone dared invade its domain.

"Okay, Iris," I heard myself say aloud. "What's your treasure? What were you hiding in here?" I shone the flashlight around the area, focusing on the darkest crevices and corners, but nothing. Then it occurred to me. The floor. So what was underneath the floorboards? In an instant I was on my knees, searching the floor of the closet, my fingers grasping at floorboards, my nails working their way into the slits. And then one gave way. I was fairly certain my heart missed a beat, and I faltered, suddenly hypoxic. I shone the flashlight on the loose board, now tipped up at the edge like a seesaw. I set the flashlight down and it rolled away, against the back of the closet, the stream of light growing thick and eerie as it did. With trembling hands, I pulled the board the rest of the way up and reached underneath. At first nothing, but then I reached farther, until I was in up to my forearm, and that was when I felt it—a sheaf of paper, rolled up and wrapped with a ribbon to make it the same width as the boards. Bingo.

My heart pounding, the papers shaking in my hand, I moved to the bed. I untied the red velvet ribbon that bound the sheets. Page after page of letters and symbols, complicated schematics and complex equations. I settled on one of the pages. It resembled something an architect might create. It seemed somehow familiar. I pulled back a little, trying to let my vision adjust to it, and then my breath caught. It was a rough schematic for a complicated sort of box. A puzzle box.

"You made it, didn't you, Iris?" I said aloud. "It wasn't some stalker boy. It was you. You made the puzzle box."

I pulled the box from the drawer beneath my bed and examined the diagram more closely. The two resembled each other, but they weren't identical. Mine wasn't the first puzzle box she'd made.

"What the hell is going on?" I said, aloud again, startling myself. Quickly I leafed through the pages. No wonder Iris's grades had slipped. She'd been an extremely busy girl. My eye caught on a page that looked vaguely familiar. It was identical in form to the note my puzzle box had contained, but the numbers were different:

R&J 2.1.75–78

            4 36 72 1 91 5 , 112 114 10 21 53 16 104 64
91 50 9 61 41 35 3 23 25 16 2 110 38 46 58 110 54
. 30 44 50 24 60 10 59 104 59 64 58 . 71 74 73 67
61 12 3 1 33 53 . 9 21 39 23 10 35 3 47 14 41 30 .
57 6 27 2 53 46 89 12 59 88 82 93 74 33 17 8 7 16
91 20 19 , 64 15 71 53 .

I had been right. They were using a key text, and these were notes for another enciphered message, only this one gave the key text in the margin of the page. R&J had to mean Romeo and Juliet. And 2.1.75–78 meant Act 2, Scene 1, lines seventy-five to seventy-eight. I scanned Helen's shelves. Somewhere she had The Complete Works of Shakespeare. She'd had it out when she was auditioning for The Tempest. It wasn't on her shelf. On a whim, I looked in her closet, but it wasn't there. I sank to my knees and was relieved to find it under her bed. How unlike Helen. Perhaps I was rubbing off on her. I pulled out the giant volume and leafed through to find *Romeo and Juliet* and the line number.

> *O Romeo, Romeo, wherefore art thou Romeo?*
> *Deny thy father and refuse thy name;*
> *Or if thou wilt not, be but sworn my love,*
> *And I'll no longer be a Capulet.*

Pulling out my pen and notebook, I set about deciphering the text. I assigned a number to each letter as follows:

O	R	O	M	E	O	R	O	M	E
1	2	3	4	5	6	7	8	9	10

O	W	H	E	R	E	F	O	R	E
11	12	13	14	15	16	17	18	19	20

The first symbol in the cipher text was 4, so I counted four spaces from the start of the key text and ended up with M. The next letter was Y. I continued on from there until I had the entire message deciphered:

MYLOVE,PLEASEGIVEMEANOTHER
CHANCE.MEETMEAGAIN.INTHEWO
ODS.MAYTENONEAM.YOURSALWA
YSANDFOREVER,IRIS.

I was overwhelmed with sadness. Iris wasn't some cold-hearted narcissist incapable of love. Iris had in fact been in love, had begged someone to meet her in an attempt to re-kindle that love. Had someone met her out there in the woods, or had she waited alone? But who was this other person? Had the secrecy been necessary or just another aspect of Iris's melo-drama, another eccentricity?

I tapped my pen against the notebook and wondered. Would this key text work for my note as well? It was worth a try. I had worked for only a few minutes when I realized I was on the wrong track. Using *Romeo and Juliet* as the key text rendered my note complete gibberish. But I was closer. No matter how far away I might be, I was getting closer. Around three a.m., I rolled up the sheaf of paper, secured it with the same velvet ribbon Iris had used, and slipped it inside my pillow. I drifted off to sleep with numbers and letters swirling behind my lids.

I didn't go to class the next morning. I figured that given the events of the previous day, the administration was bound to cut us some slack. They were probably just hoping the whole school didn't empty out. Without Helen's alarm clock, I slept in until eleven, and when I got up and opened my glass door, a breath of honeysuckle flitted into the room. I retrieved Iris's blueprints, and sitting on my bed, I began examining them. I was just starting to jot down notes when Mr. Reilly knocked on my window. I gathered up Iris's pages and, slipping them into my notebook, beckoned him in. I wondered how much he'd seen.

"So, Cally," he said, and with a bitchy grin spread across his

229

face, he took a seat on Helen's bed. "Did you forget what day it was?"

"No," I said, picking up my notebook again.

"Are you ill?"

"No," I said, anger surfacing, my head growing hot and jumbled with it.

"Then why weren't you in chemistry?"

"I don't know. Maybe it has something to do with that bag of bones you guys found in the woods."

"True. We're all suffering here, Cally, but we can't let tragedy overrun our lives. We can't let it win."

"Let tragedy win? What are you even talking about? There was a bag of children's bones up there."

"Look," he said, sighing, bringing his palms together and lifting his fingers to the tip of his nose as if to pray. "I don't want to argue with you. I just want you to know that you're not exempt from the rules."

"I am when the rules are stupid."

The color started to rise in his cheeks. "That kind of attitude is not going to get you asked back to St. Bede's. You guys . . . ," he said. His face flushed completely crimson, and for a moment it looked like he really might lose it, but then he did his best to swallow down his rage. "You have no idea the kind of work we do for you guys, the sacrifices we make."

He had that whiny, overly familiar tone I'd heard him take with other students when he wanted to play with the power dynamic. It made my stomach ache.

"I don't know what you're talking about," I said, smiling,

hoping to irritate him out of my room. "I love St. Bede's. I find it rigorous, yet nurturing."

He shook his head. "Whatever, Cally. I'm not going to reach out to you if you won't meet me halfway. This dialogue is over. Here," he said, retrieving a note from his pocket. "Dr. Harrison wanted me to give this to you."

"Thank you," I said brightly, placing it beside me on the bed.

He started for the door but then paused and stared at me with such loathing in his eyes that I almost asked him why he hated me so much. Was it because I wasn't frightened and pliant like Shelly Cates? Or maybe he just didn't think I was pretty.

"You only get one slip with me," he said, raising a tensed finger. "You miss my class again, and I'll have you kicked out. Understood?"

I nodded.

"One slip," he said again, and then jostled himself out the door.

When he was gone, I read Harrison's note. It offered condolences and invited me to drop by his office if I wanted to "process things." He'd also arranged a weekly appointment with the school counselor. It was sweet, really, but I wasn't looking forward to the therapy time-suck. I slipped the paper into my drawer, then opened my notebook and got back to work.

"This is unbelievable."

Sophie sat and I lay under an oak tree near the front edge of campus. She leafed through Iris's papers, which I'd concealed in a binder. She shook her head. "I just can't believe this. If Iris made it, then who left it for you?"

I shrugged and bit my nail. I'd taken to doing that lately. It was better than taking up smoking.

"Do you think it could be from the killer?"

"Not necessarily," Sophie said, squinting into the afternoon sun. "It could be from this person, from whomever she was secretly dating, and that person doesn't have to be the killer."

"But why give it to me?"

"You're right. It doesn't really make sense, does it? You tried using *Romeo and Juliet* on our note?"

I nodded. "No luck. And I can't make sense of the rest of her papers. Can you?"

"Not off the top of my head, no. Mostly they look like building blueprints. I don't think we're going to get new information out of them, but I'll take them back to my room and have a look if you want."

"Thanks." I nodded. "Don't let anyone see them, okay?"

"Of course not."

"Not even Jack."

She nodded and closed the binder. "What I don't understand," she said, "is why she would need the puzzle box to communicate with her secret boyfriend. I mean, clearly she was using it to send notes to plan a rendezvous, but why go through the effort? Why not just leave the note on his bed?"

"I know!" I said, sitting up. "That's what's been driving me crazy. Why do that? It's like she couldn't even risk anyone thinking it was a note. It seems crazy."

"It does seem crazy, but it also seems like something she would do. And also, if her secret boyfriend thought this kind of thing was cool, maybe she did it to impress him."

The term *secret boyfriend* made me flinch. It reminded me too much of Jack and whatever he was hiding. What was it about boarding school that made everyone so goddamn secretive? I was just beginning to compose a self-righteous aphorism in my head about honesty when I remembered that I wasn't exactly a saint.

"Something is really off about this whole thing," I said, relieved finally to have someone to talk it over with. "I mean, why would she need to hide her relationship?" I pulled at a blade of grass, something percolating in my mind. "God, it could have been an adult. It could have been a teacher."

"God," Sophie gasped. "I bet you're right. Things like that have happened before."

"Gross."

Sophie started to speak, but then she closed the notebook abruptly. I looked up to see Alex approaching. He sat down across from me on the grass. Barely acknowledging Sophie, he took my hand. She rolled her eyes and, taking the binder, got up to go.

"I'll see you later, Cally?" she said, and then walked off.

"Why haven't you come by?" Alex asked, completely oblivious. "I've been going through a lot lately."

"That was really rude," I said, taking my hand back. "You just totally ignored Sophie."

"Yeah, I don't like her."

"What?" I said, wincing. "How can you not like Sophie?"

"I just don't." He shook his head, clearly annoyed with me. "Don't you even care about what happened to me? I had the shock of a lifetime. Every girl in the school is coming by my room offering to comfort me, and where the hell is my own girlfriend? You're off with your bestie gossiping about shoes."

"Wow," I said, my head numb, my heart tender from the blow. "You are being a total dick. How can you talk about her like that? What, she's not one of the cool kids, so she doesn't even rate as a human being to you?"

He stared off toward the dorms. "Sorry. I didn't mean to be rude to your friend. I'll try to be nicer. I've just been really upset, and, like, hurt—no, alarmed—that you haven't even come by my room."

I didn't know what to say. I was incredibly annoyed with him, but I also didn't want to have a big fight. I had neither the time nor the stomach for drama, so I lied to get us off topic. "I've been dealing with some stuff back home. It's been really intense."

"Oh," he said, staring at me as if I were a total stranger. "I guess it's cool, then." We went up to dinner after that and ate side by side without talking.

CHAPTER SIXTEEN

WE HAD HALF-DAY CLASSES THAT Saturday. I'd just tossed my books onto my balcony and was heading to the dining hall when Freddy called to me. I turned and saw her lingering by the mailboxes, chewing on her cuticles. I nodded to her, then continued on to lunch. Freddy had really pissed me off, and I didn't relish the prospect of dealing with her.

She caught up with me on the stairs. "Can we talk?"

"Depends," I said, not bothering to keep the annoyance from my voice. I kept walking and could feel her trailing behind me.

"I'm sorry. Hold up, okay? I can explain. I just need to talk to you."

"Why?" I spun around to face her. "What could you possibly have to talk to me about?"

"I'm sorry about the other day. I wasn't expecting you to ask me anything about the phone call. I panicked. I can get kind of defensive when I feel threatened."

I tried to maintain my anger, but she looked so pathetic that I found it subsiding. "Yeah, I noticed."

"Come on," she said. "Let's just go for a walk and have a chat, shall we? I think we might be able to help each other out."

I nodded and headed down the path that led away from campus.

"Okay," I said when we were far enough out not to be overheard. "What do you want?"

"I want to know why you were asking about that phone call. Who told you about it?"

"Look, Freddy," I said, my hand on my hip. "I'm not telling you anything until you tell me who that phone call was from. I know you remember."

"God," she snapped. "Don't be such an idiot, Wood. There *was* no phone call." I froze, overcome by an odd sense that something bad was happening. She went on. "I made it up because I needed to talk to Iris privately. I knew she was doing her work-study in the bio lab, so I walked over to talk to her, and when I saw Ms. Snow, I made up the phone call so she could leave. Okay? Satisfied? Now you know my big secret. And I need you to do me a favor. I need you to tell me who told you about it."

"There wasn't a phone call? What the hell, Freddy?"

"I needed to talk to her alone, so I lied. I didn't think it would ever amount to anything. When the police asked me about it in October, I froze. I told the police I couldn't remember. But that was when I thought she'd run away. I had no idea it could become important. But when you mentioned it the other day, it occurred to me that if they wanted to, the police could check the dorm phone records. They might find out that I lied."

"So?"

"I don't want to get mixed up in something. I have everything set up just the way I want it, and then you asked me about the phone call and my mind went wild imagining all these possibilities. I started thinking they knew I lied and that it had gotten out somehow and was all over school."

I shook my head. "It was just Alex. He was in the lab when you came in to get Iris."

Color rushed into her cheeks and she looked incredibly satisfied. "Just Alex?"

I nodded, and she exhaled, then looked at me with sudden suspicion.

"Why is this so important to you, anyway? Why do you want to know?"

"Look," I sighed. "You asked me to trust you once and I did. I went along with your plan even though it went against my principles, and I did it as a favor to you. And if I remember, you even said you'd owe me. Well, this is it. This is what you owe me. This is my favor. I want you to tell me why you made up that phone call."

She sighed and her shoulders fell.

"Okay," she said with some effort. "Fine. I made it up because I needed to talk to Iris because I needed some weed, and I knew she had some."

"What?" I was so shocked I almost laughed. "You had, like, a pot emergency?"

"Yes," she hissed. "I did. I need it to be normal, okay? If I don't have it, I get completely uptight and anxious. I get incapacitated."

"Too bad you can't smoke it every day."

"Cally, I do smoke it every day."

"What?"

"I mean, I don't *smoke* it, I'd get caught, but I keep a stash of lollipops. I usually just need a little bit in the morning, but that day I knew I'd need more. I had a math competition the next day, and I get terrible performance anxiety. I needed it, and my connection fell through. I knew Iris usually had some, and if I asked nicely and actually hung out with her, she'd smoke me out for free."

"You used her for pot?"

"Yes, Cally. I used her for pot. I guess that makes me a total bitch," she said with a cold smile on her lips.

"So that's it? You lied because you didn't want to get caught about smoking pot?"

She nodded. "It wasn't premeditated. I didn't think they'd know about the phone call, so when they asked me, I didn't have time to make something up. I just said I couldn't remember. I hadn't even planned on making up the call in the first place. I only did that because she wasn't alone in the lab like I thought she'd be, and I needed to talk to her. So that's it. Please don't tell anyone."

I stared at her a moment, taking in the whole pathetic mess of her. "Fine," I said, and then motioned that we should head back to campus, but she just stood there looking strangely fragile. My stomach was starting to growl.

"Wait," she said. "There's more."

I turned around, exhausted.

"I need to talk to someone about it, and Tanner's been no help."

"Tanner?" I mused, the obvious now apparent to me. "That's your regular connection, huh?"

"What?"

"Tanner. He's who you normally get it from. Is he who gave you the stuff we smoked in the cave?"

She shifted her oxfords in the dirt and nodded. "It was special. His sister sent it to him from Humboldt. That's why I wanted to delay telling the police. I was trying to create some distance between us smoking up in the cave and Tanner getting the package. I thought someone might put our expedition together with the package he got, and look into him. He's usually way more careful than that."

I tried to ignore my growing hunger. "Okay, so what's up, then? What hasn't Tanner been any help with?"

She sighed. "I'm not saying that I think you'll help me. I know we're not, like, best friends, but I need to talk to someone. I need advice."

"Advice? From me?" With some effort I tried to keep the disbelief from my voice.

She nodded. "That night, the night she disappeared, everyone had left for fall break except the Math Bowl kids. So Iris smoked me out in her room, and I fell asleep in Helen's empty bed."

"Oh," I said, wheels starting to spin. "Oh man. So you were the last person to see her alive, then?"

She shook her head. "No. That's the thing. I wasn't. That night, after I fell asleep, I thought I heard a voice outside calling her name. I was ridiculously high and still mostly asleep, but I thought she left when she heard the voice. When I woke up in the morning, she was gone. I cleaned up our mess and skedaddled. I didn't know something was wrong until we got to the meet. And then I figured she ran off with some guy. That's what it seemed like."

"Oh my God," I said, a cold shock running down my spine. Had Iris left willingly with her killer that night, and had Freddy been a witness?

"I know," she said, trying to suppress tears. "And I didn't say anything because I didn't want to get in trouble. I thought she ran away. I thought, if anything, I was doing her a favor by keeping quiet. But really, it's like I just let her die. And looking back, I feel like I should have known. She was acting crazy all night. I blamed it on the pot and on her, you know, general Iris-ness. She kept worrying that someone was watching us, she kept hearing noises. She left several times to go make phone calls, but she wouldn't say to whom. Then she told me something really upsetting, only at the time I didn't realize it was important."

I nodded for her to go on, trying to suppress that familiar grieving chant of *if only*.

"She told me she'd found something out that she could use against someone. She'd found something really disturbing, really bad. It sounded to me like she was talking about black-

240

mail. I blew her off at the time, because how lame, but looking back on it all now, it's terrifying. What if she really did find something out, and she was going to use it to blackmail someone? What if that person was watching us all night? What if that was the person she left with? What if she thought she had the upper hand with this person, but really they were planning on shutting her up before she could do anything?"

"Oh God. Did she say when she found out whatever it was?"

"That day," she said, her eyes wide. "She found out that day, and she disappeared that night. If you think about it, I might know who the killer is. I can't remember the voice, but I know I recognized it. If anyone finds out I was in that room with Iris that night, I mean, what's to stop them from doing the same thing to me?"

"Oh God," I said, closing my eyes. I felt a headache coming on. "You're right, Freddy. You need to tell the cops. You really could be in danger."

"I know, but I can't. If I tell them, they'll know about the pot, they'll be pissed about me obstructing their investigation, and it'll all get back to Harvard. They'll rescind their offer, and I'll be screwed."

I looked at those cold green eyes, unable to believe she could still be thinking about Harvard.

I shook my head. "You don't need to tell them the whole thing. Tell them you called her out of class because you wanted to spend the night so you could, I don't know, talk about a boy or something. Tell them you lied to them because you didn't want to get in trouble for sneaking out of your dorm that night. You're a heavy sleeper, that's why your head was fuzzy, and you can't remember more details. And then you tell the rest like it really happened. You just omit the pot and apologize profusely for lying to them in October. The fact that she left of her own volition lends credence to the idea that she ran away. It's not totally crazy that you thought that."

"Yeah. Yeah, I guess you're right. I think I'll talk to them. Thank you," she said, reaching out as if to pat me on the shoulder, but stopping herself. "Thanks."

We walked up to lunch in silence.

I ate quickly, unnerved by what Freddy had told me, and started toward the library. Her story changed things significantly, and it would require some thinking. I'd lost the phone call but gained what was possibly the biggest lead yet. It was looking very probable that Iris had known her killer and gone willingly with him. He was someone she'd known and most likely someone I knew too.

But I never made it to the library. As soon as I left the dining hall and saw the senior lawn, it was clear that something had gone down. Groups of kids and teachers were scattered across the lawn, and everyone kept their voices eerily low. I saw Helen and Pigeon coming up the steps. Helen looked confused, and Pigeon looked deathly pale, as if she was on the verge of being sick.

"What's going on, you guys?" I asked.

Helen shook her head, incredulous. "They just came and took Mr. Reilly away. Someone said they're going to charge him."

"What?" I said. "No, that's not possible."

"It's true. I heard the bag that the bones were in was Mr. Reilly's, and they found fibers on the bones that matched something from his apartment—a rug or something," Helen said, still shaking her head as if she couldn't believe what she was saying.

Pigeon just nodded, for once unable to speak.

"Reilly wasn't even teaching here ten years ago," I said. "And he couldn't have been living in that apartment for sure. I mean, he would have been fifteen."

"No," Helen said. "But he did go to high school an hour south of here. And apparently the grave site was pretty recent. People are saying he's had the bones with him all this time, like carrying them with him from place to place. I guess when he killed Iris, he freaked and decided to get rid of them. It's so disturbing."

I shook my head, uncertain what to say. It felt wrong. It felt all wrong to me. No matter how thinly you stretched the logic or what a creep Reilly was, I couldn't believe he had killed my sister, forensic evidence or not. But it seemed that for everyone else, this was precisely what they needed. The floodgates had opened, and however illogical the catalyst might be, relief was pouring out.

Time seemed to move slowly after that. It seemed like no one wanted to be alone. We stood around, gathered in little groups on the front lawn. Someone said something about a vigil, but nothing ever came of it. Asta and I hugged each other.

"It's over now," she whispered. "We can finally let them go."

It was like a morbid kind of party, everyone sort of milling about, some laughing, others crying. When I saw Sophie, she gave me half a smile.

"I don't buy it," I whispered. "He didn't have a motive or

an opportunity. Maybe he could have been involved with Iris, but what about my . . ." I looked around to make sure no one was listening. "Ten years ago, he wasn't even able to drive, and Helen just told me he lived an hour away. Did he take the bus up here and kill two little girls for no reason and then hide the bones for ten years? What, did he take the evidence with him to college?"

Sophie shrugged. "I hear what you're saying, but you don't have all the information. You can't know what kind of evidence the police have against him. Just try to chill for a bit."

"So you think he did it?"

She thought for a moment, and then shook her head. "I don't know, but obviously we don't have access to whatever evidence the police have."

"What about the puzzle box? Do you think he sent it to me?"

"Dude," she said, holding up her hands. "I don't know. Maybe he did, and maybe he didn't. There hasn't been a trial. What did the police say about it?"

"They, um . . . ," I said, but then Freddy walked up, and I stopped myself.

Just before dinner, I was talking to Drucy and Shane when something strange caught my eye. Across the lawn, I saw Asta standing with Noel. They were side by side like sisters, closer than I ever saw Noel and Helen. Asta's hand was on Noel's forearm, and then she leaned in and whispered something in her ear, and Noel went pale. Her jaw dropped, and she shook her

244

head. She looked like she might cry. Then Asta's eyes caught mine, and she pulled away. She patted Noel on the back and walked over to the French teacher, leaving Noel there shivering like a lone dandelion. I started moving through the crowd to her, but by the time I reached the other side of the lawn, she was gone.

That night when I went to bed alone in my room, an uncharacteristically fragile Helen having gotten special permission to sleep on Noel's floor, I locked the door and said my heathen version of prayers. *Please, Universe, don't let anyone kill me tonight.*

It had been a strange day, and I found myself wondering just how much stranger things would get. There had been a lot of relief—a feeling that we could finally let our guard down. The sense that the entire campus had just exhaled was mixed, though, with a kind of morbid fixation on what if it had been one of us. I worried that it still could be.

I could see Reilly killing Iris. I could create a scenario in which that made sense: *They have an affair; she gets obsessed. He breaks it off with her in the spring because he comes to his senses. She's so distraught she has a nervous breakdown. Then there's a stretch of several months where nothing happens. She goes home and starts to get herself back together, but when she comes back to school, she's still in love with him. And then something happens. The day she dies, she finds something out, maybe that she isn't the first student he's taken advantage of. Maybe she finds out there have been—or are—others, and she freaks out. Totally enraged, she threatens to go to the police. She blackmails him. He comes by her room to talk some sense into her. They go somewhere secret—up to the cave. He gives her mushrooms, and she draws her dragon because . . . I don't know, because she likes* to draw dragons. . . . *Maybe it doesn't even mean that much. Maybe she just likes to draw it. He thinks he'll be able to talk her out of going to the police, but high on mushrooms, she's unreasonable. They argue, things get out of hand, and in the heat of the moment, he strangles her.* I could see it. I could see it all. But what about my sister? That made no sense. He hadn't come up here and killed her for no reason.

But what if there were two killers?

What if Clare and Laurel's killer knew about Reilly and Iris and suspected that Reilly had killed her? What if he then used the opportunity to frame Reilly for Clare's and Laurel's murders? It would be easy enough. Take Reilly's gym bag, plant some fibers from his apartment. Reilly hadn't been sitting on those bones for ten years, but someone had. Someone had kept them close and then buried them out in those woods. Whoever it was, the killer was still out there watching—watching me.

I pulled up the covers and sank into opacity. I don't know how long I slept before I heard the sliding glass door shudder. Adrenaline rushed through my body and I sat up in bed. I heard a faint knocking and a cracking male voice.

"Woodsy, it's me."

Jack.

I opened the door and he came in, quiet and strange. He sat on Helen's bed.

"Is this okay?" he asked, his voice still wavering. He'd been crying. He was exhausted.

"Are you okay?"

"Yeah. Fine," he said, putting his head in his hands. "Or, I don't know. Maybe I'm not."

I could smell something strange on his breath. Whiskey? Jack didn't drink whiskey.

"Jack, what's going on?" I asked, shivering a little. "Where have you been?"

He shook a finger at me. "Ah ah ah," he admonished. "Can't tell. Part of my great big secret."

"The other person? The person you're seeing?"

He nodded.

"The thing is, Wood, I've been with this other person all night, but I didn't want to be. I wanted to be with you."

"Jack, what are you doing here? You're going to get in so much trouble if someone catches you."

"I don't care. I can't stop thinking about you," he said. "I wanted to make sure you were safe."

A part of me felt a pull to him so strong I thought I might break. I wanted to go to him. I wanted to say things to him I knew I'd regret. I wanted to hold him, but all I could do was say, "I don't need anyone to keep me safe, Jack."

He started to speak, but then paused. His voice cracked when he finally spoke again. "Can I . . . can I stay here with you tonight?"

When he said that, it was like part of me simply went numb. I felt cold, as if I'd never had a single normal emotion in my life. I wanted to say the right thing, but suddenly I didn't know what that thing was. I didn't know who I was.

"I don't know," I said.

"You don't know?" he asked, running his hands through his hair. "You'd rather be alone than have me spend the night with you?"

"I didn't mean it like that," I said.

"No, I'm sorry, but this is weird, right?" he asked, his voice wavering.

"What?"

"Us. Sneaking around. Hooking up, but nothing else."

"I thought that was what we both wanted."

"I know, but after what happened the other day, I'm confused. I don't think I'm okay with this anymore. I want . . . I don't know, I want more."

"I have a boyfriend, Jack."

"Well, *don't* have a boyfriend."

"I really like Alex."

"Then why are you cheating on him?"

The question hung heavy, and I closed my eyes, as if that could protect me from it.

"I don't know," I said. "I like you both."

"This isn't a buffet, Wood. We're people. Alex and I are both people."

"You're the one who suggested this."

"I know, but I was wrong. It's fucked up and it hurts."

"But what about you? What about your secret girlfriend? What about that whole thing?"

He shrugged. "The thing is that this person, every time I saw them, I used to be so, I don't know, excited or something, but now every time, every time they leave the room and come back in, for a second, just a second, I think it's going to be you. But it never is. It just isn't you. And I can't explain it, but that, like, hurts me."

My breath caught. I didn't know why, but his words made me feel funny, warm and silky, and I realized that all along that was what I'd wanted to say to him. But now that the words were out there, I found I couldn't respond. I just sat there, frozen.

He shifted uncomfortably. Moments were slipping by and I had no way of catching up to them, of getting them back. He cleared his throat. There was no going back. I knew that. I just didn't know what that meant.

"Climb in," I said quietly, throwing back the covers.

"Really?" His voice was soft, lonely.

"Yeah," I said.

He hesitated a moment, then slipped in, folding me into his arms, my head on his chest. I didn't know I could be this comfortable. We fit together perfectly. And the strange thing was that despite all we'd done together, for the very first time, I felt embarrassed in front of Jack Deeker. I tried to quiet my breath, afraid of drawing too much attention to myself. His chest rose and fell awkwardly as if he was attempting the same strange feat. We lay there in silence, the darkness beating around us.

I awoke just before dawn, my head still nestled into Jack's wrinkled dress shirt. I looked up at him sleeping and was shocked by what I found. So much of Jack Deeker was put on. All the hardness, the danger, the recondite sexuality. Asleep, he looked like a child. The feminine arch of his cheek, his long dark lashes, the little crescents of resting eyes. He was beautifully fragile in a way I'd never noticed. Lying there, staring up at him, I was reminded—coldly, starkly reminded—of how much of a child I still was. No matter what I might do or try, I was still a work in progress, and I was raw and aching, straining to make myself fit into something stable when the world around me was constantly morphing.

He opened his eyes. His lids fluttered as he took in his surroundings. Then he turned to look at me and I felt a rush like when I was a kid and I'd swing so high it seemed like the chains might break. He smiled so wide he looked almost goofy.

"Hi," he said.

"Hi," I said.

"That was really nice."

"Yeah."

We lay there, staring into each other's eyes.

"Wood," he said. "I think I might love you." And then he reached up to touch my bleached spikes, gentle as if he were touching a newborn's fingers.

For a moment, I felt a surge of something warm, a kind of peace, but then I was back on those swings again, fear pushing me higher and higher. The trouble was that this time, the chains did break.

I plummeted to the earth. I went cold again. I went numb.

"You'd better go before people wake up," I said, dropping my eyes and pulling back the covers.

He was almost silent, getting out of bed, slipping on his shoes. He smiled at me, his lips twisted with a quiet kind of pain.

"Bye," he said.

And then he was gone.

CHAPTER SEVENTEEN

MONDAY MORNING, OUR ALARM DIDN'T go off.

"Piece of shit," Helen whined, and threw it across the room. She wasn't used to objects disobeying her. I'd spent Sunday hiding in the library and wasn't eager to reenter the world. I pulled on my clothes and sat on my bed, waiting for Helen.

"Noel's spending a lot of time with Asta lately," I said, watching Helen brush her hair.

"She always does."

"No, but this is like more than usual. She seems to be the only one Noel talks to these days."

"She talks to me, thank you very much."

"It just seems weird to me, spending all that time with a teacher."

"Don't tell me you don't like Asta. Everyone just *loves* Asta."

She arranged her hair into a neat chignon, then rolled her eyes and started over.

"I know, I know," I said. "You don't like her."

"It's not that I don't like her." Helen shrugged. "I just think she's a phony—all that pseudo-pagan new age crap. I think it's bullshit."

"Why?"

"I don't know. I just think she's full of shit. Some people are like that, you know—just totally full of shit. But I wouldn't worry about Noel and Asta. Asta's her mentor, or whatever."

"It's just that I saw something weird."

"What?" Helen faced me.

"It was right after they took Reilly. When we were all standing around on the lawn, I saw Asta whispering to Noel, and whatever she said, it really upset her."

Helen laughed and started re-twisting her hair. "Yeah, I'm sure Mr. Reilly being a murderous psychopath had nothing to do with why Noel was upset."

I shrugged. "It just seems like their relationship is a little weird, like unhealthy."

"Don't be melodramatic."

"She told me she tells Asta secrets, secrets no one else knows—not even you."

"What's wrong with that?" She snapped the clip into place, nodded at herself, then grabbed the books on her desk.

"It just seems weird to me to be telling a teacher your secrets," I said as we headed to class.

"Cally." She smiled and punched my shoulder. "You worry way too much. That's your problem. You have to lighten up.

Noel's fine. Asta's fine. You know who's not fine is Reilly. That's who you should be worried about. That sucker's gonna fry. Hey, this is me," she said when we reached the math classrooms.

"See you," I said.

"Fight the power," she said, raising a fist in the air.

I headed to English class with a lump in my throat. I hadn't seen Jack again at all on Sunday. I figured we were both trying to play it cool, but now there was no avoiding him. A slight tingle ran along my arms when I walked in and saw him bent over his book, underlining. He looked up and smiled at me like he wanted something. I nodded to him and took a seat next to Sophie.

That morning, Ms. Harlow allocated the first half of class to the half-cocked and potentially morbid exercise of writing a memoir from the point of view of the woods, while she quietly cried, scrunched up at her desk like a withered bean. When we'd finished, she didn't make anyone read their pieces aloud, but instead thrust us headlong into a discussion of A Midsummer Night's Dream. By the time class was over, I was a wreck. I barely made it through the rest of the day.

Noel was especially quiet during sports that afternoon. For a while now she'd been distant, but that afternoon she was noticeably withdrawn. After signing in, we parted ways and I headed over to the mailboxes, wondering how I was going to get any homework done. I was rounding the corner when I saw Jack in the distance talking to Pigeon. He didn't see me, and the way he was talking to her seemed unlike him. He leaned in, laughing at her presumably dumb joke. And when she talked to him, she didn't look like Pigeon. She didn't make any of her annoying little Pigeon faces, and for the first time, I saw what boys saw in her. She was gorgeous, absolutely radiant when she talked to him, her dark eyes wide with admiration. She tossed her silky hair over her shoulder and turned to walk. He fell in step alongside her, and just before they disappeared around the corner, I saw him place his hand on the small of her back.

I steadied myself against the mailboxes. For a second, I was filled with a kind of raging jealousy. Was this the girl Jack was seeing? Was I sleeping with Pigeon's secret boyfriend? Pigeon? *Pigeon?* But behind the anger, behind the jealousy, there was a cushion of relief. I didn't like jealousy. I didn't know how to navigate it, how to understand who I was when it inhabited me. I didn't understand what I felt for Jack, but it scared me, and I wanted it to stop.

I needed to clear my mind, so I headed up to the library.

Carlos was in our spot, staring out the window. He smiled when he saw me.

"How's it going?"

I slumped into my chair and shook my head.

"That bad?"

"I'm feeling kind of homicidal right now. Tell me something. Do you think Pigeon's pretty?"

"You mean Paloma?"

"Yeah, Paloma, whatever."

He furrowed his brow. "I don't know how to answer this question. I'm afraid it has something to do with your being homicidal."

I leaned my head back and closed my eyes.

"Oh, wait," he said, "I've figured out how to answer it. The answer is: not as pretty as you. Is that correct?"

I nodded.

"Oh, fuck it," I said. "Hey, Carlos. Different question. You ever hear of anyone here selling mushrooms?"

His eyes widened. "Calista, I really don't think you're in any shape to take mushrooms right now."

"Not for me," I said, laughing. "I'm just interested."

He shrugged. "I hear all sorts of things like that. That's what I was trying to hint at a while back."

"You?" I asked, shocked, leaning forward.

His cheeks flushed, and he shook his head. I'd never seen him embarrassed before. "God, no. Tanner. Tanner sells them, but he keeps it relatively quiet, unlike his little pot operation."

"Tanner sells mushrooms? Really?"

"Sure. I hear him through the wall."

"You don't remember him selling mushrooms to anyone around the time Iris disappeared, do you?"

"Of course I do. I remember it well. It was the morning of."

"Really? You really remember that? You must have a crazy memory."

"No," he said, shaking his head. "Not really. I wouldn't have remembered at all except that it was Iris. It was the last time I saw her."

"What?" My head was numb. "Did you just say Tanner sold mushrooms to Iris?"

"I did, yeah. The day she vanished."

"Oh my God," I said, shaking my head. "Oh my God."

"What?"

What if Reilly hadn't given Iris the mushrooms, but it had been her decision? She'd decided to take them. This was important. This meant something big. I knew it; I just couldn't tell what it was.

"Did you tell the police?" I asked.

His eyes widened. "Are you insane? No, I didn't tell the police that one of the most popular kids on campus is dealing drugs out of his room. Do you have any idea what would happen to someone like me if I did that? Besides, she bought from him all the time. It was nothing out of the ordinary."

"Was she buying from him her freshman year?"

He raised his hands. "I can't speak to that. I just know what happened last semester. I was living in Stanton House before that."

I chewed on my finger a bit, and then I decided to pay Jack Deeker a visit.

"I'll be back in a minute, Carlos," I said, and he waved me off.

Jack wasn't in his room, so I climbed over his balcony and grabbed a pen and a piece of paper and scribbled:

Need to call off our "chemistry project." Going to continue assignment with Alex instead.

—C

I headed back to the library. I wanted to ask Carlos more questions about Tanner, but he was gone when I got there. I sat for a moment and stared out the window into the darkness.

How had I allowed myself to get so caught up in boys? That wasn't like me. My grades were crap, and I was no closer to figuring out what had happened to my sister. They were still holding Reilly. There were so many things that didn't add up. Who had sent me the box? I knew there had to be more to do with it. I knew it held more answers, but I couldn't figure out how the hell to get to them. Then there was Asta and her recent odd behavior, her lies about being out in the woods the night my sister died. If they hadn't died in the fire, then what had happened to them? Had they really gone out of the house of their own volition, or had someone come in and led them away?

The answer was close, but it was like there was a thick fog obscuring it. I decided to go back to my room and have another look at the puzzle box. Something bothered me about that logo. I knew there had to be something more to it, but I couldn't figure out what it was. Those letters: upside-down Y, O, T, backward E, I. Could they be another code? An anagram, maybe? Mentally, I tried to rearrange the letters, but even if I assumed that the first letter was a Y and that the E wasn't backward, the letters didn't generate a single English word. I was sure of it.

I had just left the library and was about to walk around the corner and through the hallway outside the Prexy classrooms when I heard something that made me stop short. It was Helen's voice, but there was something wrong with it. There was a strange note to it that made me hang back. Gone was her typical nonchalance, and in its place were a pulsating anger and, if I wasn't mistaken, fear.

"I know because Cally told me," she hissed. "I'm not going to tell you again. You can't trust anyone. Not Asta, not Cally—especially not Cally. I'm serious. You have to listen to me and do what I say. I'm not joking around here."

The next thing I knew, Noel came around the corner, her face flushed, her cheeks smudged with eyeliner and tears. She didn't see me, and I ducked into the library and leaned against the wall, trying to think over the beating of my heart. What was going on? When I'd steadied myself, I headed back through the library and out the front entrance, but when I got to the dorm, I saw Jack waiting on the lawn outside my room.

He waved the note at me.

"Um, Wood?" he said. "What the hell is this?"

"I really don't have time to talk right now," I said.

"Yeah, well, make time, okay?" he said, his face flushed with anger.

I sighed and motioned for him to walk with me. "Not here, okay? Come on."

I couldn't have this discussion in public, so I led him behind the music classrooms. He didn't speak while we walked, but once we'd stopped, he looked at me with wounded eyes and slapped the note with the side of his hand.

"This is a joke, right?" he said.

I shook my head, afraid of what I was saying, what I was doing. "I still want to be friends."

"Friends? After the other night? Christ, Wood, I thought you were going to break up with Alex. I thought things were going to be different."

My heart was racing, and in one deft motion, my brain disconnected itself from my heart. Because the truth was I didn't know how to be with someone else—not with someone who would need things from me, someone who would ask me for promises. I couldn't do that. I was terrified of loving Jack. I was terrified of wanting him to stay.

"I know about your little secret," I said. "I saw you and Pigeon down by the mailboxes."

"What? So?"

"You had your hand on her back."

"You think I'm seeing Paloma? That's ridiculous. She's my friend. She's a good kid, but I swear to you, there is zero going on between us."

I knew he was probably telling the truth, but I also knew that I had to end things.

"Look, Jack, seriously. You are one of my best friends. It's just that I choose Alex."

"What?" he said, his voice too loud, fear in his eyes. "Why?"

"I don't have to give you my reasons, Jack. Sorry. That's just my choice."

He opened his mouth, then closed it. He furrowed his brow and pointed at me, then shook his head. "So that's how it is, then? You're serious?"

I nodded.

"Fine, Wood. Then good luck with that." He turned on his heel and started up the path.

"I still want to be friends," I called, but he didn't turn around again.

*　*　*

259

I avoided talking to Helen that night. I didn't understand what I'd overheard, but I knew I didn't like it, and I knew there was no way I could ask Noel about it. She would do what Helen wanted, and for some reason Helen didn't want her talking to me.

What was it with this place? It seemed like the whole school was nothing more than a collection of terrible secrets. Maybe that was just what happened when you put a bunch of adolescents and young teachers together, overworked everyone, and trapped them on campus. Maybe everyone went a little crazy, and bad decisions, and the secrets they generated, were the inevitable outcome.

The next morning in English, Jack made a big deal of sitting across the room from me, and when Sophie came in, she chose to sit with him, not me. I kept my head down and doodled. Fortunately, Ms. Harlow left me alone.

Chemistry was strange without Mr. Reilly. Dr. Harrison was substituting, and the whole of his pedagogy seemed to consist of reading aloud the steps of our experiment and then cowering at his desk as if he expected something to explode. Jack switched partners on me and was now paired with Cara Svitt, because apparently the prospect of sharing a Bunsen burner with me was too odious. He also made a big display of laughing with her, presumably to show how she was just the best chem partner ever. It made me want to puke.

To make matters worse, my new partner was Shelly Cates, and she had all the personality of a taxidermied otter. What was wrong with everybody? Asta was a psycho, Ms. Harlow hated me for some mysterious reason, Helen was talking shit behind my back, and Jack was running around touching every girl in sight, which, honestly, kind of made me want to stab myself in the eye with a micropipette.

I was first out of the room when the bell rang. Anger made me hungry, and I didn't want to have to stand in line to get a hot lunch. I'd have to eat quickly if I wanted to finish my math homework, because my free period was to be spent with the school counselor. It was going to take all my willpower not to beat the poor woman to death with her sand tray.

CHAPTER EIGHTEEN

DURING OUR AFTERNOON WALK, I regaled Noel with tales of my free period spent with Gibby, the counselor, an anemic scarab of a woman who quoted extensively from *Chicken Soup for the Soul,* took a minimum of twelve packets of Sweet'N Low in her coffee, and, despite my being sent to her for grief counseling, promptly diagnosed me with anorexia nervosa.

I had been forced to make a wellness collage and had spent half an hour cutting phallic shapes out of a magazine and pretending not to know what I was doing. Gibby had seemed happily troubled by the final product and told me we were making great progress.

But throughout the walk, Noel remained quiet, and strangely distant and unappreciative of my Gibby jokes. I assumed this was Helen's doing. When we went to sign in, Ms. Sjursen looked at me and shook her finger.

"Noel, dear, you haven't signed in properly."

"What?" I said. "Are you talking to me?"

"Your name's Noel, isn't it?" she chastised.

"No," I said, shaking my head. "No it isn't. She's Noel."

Ms. Sjursen raised a hand to her mouth. For a moment she was confused, but then her confusion bled into irritation, and she snapped at Noel. "Well, then you have made a mark outside of the box, and you know how I feel about marks outside of boxes."

I stood there a moment, watching Noel appease Ms. Sjursen, and I realized this wasn't the first time she'd mistaken us.

"Noel," I said as we walked back to the dorms. "There's something kind of weird I need to talk to you about."

"Yeah?"

"Yeah. A while back someone left a package with Ms. Sjursen. She gave it to me, but now I'm wondering if maybe she meant to give it to you."

Noel stopped in her tracks and stared at me. "What was in the package?"

"This weird box. It was a puzzle box."

Noel laughed her same easy laughter, but just for a second, I thought she'd gone too pale.

"A puzzle box? I don't even know what that is. I'm sure it was for you. Ms. Sjursen's batty, but she's right about people a good sixty-five percent of the time."

She started walking off to her dorm.

"Wait, don't you want to see it?" I called after her.

Turning and smiling, she shook her head. "Like I said, I don't even know what a puzzle box is. I'm sure it was meant for you. I'll see you at dinner, okay?"

But I didn't see Noel at dinner. I ate alone; I had lasagna and garlic bread, but it was hard to find my appetite. I needed to talk to Sophie. I wanted to tell her what I'd overheard Helen saying to Noel about me and Asta. I had no idea what to make of any of it, but I was pretty sure Sophie would have some solid theories. I was just leaving the dining hall and walking across to her dorm when she caught my arm.

"We need to talk," she said, a hint of anger in her voice.

"Yeah?" I disengaged my arm from hers. "What's up?"

"Come with me," she said, and spinning on her heel, she marched up the stairwell toward her room. Inside, she waited for me with arms crossed, glaring. I took a seat on her bed and she closed the door behind me.

"Cally." She shook her head. "Cally, how could you? I know you're going through some terrible stuff, but that doesn't excuse you. How could you stab me in the back like this?"

"What's going on? I have no clue what you're talking about."

"What do you think I'm talking about? Were you ever going to tell me? I had to hear it from Jack?"

I searched my mind. "This is about Jack?"

"Of course it's about Jack. It's always about Jack."

The way Sophie stared at me made my muscles tense up. I looked at her, and I knew I had done something wrong, something irrevocable, but I had no idea what it was.

"I'm sorry. I know you're mad, but seriously, I don't understand why."

"You don't understand why? Oh, well, I'm just so sorry, poor little Cally is bewildered. How adorable. Well, screw you."

"What did I do?"

"I had to hear it from Jack? I had to hear from Jack that you guys have been seeing each other—that you slept together? I have to deal with Jack coming to me, crying to me about it? What the hell, Cally, how could you do this to me?"

"I'm sorry," I said, trying desperately to find some kind of footing, some road map to tell me what to do, how to salvage things. "I know I should have told you, but we had to keep it secret. Jack wanted to. If it had been up to me, I'd have told you."

"It's not about that," she said, her eyes wide with pain. "It's not about telling me."

"Then what's it about?"

"It's about doing it, Cally. You weren't supposed to do it. You should have known."

"What? Why?"

"Why do you fucking think? Isn't it obvious? Isn't it painfully obvious to everyone in the entire fucking school that I'm in love with him?"

I stared at her, my energy slowly draining away. I should have known. On some level I should have known. The way she and Jack were together wasn't normal. There was more to their friendship than I'd been willing to admit. And all along I'd felt like an intruder. I'd felt like an intruder because I was one.

"Sophie, I'm sorry. I didn't realize. You said he wasn't your boyfriend that first day."

"Well, you should have known. You should have known."

I sat there, cold and numbness spreading across my brow. I couldn't lose Sophie. I'd be lost without her. I'd never had a friend like her before, and now I'd destroyed it.

"Please, Sophie. I'm sorry. Please don't make a big deal out of this."

"It *is* a big deal."

"It doesn't have to be."

"It does. Do you know how long I've waited around for my chance? Do you know how long he's been seeing Courtney? And I've waited the whole time, dying inside whenever he'd talk about her, and then you come along and slip right in there. Whoop, she's out, Cally's in, just like that. It's not fucking fair."

"Okay, but . . . wait. Courtney? Who's Courtney?"

Sophie leaned against the door, a smile playing on her lips, her eyes moist with the tears she refused to unleash.

"Oh, you didn't know about her?"

"Sophie, who's Courtney?"

"She's Jack's girlfriend. His real girlfriend—since the beginning of sophomore year."

"Courtney?" My mind searched all the possibilities. There was a freshman named Courtney Vance, but that didn't make sense. "Who's Courtney?" And then I suddenly understood. "Ms. Harlow?" I gasped, knowing I was right.

She smiled, and she looked beautiful standing there, exacting her revenge.

"Gross," I breathed, but even as I said it, I knew it wasn't exactly gross. More like weird and sad, and as I thought about it, I found myself growing increasingly jealous. Ms. Harlow was like twenty, fresh out of Harvard, pretty as could be, and lonely. Jack truly had been living the dream. "But . . . but he was like fifteen."

"Sixteen when it started."

Suddenly I felt sick. My head was pounding. I was angry at Sophie, angry at Jack, angry at stupid Ms. Harlow and her movie-star ringlets. As far as I was concerned, they could all piss off. I stormed out of the room and slammed Sophie's door behind me. I headed out into the early evening, down and through the bank of mailboxes.

I passed a sophomore girl, one I'd never cared for, and just then, she let out a crazy scream when she peered into one of the boxes. It was like a call to prayer, and people started popping up here and there, filtering.

"Oh my God," the girl wailed, unbridled joy infusing her tremulous alto. "Tanner didn't even get into Berkeley."

"The UC's are here!" someone else screamed, and then everything went insane. Seniors pushed each other aside, diving for their mailboxes, pulling out envelopes big and small, and depending on the envelopes' sizes, they issued little cries of despair or relief. And around them, like predators, circled juniors, sophomores, even freshmen who were delighting in the news of rejections and shouting it out for each other to hear. Brody clutched a rejection letter from Yale. He stood staring at it as if his will alone could change its contents while two freshman girls who had previously worshiped him snickered and

267

turned away in disgust. This was what Helen had been talking about. College acceptance week was a bloodbath. I had to get out of there. I practically ran back to my room.

I was so upset that I almost screamed when I ran into Helen in the dorm bathroom.

"Christ, you scared the crap out of me," she said, holding a hand to her chest.

We stared at each other, silent, and she cocked her head to one side.

"Are you okay?"

"Yeah. Sort of. The scene at the mailboxes was terrible."

"Oh," she sighed. "Are rejections here?"

"Yeah. It's ridiculous. You'd think people would let them have some privacy."

But Helen just stared at me. "Why?"

"I don't know. It's just so, I don't know, mean."

"I'm gonna go check it out," she said. "I was heading up to the rec for Sno Balls anyway. Do you want anything? My treat."

"Yeah, I guess. Um, ramen," I said, and headed back to my room.

During study hours I found myself completely unable to concentrate. I couldn't stop seething. Ms. Harlow? Jack had been seeing Ms. Harlow all this time. Ms. Harlow, all perfect with her peasant shirts and her belly ring. And then there was Sophie, who'd known all along. Sophie, my closest friend, who was no longer my friend at all because I was not a psychic mind reader.

By eight-fifteen I couldn't take it anymore. It was like

something inside me was burning. I had to get outside. I had to move around. I closed my book and headed out the glass door.

And then I did something I hadn't anticipated. I walked over to Freddy's room and bought one of her lollipops off her. She didn't know what to make of me, but she was happy to oblige. Then I went over the side of the hill and I sat by myself, looking into the night sky, quietly licking my lollipop. I sat there until in-dorm time, and while I did, I told myself I was okay. I told myself that everything was going to be all right. I told myself all the things I couldn't wait for someone else to tell me.

When the bell rang, I stowed the lollipop in my pocket and headed back to my room. Luckily, Helen was in the bathroom when I got back, so there was no witness as I fumbled on my pajamas. When I was dressed, I climbed under my covers and turned out my light. I was asleep before Helen got back from the bathroom.

The next morning my mouth felt like it had been packed full of cotton, and my head and body felt heavy and strange from excessive sleep. I headed up to the dining hall early, hungry as hell, but feeling uncharacteristically happy. Alex was leaving just as I entered. He smiled at me.

"You're up early."

I looked at my watch. "Kind of."

"Well, you're up early for you."

"I'll give you that," I said, laughing.

"Whoa, look who's in a good mood."

My brain deliciously foggy, I just kept smiling, delighting in tiny details, like the way the early-morning sun was lighting up the tips of the grass blades.

"Yeah."

"Hey," he said, looking a little too much like a peacock. "I got into Yale."

"Oh, hey, congratulations. Are you going to go?" I asked, my mind falling back to Brody clutching his letter.

"Yeah." He smiled. "My brother's going to be a junior there next year. We're going to tear it up."

He'd never told me he had a brother. Or maybe I'd just never listened. I didn't want to risk seeming like a total dick, so I just nodded and smiled some more.

"So, prom," he said.

"Huh?"

"Prom's in three weeks."

"There's a prom?"

He laughed, an edge to his voice. "Of course there is. God, you are always so checked out about stuff like that. It's like you're not even a real girl. Whatever. Anyway, I figured we're going together, but I thought I'd remind you. I know you're not good at the romantic stuff."

"Oh," I said, nodding too much, still smiling. "Do I need, like, a dress or something?"

"Yeah, Wood. People typically wear dresses. I mean, the girls."

"I don't think I have anything."

"Borrow something. It looks to me like everyone just passes

their dresses around year to year. I'm sure someone will lend you something."

I nodded again, not giving a shit, and prayed—literally prayed to God—that there would be Froot Loops in the dining hall.

CHAPTER NINETEEN

IT WAS RAINING THE NEXT night when just after study hours, I got a call from Danny. I cried when he told me he was back home. He sounded good, if characteristically taciturn, and promised me he'd try to stay out of trouble. I was possibly too vociferous when I told him I loved him, but he seemed happy about it. When he asked how I was doing, I couldn't think of anything to say. I didn't want him to worry about me, so I told him about Freddy and her lollipops, and he thought that was funny.

I hung up the receiver and walked back to my room, unable to keep from smiling. When I walked in, I found Pigeon going through my clothes while Helen reclined on her bed.

"Pigeon's raiding your closet," Helen said. "I couldn't stop her."

"I want to trade dresses for prom. You're small like me and

you have a black one that I like. I want to see what else you have. You can borrow mine too."

I was appalled and started moving to stop her, but Helen put a hand on my arm.

"She has a vintage Givenchy in her closet," she said, winking. "Don't look a gift horse in the mouth."

What's a Givenchy? I started to say, but just then there was a knock on the glass door and Alex ducked inside. He was beaming.

"They released Reilly," he said, wiping stray droplets of rain from his smiling face. "Someone came forward with an alibi."

"What?" Helen gasped.

"Whoa, whoa, whoa," Pigeon cried, waving her hands in Alex's direction. "No boys allowed in here. I'm not decent."

She was swimming in the oversized red sweaterdress I'd taken from Kim's closet. I was pretty sure it was from 1982.

"Oh my God. What the hell am I wearing, Cally? Did you actually buy this?" She winced at herself in the mirror.

"That's great," I said to Alex. "Is he here? Have you been to see him?"

"Not yet. I was thinking you might want to come with me."

"Yeah," I said. "Yeah, sure." Reilly wasn't my favorite person, but I was happy for Alex, and happy an innocent man wasn't going to go to jail.

Pigeon was on her knees, rummaging through the clothes at the back of my closet. A moment later, she emerged with my army jacket.

"Ooh, can I borrow this too?"

"Sure," I said. I was just starting to walk out with Alex when Pigeon let out a shriek.

"Oh my God, you guys!" Her eyes were wide. She held something in her hand. "No physical intimacy. It's a school rule." And then she let out a peal of earsplitting laughter.

And that was when I realized she was holding an open condom wrapper. It was one of those moments when time stopped and you knew nothing would ever be the same again. I couldn't believe what was happening, and that it was my own fault. I'd been so confused that day with Jack. My mind had been far away from my body. I'd shoved the wrapper into my pocket, intending to dispose of it, only apparently I never had.

The room was silent. Alex stared at the wrapper, anger burning in his eyes. Helen looked at her feet, but Pigeon just stood there like a child trying to understand a grown-up joke.

"Why are you being so weird? Everyone knows you guys do it. I mean, come on." She laughed.

I stared at Alex, and he stared straight ahead.

"Alex," I said, reaching for him, but he pulled away.

Slowly he turned to face me, rage simmering in his eyes. "Give me one reason why I shouldn't break up with you."

"I don't know," I said, panicked. "Because you did the same thing to me?"

He shook his head. "This is different. We didn't even sleep together."

Without making a sound, Helen slipped out of the room, and Alex and I were left staring at Pigeon.

"Oh, wow. Oh my God," she said at last. "I'm gonna . . . I'm gonna go." But just as soon as she'd left, she darted back in again. "Is it still okay to borrow the jacket?"

Incredulous, I nodded, and she bounced back out the door.

"Alex," I pleaded.

"It's Jack, isn't it?" he said, looking at the bed, at the closet, anywhere but at me. "No, I don't want to know. I don't even care. It's not worth caring about."

"I'm sorry."

"You messed up, Cally. You really messed up."

"I know. I don't know what to say."

"There's nothing to say," he said. "We're finished." He started to leave, then stopped himself. He looked me directly in the eye for the first time. "It was Helen," he said. "The person I hooked up with, it was Helen."

"No," I said, trying to laugh, trying to make it be a joke. "It was someone from home."

"No it wasn't. It was right before break, and it was Helen. I just thought you should know the kinds of friends you think you have."

Then he was gone. Stunned, I sat on the edge of my bed. I felt like my whole life had just exploded in my face. How could Helen do something like that to me, and how had things gotten so out of control with Alex? How had it come to this? I tried to remember that day at the pond, him gentle and kind, me shy and infatuated. What had happened to those people? Where had they gone? Somehow, despite all the time Alex and I'd spent together, we'd never managed to find them again.

I climbed into bed, turned out the lights, and pulled the

covers over my head. When Helen came back, I pretended to be asleep. She knew that I knew. Otherwise she would have woken me up to find out what had gone down with Alex. She changed quickly and got into bed, pretending to be asleep as well. I lay there for hours, listening to the darkness, dreading the morning.

CHAPTER TWENTY

THE ROOM WAS QUIET AND empty when I awoke, the sunlight filtering through our dusty beige curtains, infusing the room with a velour kind of white. I made my bed only to sit back down on top of the comforter. I had just tucked a pillow behind my back and leaned up against the wall when Helen slipped in, emerging from behind the curtain in a lovely yellow chiffon dress, her hair in a neat bun and, unless I was mistaken, tiny diamond teardrops in her ears. Behind her the day swept into the room, all beautiful and blue.

"Hey there, *Never Mind the Bollocks,* why aren't you dressed? We're supposed to be ready in ten minutes. God, what are we going to do with that hair?"

Pain tore across my chest. I stared at her, my eyes filled with tears, but she turned away, pretending not to see. I wanted to hide. I tried to put on a fake smile, but my voice was flat. There was nothing I could do about it.

"What are you talking about?" I asked.

She rolled her eyes and thrust her jaw out for effect. "Your head is always in the clouds, I swear. Brunch, remember? Pigeon's mom's in town. We're having brunch at the Coeur de Lyon."

She placed a hand on her hip, and I noticed she was shaking, tiny little tremors sweeping through her suntanned shoulders.

I had a vague recollection of something involving Pigeon's mother and food, but it had been so long before that I couldn't quite get my head around what that meant for me.

"Yeah, I kind of remember. We're going to brunch?" I stared at her, searching for any sign of acknowledgement.

"She's been planning this for months," she said, turning from me, pretending to rifle through her desk for something. "She's here from Spain and she's taking us to brunch at her hotel. It's pretty much the only decent restaurant between here and San Francisco. Don't tell me you haven't got anything to wear."

I closed my eyes, trying to process the information, trying to remember if I had anything to wear. I certainly didn't have anything approaching what Helen was wearing.

"How fancy is this place?" I said, clearing my throat, trying to get myself together.

"Really fancy. Wear your black cocktail dress."

"It's dirty. I wore it to formal dinner." I shook my head, staring at her.

"Yeah, like three weeks ago." She laughed, still averting her eyes.

Helen rifled through my closet, wincing and holding articles of clothing at a distance. She found the black dress and laid it out on the bed, trying to dust and pat it into shape.

"God, Wood, is this avocado?"

"I know. I need to get it dry-cleaned or something," I said, unable to keep the wonder from my voice.

How could she act like this? Like everything was completely normal. She had to know that I knew. But she didn't say a word about it. Instead she held her arms akimbo and shook her head from side to side, slipping more comfortably into her disappointed-older-sister role, then turned to her own wardrobe.

"There's got to be something in here that will fit you," she sighed, and emerged with a dress. She held it out to me, and for a second I considered not taking it, not going at all, but I didn't want to be rude to Pigeon's mom. I took the dress and tried it on in silence.

It was a powder-blue A-line strewn with white polka dots, and to say it didn't suit me would be a vast understatement. Helen had this habit of purchasing hideous clothes that only she could look great in. It was way too long, and bulky in unexpected places. The tag read *Dior*. When she'd finished with me, Helen stood back and appraised her creation, pleased with her paper doll. I refused to smile at her, and she avoided eye contact.

When we met the other girls on the lawn at the top of the school, none of them acknowledged me. Standing there with them, I felt strangely ashamed of myself, cast out, even. They all looked ideal, of course, Pigeon especially, in a white strapless eyelet dress that emphasized the bronze sheen of her skin and hinted at her minuscule waist. I'd never seen her so happy before. She was so excited to see her mother that all the annoying had been siphoned off and drained away for the day. Still, there was a definite chill to the air. Why were they all giving me the silent treatment?

"What's going on?" I asked, and Noel looked away.

"Cally," Helen snorted, embarrassed by me.

"What?" I said. "Did I do something to you guys?"

Freddy raised her eyebrows, patrician nastiness settling onto her like a little lace shawl.

"We just think what you did to Alex was really uncool," she said as if coolness were one of the lesser-known beatitudes.

"What?" I laughed. "Why does that have anything to do with you guys?"

"It just does, okay?" Freddy said. "There are lines you don't cross. There are things you simply don't do. Let's just leave it at that."

"Wait a minute," I said. "Since when am I Hester Prynne here? So I've been having some boy trouble lately. So I kind of messed up, and I'm sorry, but I'm sorry to Alex, not to you guys. It's not like I pledged to uphold some ridiculous idea of decorum when we became friends."

"I wouldn't call us friends exactly," Freddy said.

"What? What about you, Freddy?"

"What about me?"

"You've been sneaking around with Cara Svitt's boyfriend for months. That's okay?"

"That's really different," she said, completely convinced of her own moral authority.

"How is that different?"

"It just is," Pigeon said, nodding sadly.

"Seriously, Cally," Helen said. "What you did to Alex was really lame, and I think we're all just feeling a little uncertain about our friendship right now. But let's not mess up Pigeon's lunch. Let's not make this all about you, okay?"

"And you," I said, turning on her. "You hooked up with Alex."

She stared at me, not admitting a thing.

"He told me," I said.

A car was heading up the hill. Pigeon's mom would be there soon, and I felt like screaming.

"You're not going to admit it?" I asked. I looked to Noel, who'd been silently staring at her feet the whole time. She wrapped her arms across her chest and looked like she might cry.

"Admit what?" Helen asked, smiling at me.

"I can't believe you. He told me. I thought you were my friend."

Just as the limousine pulled up in front of us, Helen sighed, put her hands on her hips, and looked at me with meretricious pity. "Oh, Cally, you know, I am so tired of living with you."

That was it for me. The four of them and their fancy brunch could fuck off. I headed up to lunch, practically storming into the dining hall. I grabbed two slices of white bread, slapped some bologna inside, and headed out to the porch balcony.

I sat alone out there, unable to eat, burning with anger. Why did it have to be like this? Was there something wrong with me? It couldn't just be that every single person in my life was an asshole. I had to bear some responsibility. I must be doing something wrong. I couldn't believe that I was simply unlucky. I gave in to the sadness swelling within me, bursting in my chest, and the tears began to flow. Soon my body was crumpling into sobs, finally defeated by grief.

I pulled myself to sit upright and wiped my eyes. The afternoon sky was growing dark, flushed with an odd mixture of dark clouds and bursts of bright white sunlight. A wind picked up, and I wrapped my arms around my knees to protect against the chill. And then I heard it. At first I thought it was the wind thrashing leaves against the roof above me, but then the noise revealed itself to be the beating of great wings, and as if from the heavens a giant creature descended and circled out above the side of the hill, gliding, and then with a final beat of its wings, it came to perch before me on the railing of the balcony. For a moment I took it to be an angel, something not of this world, but then I perceived its remarkable white neck, a wonderfully serpentine thing that glided up to a set of obsidian eyes and a dagger of a beak. A heron. I'd seen one once, a long time before, when my father had taken us to a pond near his childhood home. That one had been larger, with cool gray feathers and a black-streaked head. A great blue heron, he'd called it. The bird before me was less blue, and a touch smaller, but it would do.

"Hi," I whispered without really meaning to.

It stared at me, and as the clouds shifted, shafts of sunlight illuminated the gray-blue of the creature's downy wings. The bird held my eyes, and for a moment I almost felt it was communicating with me. A calming liquid warmth rushed through me, and I was overcome with the desire to keep the bird with me forever, to take it back to my room, to make it be my friend. And then a noise from below, a girl laughing, and the bird reacted, an undulating feathery spasm spreading through the torso and out into its wings. The heron turned, pushed forth, lifting off with one great beat of its wings, and glided down into the ravine and out of sight.

I sat there for a moment, stunned, unsure of what had just passed. Maybe other people had moments like this all the time, but I didn't, and I couldn't help thinking it was some kind of message, the universe trying to help me out when I was too paralyzed to do it myself.

Sometimes something or someone comes into your life, and it's like their presence shocks you out of a bad dream. You hadn't been looking for them—you hadn't even known something was missing—but once they were there, you wondered how you ever could have gotten by without them. I didn't make friends easily, not close ones, not ones to whom I revealed my heart without fear of criticism. There was just Sophie, but somehow I'd ruined it. Maybe, though, it didn't have to be ruined for good. Maybe there was some way to fix it. It was worth trying. I cleared my eyes and pulled myself up. I headed over to her room.

"Come in," she called when I knocked on her door. She was sitting on the floor, leafing through her vinyl collection.

"Hey," I said.

"Hey," she said, avoiding my eyes. She chose Etta James, pulled it from its sleeve, and set it on the turntable.

Slowly Etta swept into the room, thickening the air, opening the channels for peace.

"I want to say I'm sorry. This is going to sound weird, but your friendship means the world to me, and I don't want to lose it. I don't want to lose you," I said.

She looked up at me, her forehead creased with emotion. "I don't know that I want to have this talk."

"Please just hear me out. I am so sorry about what I did. I am sick with regret about it. I'm sorry about not telling you. I'm sorry about doing it, but most of all, I'm sorry about not knowing. A better friend would have known."

She shrugged and wiped her eyes. "I don't know. Maybe I was being melodramatic."

"No," I said. "That first day, I could see what was between you guys. I saw the way you looked at each other. It was the first thing I noticed about you, but I chose to ignore it, because I liked him too, but I shouldn't have ignored it. And I promise you, whatever we were doing, it's over now. I swear."

She shook her head. "No, maybe I was being kind of crazy. That's asking too much of a friend."

"Maybe it isn't," I said. "Can we start over?"

"I would love that," she said, standing to hug me. "I know

it hasn't been that long, but I've really missed you. There have been so many times when I wanted to tell you something, but you weren't there to tell."

"I know," I said, wiping my eye. "Me too."

"Oh my God," she said, her eyes suddenly wide. "Did you hear about Reilly?"

"Yeah. I heard he has an alibi."

"Okay, but did you hear who the alibi was?" She waited for me to shake my head. "Mrs. Harrison."

"No way."

"Yeah. Pretty awkward, right?" Sophie winced and smiled at the same time.

"Mrs. Harrison and Reilly? But I like her. She calls me sugar."

"Everyone likes Mrs. Harrison. Apparently Mr. Reilly does too."

I started to laugh, but just then there was a knock at the door, and Cara Svitt started talking to Sophie about prom decorations. Sophie gave me an apologetic cringe.

I got up to go. "Let's hang out later, though, okay?"

"I'd love that," Sophie said, smiling at me as I left.

Though I was relieved to have resolved things with Sophie, my thoughts fell to the other girls, and anger started to well up inside me as I walked down the Prexy steps. How hypocritical of them to turn on me like that when Freddy and Helen had done basically the same thing. And I didn't see anyone shunning Tanner for what he was doing to Cara or, for that matter, Alex for cheating on me. But a girl making the same mistakes as boys was apparently more than people could handle, and lessons had to be taught. When I started down the path to my dorm, I waved to a couple of sophomore girls I knew through Carlos. They ignored my greeting, putting their heads together and whispering without taking their eyes off me. Wow. So that was how things were going to be. Apparently the news of my wantonness had spread far and wide. I ducked my head and hurried to my room, fighting back the tears.

I didn't breathe easily until I'd closed the door behind me. I changed my clothes and tossed Helen's dress in the general direction of her closet. I had to get out of this place. There was no way I could live with Helen anymore. Blood beat inside my head with metronomic certainty.

Getting on my knees, I opened my bottom drawer, shoving aside Iris's crumpled papers. My hand lingered on the puzzle box. I took it out and, setting it in front of me, tried to stare it down. I knew there had to be something more to it, and I had an idea it had something to do with the logo—those two circles separated by a *T,* but I didn't know what it could mean. The letters certainly didn't signify anything. I'd tried to make some sense of them and had come up with nothing.

"Oh, fuck it," I said, sick of waiting around for something that would never happen. I flung open Helen's closet and reached inside for her tool kit. I extracted her hammer and returned to the box.

"Sorry," I said. "It's nothing personal." And then I slammed the head of the hammer full force into the back of the box, cracking it down the middle, the resulting trauma causing a cascade effect of screeching wood and a single pop as one of the circles on the bottom of the box popped out. I picked up the box and examined the circles, finally seeing them for what they were: two tiny grooved dials.

I dug my fingers in and turned them, thinking if I could move them to the right position, something might happen. And then I saw it: the letters hadn't seemed to signify anything because they weren't Roman letters. They were ancient Greek. And suddenly I knew what to do.

"Oh my God," I gasped, my fingers shaking. I turned each dial clockwise one half turn, until the letters spelled a word: *ΟΥΤΙΣ. Nobody.* Ms. Harlow's favorite word had certainly made an impression on Iris. *Nice, Iris. Very nihilistic.* I shifted the second dial until it was perfectly in place and then something clicked. A lever gave way, and a tiny compartment sprang from the side of the box. Inside was a tiny slip of paper and on it was written:

Fagles, IV, 304–308

I looked again at the top of the puzzle box. The Fagles translation of *The Odyssey*, book four, lines 304 to 308. I pulled Helen's copy down and turned to the passage.

> *What a piece of work the hero dared and carried off*
> *in the wooden horse where all our best encamped,*
> *our champions armed with bloody death for Troy . . .*
> *when along you came, Helen—roused, no doubt,*
> *by a dark power bent on giving Troy some glory*

The Trojan horse. How fitting. *Nice work all around, Iris.* Pulling out my notebook, I set about deciphering the text. It was going to take me a while, but I finally had the key. I felt suddenly giddy, knowing that the answer was at my fingertips. Now all I needed to do was plug in the letters and I'd have the last piece to the puzzle.

My pen flew across the page as I worked, the message slowly revealing its secrets. When I had finished, my head starting to pound, I read the deciphered note in its entirety.

RICHARD,AFITTINGMETHODOFCO
MMUNICATION?NOWIAMTHETRO
JANHORSEINVADINGYOURCITY.LE
AVEMAGDAORIWILLBURNYOURCIT
YTOTHEGROUND.YOURSALWAYSA
NDFOREVER,IRIS.

Richard? Magda? Iris had been having a secret affair with Helen's dad? I sighed and leaned back against the base of my bed. I was disgusted, but if I'd learned anything lately, it was that you never knew what people were capable of. So this was what Iris had been doing at the Slaters' lake house the past spring. She must have been out there seeing Richard when Chelsea thought she was visiting Helen. The scenario I'd created with Reilly and Iris could also apply to Iris and Richard Slater. Had he broken it off with her and then started messing around with someone else? Chelsea, maybe? Had she threatened him with blackmail and he'd killed her?

I sat there, trying to get my mind around it. I was sick with the possibility, but I didn't have much time to think about it, because I saw Helen descending the lawn, Noel a few paces behind her. Quickly, I shoved the deciphered note under my pillow, but not before it registered in Helen's eyes. She flung open the door, her face lovely, sparkling, her starlet smile lighting up the room, and then her gaze settled on the demolished dress I'd tossed in the general direction of her closet.

"Wow," she said, raising her eyebrows. "Thanks."

"No problem," I said, staring at her.

She picked up the dress and examined it from a distance. Noel entered quietly, refusing to meet my eyes.

"Brunch was amazing." Helen laid the dress over the back of her desk chair, her eyes drifting to the box that lay in pieces on the floor.

"Ah," she said when she saw it, and then her eyes shifted to my pillow.

I slowly inched back toward the pillow, but she pushed me out of the way, and before I knew what happened, she had the note crumpled in her fist. I jumped up to face her, but she stepped back, holding the note against her chest.

"Helen!" Noel gasped. "What are you doing?"

Helen's eyes moved over the paper quickly, a slight color rising in her cheeks.

"What is that?" Noel whispered.

When she'd finished reading, Helen smoothed out the paper, folded it up, and held it between two fingers like a stylish cigarette.

I just stared at her, not knowing whether to be angry or afraid.

"You think I didn't know about this?" She laughed.

I was shocked. "You knew?"

"Of course we knew."

"Iris?" Noel gasped.

"Who else?" Helen laughed, throwing her arms into the air in a theatrical display of exasperation. "Even from beyond the grave she torments us."

"How did you know?"

"She told us. It's a lie, you know. He never touched her. She was delusional. She was crazy and obsessive."

"Helen, what are you doing?" Noel cried.

"So juvenile," she sighed, a hand on her hip. "Codes and secret liaisons. It's so, like, wannabe James Bond or something. So sad."

Noel was staring at her feet, barely breathing, it seemed, and Helen smiled at me, triumphant.

"Very romantic, don't you think? You should have seen the *Romeo and Juliet* one she made him after we read it in class. So embarrassing. My dad keeps it locked up in his desk at home. He pities her. God, she was such an idiot."

"How can you do that?"

"Do what?"

"Make fun of her like that. She's dead. Your father killed her."

"My father didn't kill her," she said, laughing.

"How do you know that?"

She stood there, smoothing her hands like a cat preening, and then replaced one on her hip and stared at me with cold precision. "Look, I know for a fact that he didn't kill her, okay?"

Suddenly I felt very cold.

"Oh my God, Helen. You didn't. You didn't . . . kill Iris, did you?"

She just smiled at me.

"No." I shook my head. "You wouldn't do something like that. Please tell me you didn't do . . . that. Please tell me, Helen."

"Let's just say I'm glad she's dead and leave it at that."

"No. You can't leave it at that. This is a life we're talking about. It wasn't yours to take."

I noticed Noel was shaking. "Oh my God," she said. "Oh my God."

A moment later Noel was gone, the curtain slapping gently against the frame as the wind picked up.

"Cally." Helen laughed. "Please don't be a total fuckwit. How could I have killed Iris? I have an alibi, remember? I was at my party all night with like thirty other people. Noel was there too. She went to bed early, remember?"

I sat down on the edge of the bed and looked to the window. Why did I feel like I was drowning?

"Noel?" I heard myself say.

Helen raised her eyebrows and tilted her head to the side like she did when she was bored. Then she smiled to herself, clearly pleased at the chance to reveal a secret.

"No. Noel wouldn't do that," I said.

Helen shrugged. "Accidents happen, Cally. I'm telling you this so you don't push things any further. I know you care about Noel too, and you'd never do anything to hurt her, so let's just drop it, shall we? Only, I do need to know one thing. Where did you get the box, Cally?"

"No, Helen," I said. "Tell me what happened that night. You said it was an accident. What kind of an accident?"

Helen sighed, feigning exhaustion. "God, all right, Cally. I'm telling you this because I know you'll make a big stink about it if I don't, but I need your word that you won't go tell anyone. This is really serious."

She raised her eyebrows at me, and I nodded.

"Okay," she said. "Here's the deal. Iris was psychotic. She was obsessed with our dad. She even pulled some strings to make sure we were roommates, because she thought it would put her one step closer to him. By October I kind of thought she was over it, and then the day of the party she told us she'd been sleeping with him, and that they were in love, but that they broke up last spring because of my mother. It was obviously a lie," she said, shifting her eyes to the side. "But she made a big deal about how we needed to talk to her about it or she was going to tell everybody. She wanted us to invite her to our place for fall break so she could try to win him back. Can you believe it, the audacity? She kept calling us, wanting to come to the party so we could discuss. Obviously she couldn't come to our house. What was she thinking? And I couldn't leave the party and go deal with her, so I sent Noel. She pretended to feel sick and go to bed early, but really she went back to deal with Iris."

"And Noel took her up to the cave?"

"No," she smirked. "That was Iris's idea. She was like that.

Cally, you didn't know her, but the girl was a serious nutcase. She took Noel up to the cave and gave her mushrooms. She was trying to bond with her, to get Noel on her side."

"And Noel ate them?"

"Noel will take whatever someone gives her. I don't think you realize how malleable my sister is. She just goes along with whatever anyone tells her. Fortunately, that person is usually me. In this case, though, she wasn't so lucky."

"So they just went up to the cave in the dark and took mushrooms the night before the math competition? What the hell?"

"My sentiments, though to be honest, I doubt Iris gave a flying leap about that math competition. She gave up caring about school a long time ago. So they go up to the cave, chill out, Iris draws her crazy dragon, and Noel does God knows what, and then at some point Iris gets really weird and delusional. She tells Noel that she wants her on her side. She wants Noel to get our dad to divorce our mom. Can you imagine? What a pathetic psycho. She showed Noel that stupid box she'd made him like she was that woman from *Fatal Attraction*—like the box was proof that it was true. Noel tried to take it from her, and Iris, like, attacked. Noel had to push her off. That's when it happened. Iris fell back and hit her head on a rock. And Noel booked it out of there. Obviously, she had no idea that Iris could die. She was alive when she left. Her head was bleeding, but she was fine. She ignored Noel and went back to her drawing. Honestly, we thought she ran away after that. We had no idea she was dead. We really didn't until . . . well, until we all found her that day. God, I felt like such an idiot taking us to that cave. I had no idea that was where they'd been, and obviously I didn't know she was dead. But that box, it was in the cave when Noel left."

"Wait," I said, something sinking in. "Iris didn't die of a head wound."

"Not at the time, but it can happen slowly over the course of a few hours. We didn't know."

"No, Helen. You're not listening to me. Noel didn't kill Iris, because Iris didn't die of a head wound. Iris was strangled."

"What?" Helen's face lit up, luminous with relief. "Are you sure? How do you know that?"

"Just trust me. I'm sure."

She put her hand on her hip, her joy quickly turning to calculation. "So sometime after Noel left the cave, Iris was strangled? How is that possible?"

"I think someone was following them that night. He waited outside the cave, and when Noel left, he saw his chance to be alone with Iris. He went inside. They argued, things got out of hand, and he strangled her. Then he took the puzzle box."

"Who?" Helen asked, her eyes wide. "Who did that?"

"I don't know," I said, my mind moving quickly, dancing over pieces of information, trying to put it all together.

"Okay," she said, her eyes moving over me. "Here's what I want to know. Why the hell are you involved in any of this? What gives, Wood?"

And that was when it all snapped together.

"Oh God," I gasped.

"What?"

"Oh my God," I said, starting to pace. "The box was never meant for me. It was meant for Noel. I had an idea it might have been. I even asked her about it, but I couldn't see why someone would have left it for her."

"What are you talking about? How did you get it?"

"Someone left it for me to pick up at sports sign-in, only it wasn't for me. Ms. Sjursen said there was a Post-it note with my name on it, but she couldn't find it, and it was never my name. It was Noel's."

Helen cocked her head to the side. "Okay, but why?"

"I don't know," I said. "We need to back up a bit. We need to consider this from the killer's point of view. What if the box doesn't mean anything to the killer? What if the box was just the link between Noel and Iris? What if the killer knows that Noel injured Iris? What if the killer's trying to lay the blame for the murder on Noel?"

"But Noel would know she didn't kill Iris once she found out Iris was strangled."

"It might not matter. If the police find out that Noel and Iris fought up in that cave, high on drugs, on the night of Iris's death, it's not going to look good for Noel."

"So where does the puzzle box come in?"

"I think it was something to freak Noel out and get her to go to the police. It came with a note that said *there is only one way out.* For months I've been trying to solve the puzzle box and see what was inside it, but that was never the point. The box itself was the point, the very existence of it. Sending it to Noel with that note was like saying, 'I know what you did up in that cave, and you're going to pay if you don't confess.' I think

295

the killer was trying to manipulate her into confessing and taking the blame."

"Okay," she said, biting down on her lip. "But how could the killer know for sure that Noel thinks she killed Iris? I mean, it's not like she's advertising it."

"I don't know," I said, pressing my fingers against my temples. "Noel didn't tell anyone else about what happened that night, did she?"

Helen frowned.

"Oh God," I said, my heart sinking. "She did, didn't she?"

She closed her eyes. "She told Asta."

"When did she tell her?"

"Right after we found Iris in the woods."

"Jesus," I said, shaking my head, thinking back to that night at the lake house. "That's Noel's secret? That's the secret she told Asta? And Asta didn't go to the police?"

Slowly Helen sank down to sit on her bed. She looked at me with dark and serious eyes. "No. She didn't."

I massaged my temples, as if it would help me extract whatever was percolating there. "Has Noel talked to you at all about going to the police?"

Helen sighed. "No. She'd never confess. She knows it would destroy our father," she said, and she looked down at her feet, her cheeks flushed with shame.

"Okay," I said, trying to keep hold of the thread. "So she wouldn't confess, but the killer couldn't know that. Unless . . ."

"What?"

"Well, the note didn't suggest that she confess. It said *there is only one way out*. Confession isn't exactly a way out, is it? It's a way to land in jail. What if that's not what the killer wanted at all? What if *one way out* means suicide? Helen," I said, barely able to speak the words I needed to say. "What if the killer knows that Noel thinks she killed Iris because Noel told her that she did?"

"What do you mean?"

"Noel told Asta."

"Asta?" Helen laughed. "No."

"Think about it, we know that Noel told Asta that she killed Iris. And we also know that she can exert an amazing amount of influence over Noel. And there's something else. A while ago I had this really weird conversation with Asta about death and fruit flies, and I was totally creeped out by it. It was like she was having two different conversations, and I'm now thinking that maybe she actually was. I think she may have been using the opportunity to goad Noel, to kind of torment her without seeming to by getting me to say certain key things."

Her eyes moved slowly around the room, her mouth opening and closing, as if she was searching for the words to say what she meant. "But that would have to mean that Asta killed Iris. I mean, think about what you're saying."

"I know. I don't want to think that Asta could ever do a thing like that, but we need to consider everything. I think Iris had found out something about her killer and was planning on blackmailing them. Asta could have been the person she was going to blackmail. And there's no way Asta could be sure that Iris wouldn't suddenly change her mind and go to the police, so she had to get rid of her. People will do crazy things if they think their freedom is at stake."

Helen shook her head and closed her eyes. "No, it doesn't make sense. Besides, it's too big of a coincidence that the one person Noel would confide in would just accidentally also happen to be the real murderer."

"What if it's not a coincidence, though?" I said, and for a moment the air hung stale and still between us. "When did Noel start spending time with Asta?"

"I don't know," she said, her eyes wide. "When she started working for her as her lab assistant."

"Which was when?"

"Um . . . October?"

"Which was after Iris was murdered," I said, shivering a little, suddenly cold.

"Oh my God," Helen gasped, fear in her eyes.

My voice was shaking as I continued, my theory forming as I went. "What if Asta took Noel on as her lab assistant so she could keep an eye on her, and when Noel confided in her, she saw her chance?"

Helen bit down hard on her bottom lip. "So, what then? You honestly think Asta's been trying to get Noel to kill herself so that she will be blamed for the murder?"

"I don't know. Maybe."

"But what could Asta be hiding that Iris could have found? What terrible crime could she possibly have committed?"

"I'm not sure," I said, suddenly cold to my core. "But I think I might have an idea."

My mind flitted to the image of Noel standing near the window, crying, and I wondered where she had gone. And then panic crept into my veins. "I think we need to find her," I said, pulling back the curtain, looking out onto the empty lawn. "I think we need to find Noel right away."

We stared at each other a moment, the air tense and electric.

"Yeah," Helen said, her lips white and shaking. "We have to find Noel. Split up and find her."

"Okay," I said, slightly incredulous. "Yeah."

"That Cryker guy, he's usually up in the teachers' lounge, right?"

"Yeah."

"Okay, I'm going to grab him and head over to Asta's house," she said. "You start with the dining hall. If you see Cryker first, send him to Asta's. I'll be waiting."

Helen was on her feet and moving toward the door before I had time to slip on my shoes. When I emerged into the afternoon sun, she was nowhere in sight. The day was strange. Clouds moved quickly across the sky, and the atmosphere was thick with electricity, the kind that precedes a storm. I started asking people, asking anyone I passed, but no one had seen Noel. I checked in the dining hall, in the library. Nothing.

I had to be wrong. Everything I'd said about Asta, it was all theoretical. It couldn't actually be true. There had to be a reasonable explanation for it. I was walking faster now, and then I saw Carlos sitting on a bench, reading one of the detective novels I'd lent him. He nodded when he saw me.

"What's up, Calista?"

"Have you seen Noel?" I asked, trying not to seem too frantic.

He nodded gravely. "Went past with Asta not ten minutes ago."

"Asta? Where were they going?"

"They went toward the woods. I asked if they were going on a nature walk and if I could come, but they said no. Must be a girl thing."

"Listen, Carlos," I said, grabbing his arm. "I'm going after them. Go find Cryker and Helen at Asta's house. Tell them where I've gone."

"Cally, what's going on?"

"Just hurry, okay?" I called over my shoulder, already jogging, then running toward the woods. I pushed my way through the fence, doing my best to choke back my fear. On the other side of these woods I might see something I didn't want to see. I might find something I didn't want to find.

I plunged deeper into the woods, the forest around me silent save for the feathery wavering leaves and the whispering growth of the massive trees, but there was something else there too—a feeling of darkness, of despair. Maybe Brody was right about some places just being bad. I pressed onward, the possibilities I'd considered seeming increasingly outlandish as I went.

A moment or so before I emerged into the clearing, I had a flash of darkness, of evil, but when I saw them sitting there at the edge of the pond, peaceful, just staring out at the water, I was finally able to exhale. I had been wrong, and that was okay. It was good to be wrong.

The sky was growing dark now, and the wind was picking up, playing with Asta's gossamer locks, lighting up her skull like a halo. From behind like that, they looked beautiful, as if they were having a gentle chat, student and mentor, but then I saw that Noel was shaking, her whole body trembling. My heart throbbed again as I took a step toward them, but a twig broke underfoot, and slowly Asta turned her head, her blond hair billowing around her.

"Cally, go back to school," she said. "You're not allowed to be out here. You're breaking the rules."

"Noel?" I said, my voice cracking. But she didn't move. Head down, facing the lake, she was shaking. And then I saw it, blood trickling down, pooling on her bare thigh. "Noel!" I cried, and rushed to her.

She looked up at me, her eyes sick and distant, the gray beneath them harbingers of a darkness closing in around us. Her face was blotchy and she was crying. In her hand she held a razor blade.

I grabbed it from her, shoved it into the pocket of my jeans, and grabbed her wrists. The blood was trickling from them, oozing like crimson-black buds.

"My God, what are you doing?" I looked for something, anything, to staunch the flow. Lamely, I wrapped my flannel around the torn flesh.

"Helen?" she asked, looking up at me with pupils dilated like saucers.

"No, it's Cally. What are you on? What did you take?" Beside her on the ground was a handwritten note—a suicide note. My focus turned to Asta. She stared straight ahead at the pond, her body perfectly still.

"I did it, Cally," Noel managed to say, her voice shaking. "I killed her. I killed Iris."

"You didn't. I know you didn't. And even if you had, this isn't the way, Noel."

She shut her eyes and shook her head. "It's better this way."

I was applying pressure to the wounds, but it didn't seem to be working, and as soon as I'd make headway with one wrist, the other would streak forth unexpectedly.

"Asta!" I screamed. "Do something. Will you fucking do something?"

But she didn't say a word. She just stared ahead into that still water. That was when I realized how quickly I needed to act. I leaned down to Noel, pretending to adjust my makeshift bandages. She peered up at me, the light seeming to cause her pain.

"Noel," I whispered. "I need you to trust me. I need you to run. I'm going to help you to your feet and when I say run, you run as fast as you can back to campus, and you get help."

She squinted up at me, screwed her eyes up a bit, then nodded.

"Okay," I said aloud. "Now, let's get you to your feet."

But as soon as I pulled her up, Asta stood and dusted off her skirt.

"Cally," she said. "I know what you're thinking of doing, and I want to advise you against it. We can work this out all together. You don't have to create a drama."

She moved toward me, and I could see something off in her eyes. And every instinct in my body told me to run, but instead I screamed, "Run, Noel! Now!"

As soon as Noel took off, loping like a wounded antelope, Asta sprang to terrible life—an ancient goddess, her hair twisting about her, lunging after Noel—and before I knew what I was doing, I found myself barreling into her, putting my full weight into her chest. She was screaming, trying to get Noel to stop, unwilling still to relinquish control. And my world was a mass of white hair and fury, rage and chiffon. Soon I had her on the ground, a knee to her chest. Fingers darted up, clawing my eyes, tearing at my cheek, heat and fire rising there, something wet and salty trickling down, and then I was holding her off with one arm while my other hand searched my pocket for the razor. In a moment I had it, and then she was biting my arm and I slashed at her, slicing her cheek, blood flowing. I sliced at her hand for something like good measure, and then she was weeping, crying like a child, and I held the razor flush against her throat.

And just like that everything stopped, all the frenzy, the raging, the screams. Suddenly she was perfectly still, glaring up at me with ice-blue eyes, the sockets of which were now pooling with blood from her cheek. And I stared at the tip of the blade resting flush against the pulsating beat of her carotid artery.

"Cally," she gasped. "What in the name of God are you doing?"

"I know you killed her," I said, a primal rage throbbing within me. "I know you killed Iris. Why? Why did you do it?"

"Cally," she said, her voice calm despite her labored breathing. "Cally, it's me. It's Asta. Please, think about what you're doing. You don't want to do this."

"Why did you kill her?" I yelled. "You argued that day. It wasn't the phone call that spooked her, because there was no phone call. It was you she was afraid of."

"Please, Cally, I don't know what you're talking about."

"You argued that day in the bio lab. She found something out about you, and whatever it was scared her. What was it? Tell me."

"Cally, it's me. It's Asta. Let me sit up and we'll talk about this like adults."

"I'm not a fucking adult. Tell me what it was. She confronted you about it in bio lab. Alex saw you arguing. She was going to blackmail you, wasn't she? You couldn't let her do that, and you had to get to her before she told anyone else. You had to act quickly, that same day, didn't you? You followed her up here and you killed her because no one could find out what she knew. What was it? What did she find?"

"Cally, I want you to close your eyes. I want you to breathe. Imagine air coming in at the base of your spine."

I was crying now, faltering. Maybe I was wrong. Maybe I was crazy.

"Good," she said in that smooth, calm voice, and part of me still wanted to please her, wanted to trust her. I looked at her, and seeing the fear in her eyes, I suddenly felt like a lunatic. I released my grip.

"Good," she said. "Now, I'm going to sit up. Put that silly blade away like a good girl. That's right. That's a good girl. Now let me sit up and I'll tell you everything. I'll tell you about Clare."

Her name pierced me. My breath caught, and I let go of Asta. She pulled herself up and wiped the blood from her eye with the edge of her sleeve as if she were removing a gnat from a glass of champagne. She steadied herself and stared out at the pond. I noticed I was shaking.

"Cally," she said. "I know what you're thinking, probably more than you do. I need to make you understand what happened. I'm a person, Cally, just like you, and I make mistakes. We all make mistakes."

I stared at her, my mind numb, Clare's name still pulsing inside me like the steady drip of a faucet. Asta focused her gaze on me, the emptiness in her pellucid eyes the only sign that something was wrong.

I shook my head and stared out at the lotus flowers lounging in that pond as if nothing had ever gone wrong. "Tell me what happened," I said slowly. "I know they didn't die the night of the fire—Clare and Laurel. Tell me what really happened. What happened to my sister?"

She put a hand to her mouth and closed her eyes. "I don't know for sure," she said. "I think . . . I think she drowned. They both drowned."

"They drowned? How is that possible?"

"If I could just make you understand . . . I saw what was happening, but I couldn't save them."

"I don't understand," I said. "Make me understand."

"It wasn't the night of the fire. They were already gone by then. It was the night before, and what a beautiful night it was," she said, her voice trembling. "It was filled with stars and strange winds, winds that would eventually lead to the fire," she continued. "And it was hot. None of us could sleep, it was so hot. I'd recently discovered jimsonweed, and I'd been experimenting with dosages, purely for personal use. I took quite a lot that night. And you see, it's hard to remember a lot of what happened. Around midnight we all gave up on sleeping because of the heat, and I told the girls to get their bathing suits on. We were going to the pond. They were thrilled, of course. How fun, you know." She smiled brightly, her eyes even farther away. "I was always doing things like that. I was a very fun mom. We headed out, and I was reacting strangely to the herb. I'd never taken that much of it before. And when we reached the pond, I lay down on my back and watched the stars. And you know, I spoke with a goddess that night. I did. I can't tell you which one, but she came to me and she whispered important things in my ear. Things about the world, about how it really works. Did you know that there is no such thing as a soul?" She shook her head, her brow suddenly creased with pain. "I must have dozed off. At some point I awoke, and I saw them there, bobbing in the water—that's what happens when you drown, you know. You don't flail about. You can't. Your arms become fastened to your sides. It's like the water nymphs are grasping at you, pulling you down to their depths, and there's nothing you can do to stop them. They were probably still alive at that point, but I was powerless to save them. It was as if I were watching them in a film. There was no way of breaking through the wall. At some point, things changed. I could move, I could act, but by that point, it was too late."

I stared on in horror. She clutched her wounded hand to her chest, smearing blood across the mint chiffon.

Her face crumpled. "I can't explain to you what any of this

was like for me. I pulled them from the water. I wept over them. I buried them out here and then, when it was safe, brought them inside with me. I prepared them. I honored them. You have to understand." She shook her head. "I still can't believe it. I still can't believe what happened to me, that the gods would be so cruel."

My mind spun. I knew I should leave it there, that pressing her further could have disastrous consequences, but I'd been waiting ten years for this. I had to know. "No. That's not true. At least one of them was strangled," I said. "One of them didn't drown. She was strangled."

Her eyes narrowed, and that horrible fire leapt into them again. "You don't know what it was like," she growled. "To hate your own daughter. She ruined my life. She gave me nothing in return. She was a monster, a wraith. What was I supposed to do? She was screaming in my face, saying I'd let Clare drown. What was I supposed to do? I had to stop her."

"So you strangled her."

"No," she said, shaking her head. Fighting off tears. "They both drowned. I told you. They drowned." In an instant she sprang to her feet and started walking, clenching and un-clenching her fists, rage burning in her eyes. I sprang up too and tried to assume a casually defensive position.

"Have some respect for a mother," she hissed. "You're, all of you, you're just like her—just like Iris. As if changing one grade was going to save her whole miserable existence."

My breath caught. So that was what Iris had been black-mailing her for—a grade? Iris had risked her life for something as trivial as a grade? That was possibly the most heartbreaking thing I'd ever heard. But of course, to Iris, the grade would have been more than a grade; it would have been assurance that she could stay at St. Bede's, that she could be near the man she loved.

"That's what Iris found, didn't she? That's what she was using as leverage, the bones you'd been hiding for ten years."

She nodded, her eyes somewhere very far away.

"She was supposed to be helping me organize my home office. She was supposed to stay in the office. I left her for fifteen minutes, and she went to my bedroom. She found the bones. I tried to explain to her, just like I'm trying to explain to you, but Iris . . . she didn't understand."

As I watched Asta try to hold herself together, her body clenching itself in abnormal ways, I wondered if Noel had made it back to campus. I wondered if Carlos had found Cryker. Was someone going to come save me, or was I going to have to save myself?

I needed to shift the dynamic. I needed to calm her. There was something wrong with her. She'd gone over some edge—an edge she'd been walking for some time. The Asta I'd known was gone, and it didn't look like she'd be back anytime soon. Given her fragile mental state, it was possible, if I kept my wits together, that I could manipulate the situation. It was also possible that I couldn't. But I was uniquely equipped to handle dangerous emotional oscillation. It was as if my whole dysfunctional life had simply been in preparation for this moment.

"Asta." I laughed, trying to keep my voice even and pleasant. "It's okay. I believe you. It wasn't your fault. They drowned."

She stared at me a moment, something frightened in her eyes, and then she nodded. "They did," she whispered.

"And I know you didn't kill Iris."

"I didn't?"

"No." I smiled and let out a huge sigh. "You couldn't do something like that."

"I couldn't," she said, and looked at her hands as if they weren't attached to her body.

"Of course not. Now, why don't we head back and check on Noel, okay? We'll sort it all out, okay?"

Despite her height, she looked small and weak standing there, her bloody hand clutched to her chest, her eyes disklike with fright. A wind kicked up and I thought I heard a rustling in the trees behind us, but I turned to find nothing. Dark clouds were rolling in now, and a chill bit at the back of my neck.

She reached out and gripped my hand, blood smearing hot and sticky between our palms.

"Cally," she said. "I'm so sorry."

I nodded, my gut churning.

She smiled and released my hand.

I wiped the blood on my jeans, and then I heard it again, something in the bushes. I turned to see what it was, but then something happened, something I didn't understand. I felt it slip over my head, and suddenly I couldn't breathe. I reached for my throat. There was something there. A cord. The cord that had been meant for Noel had she chosen not to comply. I lurched forward, strange sparkles before my eyes, and the next thing I knew, I was pushed down with a great deal of force, my head plunging into the water. I scrambled. I clawed. I kicked, but the world began to dissolve around me, drifting into aqueous confusion.

And then something else happened. A jolt. The cord released and I lifted my head from the water, gasping for air. It burst into my lungs, inflating them, and at first it burned, the sheer force of it. My vision was floating and filled with spots. I collapsed onto the dirt, and it was only then that I understood what was happening. Asta lay there stretched out in the sand—unconscious. Her head was opened into a crimson gash and the blood was starting to seep into the dirt. I followed a pair of Doc Martens up to Chelsea Vetiver. She was holding a large bloody rock.

"Chelsea?" I gasped.

"You okay, Inspector Wood?"

"I don't know. I think so." I looked at Asta. "Is she . . . is she dead?"

"I don't think so. I'm no doctor, but her chest's moving up and down there. What the hell is going on here, anyway?"

"Noel. We need to find Noel."

"I already found Noel. That's how I knew to come looking for you. She's messed up, though. I left her a ways back in the woods. I called 911 and then came back here looking for you. Good thing I did, too." She raised her eyebrows and took me in, then grimaced.

"You called 911?"

"Yeah," she drawled, hand on her hip. "Ten minutes ago. They should be here soon."

"How? How did you call 911?"

"With my cell."

"You have a cell phone?"

"Yeah, I do, because I'm not a fucking Luddite like the rest of you. Come on," she said, giving me a hand up. "Let's go see how Noel's doing."

I staggered a bit, and Chelsea had to hold my arm. Just before we reached the path, I turned back to look at Asta.

"You really just hit her with a rock?"

"Yeah."

"My God, Chelsea."

"You should be thanking me. I saved your life."

"Thank you. I mean, that was . . . that was ballsy."

"See?" She smiled. "I told you I'm a fucking art star."

I leaned into Chelsea, and we started onto the path. Lightning tore across the sky. A moment later, thunder replied, and the sky opened up in thick, lush drops. We stepped under the cover of the darkening woods, blanketed—protected.

CHAPTER TWENTY-ONE

THE EMTS GOT TO NOEL before we did. She looked terrible, but they told us they'd take good care of her. I felt fine, but I had to go to the hospital too, because apparently, being half strangled, half drowned was not an ideal health state. Chelsea stayed for a few hours and kept me updated until we were sure Noel was going to be okay. She also told me that Asta was downstairs in the hospital being questioned by the police while the doctors treated her wounds. I tried not to think about it.

Kim and Danny were driving down and were due to arrive sometime in the morning. They were taking me home, and I wasn't coming back. I didn't want to go back to school, even for a night, so I was pleased when the attending physician decided I should stay.

"You know," Chelsea said, handing me a cup of hot chocolate

and slumping into the chair next to my bed, "you're much more punk rock than I thought you were."

"I try," I said, blushing.

The rain beat hard against the window, and I felt warm and safe in my womblike hospital room. The lighting was soft and yellow, and I found the steady beep and constant thrum of the machines tremendously comforting. I set the hot chocolate down on my little sliding tray and leaned back, closing my eyes.

"Richard Slater was messing around with Iris," I said.

I could hear Chelsea move in her chair. She cleared her throat.

"So?"

"Look, Chelsea," I said, eyes still closed, sinking farther into my paper-encased pillow. "I don't know if you were serious or what that day at the pond, but I thought you should know. Just in case."

"God, Wood." She laughed. "You are so gullible. Even I wouldn't do something like that."

A moment later there was a noise from the hall. I recognized the sound of the approaching footsteps and sat up in bed. I found myself adjusting my hair and then felt stupid for doing so. Jack and Sophie came around the corner, clinging to each other like a long-married couple. There was something in the way they held each other that made me feel strange, though I couldn't quite place why. Their faces lit up when they saw me, and they rushed to my bed, kissing my forehead, my hand, my arm. They tousled my hair, laughing and emitting cloying platitudes about friendship and health.

"God, you guys. I'm totally fine."

"Um . . ." Chelsea sneered. "This is grossing me out and I have no fucking clue who you people are, so I'm gonna go see Noel now. I'll be back, Cally, yeah?"

I nodded, and she slunk out.

"Who was that?" Sophie asked, her eyes wide.

"That was Chelsea Vetiver. She's an art star. Thanks for coming, you guys," I said, pulling a pillow from my side and clutching it. They beamed down at me.

"So you're going to be okay?" Sophie asked, tears welling.

"God, yes," I said. "I am completely fine. I can leave tomorrow. I'm going home, actually."

"Home?" she asked. "Like, home home?"

"Yeah. I'm getting the hell out of here."

"No, don't go," Jack said, brushing the hair out of my eyes. "I want you to stay."

We stared at each other a moment, something strange and sad between us. Sophie backed away. "I'm gonna see if I can find some coffee," she said, and then left the room.

"You should stay," Jack said, taking my hand in his.

I shook my head. "I don't think I can. I don't want to stay here. I really don't."

He released my hand and wrapped his arms across his chest. "I'm sorry for acting like a jerk."

"*I'm* sorry," I said. "I acted like a jerk. My note was incredibly lame, wasn't it?"

He ran his hand over his head a few times, then gave me a confused look. "What happened between us, Cally? I don't really understand what happened."

314

I laughed. "I don't either."

"I thought we were gonna go out. I thought we might be in love or something."

I stared at him, trying to figure out why it hurt so much to look at him. If I could have loved someone, it would have been Jack Deeker, but I couldn't. Not yet. I had a lot of work to do before I could give someone the kind of love that Jack deserved.

But I would have been lying to say that my emotional disability was the only problem with us. All along, there had been something else—something else that had stood silently between us. And then the light came flooding in, and I understood.

"Jack," I said, words coming before I could expect them. "It's not me."

"What?"

"It's not me," I said, suddenly seeing clearly. "It's not me. It was never me."

"What's not you?"

"The person you're in love with—it's not me."

Images flooded my mind—Jack and Sophie entering the room, the way he held her arm, the way he looked at her each and every day no matter what mood he was in, that day in the bathroom, the way he'd freaked out at the mere thought of Sophie being with someone else. There was something there I hadn't seen because I hadn't wanted to.

He smiled. "I'm probably not mature enough to be in love with anyone."

"No." I shook my head. "You are. You definitely are. It's just not me."

"Okay, so who is it, then?" He laughed.

I motioned with my head toward the doorway.

"That Chelsea girl? Sorry, but she's terrifying."

"No." I laughed. "God, what is wrong with you? Not Chelsea."

"Then who?"

I met his gaze and tried to communicate everything I knew, everything I felt, everything I saw in his eyes. "Who do you think?"

"Sophie?" He laughed and rolled his eyes.

It hurt me to realize he'd always loved her. Maybe he loved me too—maybe that was possible—but not like he loved Sophie. She was his everything. I tried not to let him see my heart break as I stared at him, and he stared at me, watching me watch it sink in.

"No." He laughed, but he was clearly shaken. "Sophie and I aren't like that."

I nodded. "Yes you are."

He shook his head, blushing despite himself. "No. Even if I did, she would never. She doesn't think of me that way."

"Give it a try," I said, watching as something joyful and childlike spread across his face. "Trust me. I wouldn't steer you wrong. Give it a try."

"Give what a try?" Sophie asked as she entered, juggling three cups of coffee. Jack stared at her, pure wonder in his eyes. She laughed at him. "What's going on? Here, take your coffee."

He took it from her, his fingers, I noticed, lingering just a second too long on hers. He looked back at me and smiled, shaking his head, fantastically bemused.

"Give me one of those coffees," I said, choking back an acerbic combination of pain and joy.

"I don't know if you're allowed to drink coffee," Sophie said.

"Then why'd you get me one?"

"Because I'm awesome," she said, and handed it to me.

The hot bitter liquid was wonderful. I vowed to drink coffee every day for the rest of my life. They stayed a half hour or so, Sophie doing most of the talking. Jack hardly spoke; he just stared at her as if she were a fantastic creature—something no one thought existed—that he was seeing for the first time, face to face in the wild.

Cryker came by just before I drifted off to sleep.

"How you holding up?" he said, taking a seat in Chelsea's squeaky blue chair.

"Okay, I guess. Nothing's broken. I'm just a little confused."

He nodded. "I wanted to let you know she gave a full confession."

"What?" I sat up in bed. "When?"

"A couple hours ago. It's over now. I wanted to let you know."

"Really?" I said. "She confessed? So is that it?"

"There will be a trial, but this will make that go a whole lot smoother."

"Wow," I said, grasping at the bedsheets as if they could calm me. "Thank you for doing that. Thank you for getting the confession."

"Ptsh." He waved my compliment away. "It was like cracking a rotten watermelon. After the first strike, the whole thing came out soft and easy."

"So she admitted to all three murders?" I asked, my voice cracking.

He shook his head. "Not exactly. She admitted to Iris straightaway—killed her because she found out about Laurel and Clare, but with the girls, things get a little fuzzy. She admits to killing them, but her story keeps changing as to how she did it. First she says they both drowned, then she says she strangled them both. She admits her guilt, but she can't seem to settle on a story. My guess is that your sister drowned while Asta was sleeping, and then she strangled Laurel. Honestly, Cally," he said, shaking his head, "I'm not sure we're ever going to know the complete truth of what happened that night."

"But you've got enough, right? Enough to put her away?"

He nodded and smiled. "That we do."

"Will she plead insanity?"

He shook his head. "If she does, it won't take."

"She seemed pretty crazy to me," I said, leaning back against the pillow.

"I'm not saying she's a healthy woman, but she knew what she was doing. And she can go on about keeping the bones as some kind of sacred hoo-ha, but she got rid of them quick when she thought they might bite her in the ass. She framed Mike Reilly on purpose. Did she tell you that up there?"

"No."

"Out of vengeance, she said, over some professional slight that probably never even happened." He shook his head.

"Anyway," he said, pushing himself up to stand. "I have to get back downstairs, but I wanted you to know about the confession. I don't know, maybe it will help you get some closure or something."

I squinted up at him. "Is that a real thing, closure?"

"Eh." He shrugged. "Maybe it is, maybe it isn't, but for you, I hope it is."

He patted me on the head and walked out of the room. I closed my eyes and listened to the squeak of his rubber boots receding down the hall, eventually eclipsed by the steady hum of medical machines.

CHAPTER TWENTY-TWO

I NEVER WENT BACK TO ST. Bede's. Sometimes it almost felt like I'd never been there at all. It was easy to forget the buildings, the classrooms, the food, but the woods I couldn't forget. The woods I carried with me.

My mom showed up about a week after I got home, but she went straight into rehab again, and I moved in with Kim and Danny. I was sick of waiting for something that would never happen. I went back to my crappy school, where I could goof off and still get good grades. I went back to playing too many video games and watching too much TV.

I let go of St. Bede's nearly completely. My only remaining ties were Sophie and Jack. They'd started dating soon after I'd left. Sophie had actually called to clear it with me. I'd given my blessing and told her she should get Harlow arrested, but nothing transpired, and when school let out, Harlow informed the students she was leaving St. Bede's to get an MBA at Harvard. Sophie thought Reilly and Dr. Harrison's wife ran off together, but she wasn't sure, and I didn't really care. In general, Sophie said it was pretty much like nothing had ever happened at St. Bede's. Business as usual.

Over the summer, Helen and Noel sent me a box of chocolates and a polite thank-you note. Sophie told me that their little group had kind of dissolved when Freddy went to Harvard, which neither surprised nor interested me. I was finished with those girls.

A month and a half after I'd officially withdrawn from St. Bede's, the school sent me a letter to inform me I was not being asked back. Whether it was meant to be a slap in the face or was simply the product of bureaucratic idiocy, I had no idea, but the administration wished me luck in all my future endeavors and sent me on my way. I gave the letter to Danny, who promptly lit it on fire. We watched it burn in the backyard.

I muddled through the fall semester. School wasn't great, but at least I had Danny. I got myself a dog, a rescued mutt I named Sancho Panza. She slept on my feet and woke me up at three in the morning when she needed to pee.

Over winter break, Sophie and I went to Jack's parents' house in Vermont. Kim used her miles to fly me out. On Christmas night, they made hot spiced cider, and I was pretty sure Jack's little sisters sneaked brandy into their mugs. We ate goose near a little stone fireplace and listened to Handel. We played board games until the sisters insisted we watch them make snow angels in the dark while Sophie danced around them, sprinkling them with powder. Snow was falling in large flat flakes, the stillness of the night wonderfully incongruous with the squealing snow angels, when Jack smiled at me.

"I'm glad you came," he said, snowflakes clinging to his dark lashes.

"Me too." I smiled.

Sometimes my heart still constricted when I looked at him, but if I was sad, it was a good kind of sadness. Someday, I told myself, someday I would find what Jack and Sophie had. Maybe I just wasn't ready to find it yet.

I was at peace standing there, snowflakes kissing my cheeks, and I watched as one drunken snow angel pounced on the other, combing snow through her hair and laughing until her sister suddenly lurched up and over and puked prostrate in the snow. Sophie ran shrieking to us and threw her arms around me.

"Oh my God. Gross!" she wailed.

We all headed up to bed after that. Jack wished us good night and deposited us in our snug guest bedroom with its arched ceilings and sconces fashioned to look like candles. As we changed for bed and climbed under our covers, Sophie was uncharacteristically quiet.

"Is everything okay?" I asked.

She smiled. "Things are good. It's just . . . I've been worried about you."

"About me? Why?" I rolled over to face her.

"I don't know. You've had a tough year. I just wish you still went to school with us. I wish we could still hang out. I just don't like you being all alone."

"I'm not alone," I said. "I've got Danny and Kim. I've got Sancho Panza. And soon we'll be in college. Maybe we'll even get into some of the same schools, and then we can hang out for four more years."

She smiled. "And maybe we can have an uneventful friend-ship where nobody commits any crimes, and we can just hang out and eat pizza."

"I'd like that," I said.

She smiled at me. "I think you're gonna be all right, Calista Wood."

"Thanks," I said. "I think so too."

That night I had a dream. In it Clare and Laurel lived in a glade in a stone cottage with a white witch who taught them how to bake pies and never made them go to school. I visited them, and Clare held my hand and told me she missed me. On my way back home, I saw Iris. I wasn't sure it was her at first, but when I took a closer look, there was no one else it could have been. She stood there at the base of the woods, a puzzle box in one hand, a chalice in the other. She pointed to the trees that surrounded her, and slowly they transformed into a thick velvet curtain of bark and leaves. She pulled it back and stepped in-side, holding the box out to me like a lure. I walked toward her, reaching for it. It was a new puzzle box, one she'd made just for us, and inside was everything we'd ever wanted to know. She smiled at me with the mien of an enchantress. She had scarcely opened the box, and I had witnessed but the first glimmer, the first inkling, of the gnosis held therein, when I stopped myself, not wanting to see—not wanting to step over that threshold. The heavy curtain fell, and I turned to go.

It was time to leave the land of the dead.

ABOUT THE AUTHOR

MCCORMICK TEMPLEMAN ATTENDED A SCHOOL not unlike St. Bede's as a teenager. She then graduated from Reed College and went on to complete two master's degrees. She lives in Southern California, where she is a licensed acupuncturist and herbalist. This is Ms. Templeman's first novel. Visit her at mccormicktempleman.com